PAUL MCDONALD was born in Walsall in 1961, left school at 16 to train as a saddlemaker, completed his PhD in 1993 and is now Senior Lecturer in English at the University of Wolverhampton. His published work includes books on the fiction of the industrial Midlands, and the American writer Philip Roth. His first novel, *Surviving Sting*, was heralded as 'a voice from the Black Country as authentic as baltis and Banks's bitter' (*Time Out*). Paul remains in Walsall where, to his horror, he finds he's developing a taste for chunky jewellery and combat dogs.

# Kiss Me Softly,
# Amy Turtle

## Paul McDonald

To Jim —
with best wishes
from Paul
1/4/04

TINDAL STREET PRESS

First published in 2004 by
Tindal Street Press Ltd
217 The Custard Factory, Gibb Street, Birmingham, B9 4AA
www.tindalstreet.co.uk

Typesetting: Tindal Street Press Ltd

All the characters in this book are fictitious and any resemblance to
actual persons, living or dead, is purely coincidental.

A CIP catalogue reference for this book is available from
the British Library.

ISBN: 0 9541303 7 5

Printed and bound in Great Britain by
Clays Ltd, St Ives PLC

# *Acknowledgements*

I'd like to thank the University of Wolverhampton, with particular thanks to the English Subject Team for all their encouragement and support. I'm also grateful to Alan Mahar, Emma Hargrave and Joel Lane for their excellent editorial advice.

Many people have also helped me in my research for the novel. Those who won't mind being mentioned include: Dr Gerry Carlin, Dr Mark Jones, Ira Markov, Stephen Micklewright, Claire Moore, Wayne Stackhouse and Alexandra Witteveen. Those who don't want to be mentioned include: Mr X, Mrs X (no relation), Madame X, Dr X, Revd X, and Sister Bernadette X of X and the Immaculate X. Any factual errors are my own (and deliberate). Thanks are also due to the East End restaurant, Walsall, in whose balti-scented interior the novel was conceived.

Lastly I'd like to thank my partner, Pamela Dumont, for being witty, intelligent, perceptive, and for dictating this final sentence.

# Part One

# David *Ichabod* McVane

Waking up in Walsall is like waking after surgery to find that the operation hasn't been a success. And if you happen to wake up in Walsall's Wesley-in-Tame Hospital then there's a fair chance your operation won't have been a success. At least that's what I'd read in the *Walsall Reflector* (formerly the *Walsall Mirror*). Mind you, I was always sceptical about stories that appeared in the *Walsall Reflector*, mainly because I wrote them.

All the wards in Wesley-in-Tame are named after birds. I was admitted onto Vulture Ward at three a.m. on Tuesday 16 April 2002. It was no longer possible to be admitted onto Raven Ward at this hospital because they'd changed the name following complaints. People argued that it wasn't appropriate for a hospital ward to be named after a bird like a raven. Perhaps they'd been reading Edgar Allen Poe. Either way, it was changed; changed to Vulture Ward. I expect some bored administrator was taking the piss. I made a mental note to refer to it in my column for the *Reflector*, assuming I lived to write another one.

I was allocated Bed 1 in a ward-bay of six beds. For my admissions procedure the nurse switched the light on over my bed – it was bright enough to illuminate the entire ward and patients in the immediate vicinity groaned. It's hard enough to sleep in hospitals without admissions at three in the morning. It's doubly hard when Nurse Maud

Frigata is conducting them. She was about fifty and, I guessed from her surname, must have at some stage married a Spaniard. Judging by the volume of her voice, he was a deaf Spaniard.

'Could you give me your full name?' she said, sounding like Brian Blessed playing the part of Tamburlaine the Great.

'David McVane,' I said as quietly as possible.

'David McVane?' she boomed. I knew she would ask me if that is Mc or Mac and, sure enough, she did, at full volume. 'Mc or Mac?'

'M small c.'

'And what's your occupation, Mr McVane?'

'I'm a writer,' I said. I didn't want to let on that I was a journalist. Had I been a puppy-throttling paedophile I wouldn't have mentioned that either. People get the wrong idea.

'Hang on,' she said.

Oh dear, I thought.

'You're not by any chance Dave *Ichabod* McVane who writes for the *Walsall Reflector*?'

I cleared my throat. 'I might be.' Ichabod is the middle name I began using when I became a journalist. I thought my readers would find it memorable. It was months before I noticed that the initials spelled DIM.

'Yes, I'm Dave *Ichabod* McVane who writes for the *Walsall Reflector*,' I admitted. 'It's a fair cop.'

Nurse Frigata regarded me the way you might look at someone who'd just cheated Pudsey Bear out of his pocket money. It was a strange, unsettling look. Am I that despicable? The answer was clearly yes. The name Beverley Allott entered my mind, unbidden.

'Do you smoke?' she bawled.

'Now and again,' I whispered.

'Drink?' she bellowed.

'Moderately,' I said, again in hushed tones. I was trying to speak quietly so that she might get the hint and keep her own voice down. I was lying, though. I drank like a whale and you could use my lungs to re-tarmac the M42.

'And by "moderately" you mean?'

'Well, OK, a bit more than "moderately",' I conceded, *sotto voce*.

'By "a bit more than moderately" you mean excessively?' she queried, at window-shattering volume.

I nodded.

'When did you last open your bowels?' Her voice wasn't a voice. It was a tidal wave of sound with sufficient amplitude to vibrate the metal frame of my bed and those of the nearest half-dozen patients. She couldn't have drawn attention to our conversation more had she punctuated it with shots from a starting pistol.

I've always considered 'When did you last open your bowels?' an odd question. People who open their bowels are people who eviscerate themselves with their own swords, like the noble Samurai, say, or someone in *I, Claudius*.

'Yesterday.'

'What about your stools, Mr McVane? Do they float?'

'In the air?'

She was not the type to be impressed by smart-arse banter. She gave me a look that turned my nads to prunes.

'In the toilet water!' she thundered. 'If they're fatty stools they float and are difficult to flush away.'

A few more patients woke up. Sleeping with Nurse Frigata around was like trying to nap in the Reverend Ian Paisley's loudhailer.

'I don't look in the toilet before I flush,' I lied.

'How about sex?' she megaphoned. I hadn't the energy for the obvious riposte. I wasn't inclined to tell her the truth either. The patients whose sleep was being disturbed by my admission were now taking a keen interest in our dialogue. One in particular, under the pretence of fluffing his pillow, had cocked an ear in our direction; another had propped himself up and was blatantly staring at us. I wasn't about to let on that I hadn't had sex since 2001 (or, if the truth be told, 1996).

'No problems, thank you,' I said.

'Genital emissions?' she yodelled.

'I'd prefer a cup of tea.'

The guy who'd fluffed his pillows chuckled.

Nurse Maud Frigata's hair was shampooed and set into the style that Danny La Rue adopts when he's not pretending to be a woman. You could tell she had enough problems without being forced to listen to a bald, forty-year-old twat with stomach ache trying to be funny (that's me by the way). She was working nights. She was in the ugliest town in England. She was married to a Spaniard who'd no doubt buggered off back to Bilbao the second he laid eyes on Walsall. She fiddled with people's suppurating sores for a living. I should have been ashamed of myself.

'Could you describe the pain, Mr McVane?' she asked.

'It's as if I have a rhinoceros trying to buffet its way out of my stomach,' I said. This simile occurred to me on the spot, but it would be difficult to find a better one.

'When you say "buffet", is the rhinoceros nodding its head or shaking its head?' Her voice was as loud as ever and a couple of my fellow patients were stifling titters.

'Pardon?'

'The rhinoceros. Is it saying yes or is it saying no?'

'Are you taking the piss?'

'No,' she said, nodding her head. 'Yes,' she added, shaking her head.

If I'd thought it couldn't get any worse than this, lying in agony in a Walsall hospital being loudly mocked by a nurse who looked like Danny La Rue, I'd have been wrong. If I'd had any inclination of the torment, humiliation and horror that lay ahead I'd have taken myself, and my buffeting rhinoceros, to BUPA.

Nurse Frigata gave me a long pair of elastic socks to wear and three injections. One in my stomach to stop me getting blood clots (not as painful as it sounds); one in my leg to subdue my rhinoceros; and another in my arse to stop the one in my leg from making me vomit. She said the consultant, Mr Dunderdale, would be round to see me in the morning. She wrote his name on the white board that hung at the side of my bed. It said:

> Name: David McVane
> Consultant: Mr. Dunderdale
> Nil by mouth (Watch him he's a twat.)

I made the 'watch him he's a twat' bit up. (It actually said, 'Watch him he's a prat.')

At the end of the admissions procedure Nurse Frigata produced a form for me to sign.

'What's this?'

'It's a consent form.'

'What am I consenting to?'

'You're consenting to put yourself in Mr Dunderdale's hands.'

'And what does that mean?'

'It means that you agree to consent to whatever Mr Dunderdale deems necessary to cure you. It's a legal waiver essentially. We need your signature to protect ourselves.' She made it clear just how repulsive she found me by yelling this piece of information at the ceiling.

'I'm agreeing to consent to whatever Mr Dunderdale deems necessary?'

'*Yes!*'

'And what if he deems it necessary for me to give him a blow job?'

'Pardon?'

'I think you heard me.'

'Mr McVane, if you don't want to sign it, fine. There are half a dozen people on trolleys down in A&E who'd be glad of this bed.'

I felt the rhino horn jab at my heart. I signed.

When Nurse Frigata had gone the chap in the next bed went, '*Pssssst.*'

'Hello?'

'Yow can forget seeing Dunderdale in the morning, wack.'

'Pardon?'

'Yow can forget seeing Dunderdale in the morning, wack.'

'I'm not with you.'

'Yow've mower chance of a bed-bath from the Queen Mother.'

'The Queen Mother died the week before last.'

'Exactly. Yow've got no chance.'

'Actually I used to know someone called Dunderdale,' I said, 'many years ago. He wasn't a particularly pleasant character.'

'This one ay no saint either, wack. Not that yow've any chance o' seeing him.'

'How do you know, Mr . . . ?'

'Droppy; me name's Droppy Collins. I know everything about this place, wack. I'm a regular.'

'A regular?'

'I'm a swallower,' he said.

I hadn't a clue what a swallower was, but I wasn't sure I wanted one in the next bed. I had an uncomfortable feeling it might be prison slang. Absent-mindedly I reknotted the cord of my pyjama bottoms. 'Go on then,

Droppy,' I said, my journalistic nosiness getting the better of my better judgement, 'what's a swallower?'

'Yow'll see,' he said. He then pulled the covers over his head and lay completely still, silent except for the muted rasp of his breathing.

# Grotesquely Bloated

It wasn't a good night. Sleeping on a plastic mattress makes your buttocks sweat for one thing. Then you start thinking about all the people who've died in that very bed. The heart attacks, strokes, victims of flesh-devouring super bugs. Knackering hell. And we all know about the mortality rate in Walsall's Wesley-in-Tame. It had one of the worst records in the country. *The* worst actually. We'd run several stories in the *Reflector* about it: the recent 'Wesley's Wards of Woe' headline covered a couple of reluctant amputee outrages; our 'Theatre of the Absurd' story also addressed the growing number of surgical blunders at Wesley. One victim of over-zealous circumcision had sought legal representation and we were following his progress keenly. Walsall was a dangerous town, but few places more so at the moment than its hospital. At least that's the way it's presented at the *Reflector*. A juicy scare story about a hospital sells papers, you see, and no one at the *Reflector* was more associated with such stories than Dave Ichabod McVane. Indeed, it was hard to think what might be less popular than me at this hospital. Legionnaire's in the air conditioning? Salmonella in the geriatrics' mush?

But on a positive note: my rhino was snoozing. Thanks to the painkiller I no longer felt its phallic horn about to pierce my gut to appear, blood coated and draped in viscera, the way John Hurt's indigestion presents itself to a startled crew in *Alien*. Frigata's painkiller had done what ten Settlers, six Deflatines, five fruit-flavoured Rennies and a bottle of Gaviscon had failed to do.

Not to mention the booze: lager, more lager; brandy, more brandy.

Booze had always worked in the past. That's when I began to get frightened, when booze didn't kill my rhino. It's always been the one cure I could rely on. I've long suffered from a dodgy stomach: wind, indigestion, quirky bowels and a variety of intestinal jitters. But a twelve-pack of Dutch lager had always seen such problems off. If it was a particularly nasty bout, the twelve-pack would be supplemented by a half-pint of brandy. I'd be cured *and* ready for a party. I'd seldom get to a party of course; generally I'd wake up on my fag-burned sofa surrounded by empty cans and the most profound odour of flatulence imaginable. But I'd be cured. And the whiff of my flatulence on such mornings had a beautiful appeal akin to Robert Duvall's love of napalm in *Apocalypse Now*: the odour of victory. In the post-binge glow my guts would be anaesthetized and I'd have won a battle with dyspepsia yet again.

Not this time.

I drank the brandy and didn't get drunk. I vomited twelve quid's worth of the finest Remy Martin into the bog, while another five quid's worth splattered my bottle of Toilet Duck. My distended stomach, far from deflating, increased another inch in its already freakish girth. Clearly I was pregnant with something more sinister than indigestion.

'Severe stomach pains,' I said to Droppy Collins when he enquired about my malady. It was six thirty a.m. and the auxiliaries were bringing round the tea trolley. Not for me, of course.

'Is the pain constant or intermittent?' he asked, with the air of someone who knew what he was talking about. The word 'intermittent' was incongruous against his Black Country accent, but he was clearly comfortable with medical discourse. Presumably this had something to do with him being 'a regular'.

'Constant,' I replied, 'without the painkiller, of course.'

'Is it a sharp pain or a dull un?'

'A dull, boring pain that radiates through from my stomach to my back.' I had been rehearsing this response ready for my interview with the consultant.

'They'll probably tek yow to x-ray fust,' Droppy informed me, 'then they'll tek some blood tests and piss tests. They probably woh bother with a shit sample yet.'

'I suppose it's my consultant's call.'

'Yow've no chance of seeing Dunderdale, wack.'

'Oh, sorry, I forgot.'

'Dunderdale will be playing golf on a Tuesday morning. Yow'll see a registrar.'

I watched with envy as they gave Droppy a cup of coffee. My mouth was parched.

'Car I have a spoon, nurse?' he asked, with a twinkle in his eye.

The auxiliary, a buxom black woman called Annette, tutted and shook her head. 'Now you know I can't trust you with a spoon, Droppy Collins. I've stirred it for you.'

He turned to me and winked.

Just as Droppy predicted, Mr Dunderdale didn't make an appearance. A registrar, Dr Robin Fostus, came round at about eight. He was a pale, glum man with sunken eyes. After twenty-four hours of agony, ten Settlers, six Deflat-ines, five fruit-flavoured Rennies, a bottle of Gaviscon and forty shots of brandy, I still looked healthier than he did. I shivered involuntarily: his arrival was like a freezer door opening.

'It's a dull, boring pain that radiates through from my stomach to my back,' I said.

'What have you consumed over the past twenty-four hours?' he asked, kneading my over-inflated belly. 'Anything unusual?'

Well, I thought, apart from ten Settlers, six Deflatines, five fruit-flavoured Rennies, a bottle of Gaviscon and forty shots of brandy, nothing springs to mind.

'Nothing springs to mind,' I said.

'Is your gut always this massively distended?'

That didn't sound too complimentary. 'By "massively distended" you mean?'

'Grotesquely bloated.'

'Not really; but I do suffer from wind.'

'You've got a bit of a gut on you.'

'It's all paid for, doctor. Besides, I don't use the word gut: I prefer to call it a liquid grain storage facility.' Fostus ignored my stab at humour.

'We'll take some x-rays of your abdomen,' he said, 'and we'll have some blood and urine samples. We won't bother with a stool sample just yet.'

Droppy certainly knew what he was talking about.

After Fostus had gone there was nothing left for me to do but listen to the hospital radio. The rubber Y of the headphones reminded me of a device used for water divining but, in the spirit of adventure, I put them on. Though I'd been in hospital twice before (once with a broken nose and once for the effects of smoke inhalation), I'd never listened to hospital radio. Nothing could have prepared me for the *Tinker Lawson Show*. I tuned in just as he was announcing that this would be his last ever broadcast – despite the fact that he was a volunteer, he told us, he'd been sacked. As soon as he began playing records I could see why. He began with Radiohead's 'My Iron Lung' and followed with 'Aneurysm' by Nirvana. I was also interested to hear 'Last Gasp Death Shuffle', which, Tinker informed us, was the first single release from Kitchens of Distinction. But his favourite band was the Smiths. I liked them too but, given that they're not exactly remembered for their sunny disposition, I wasn't sure they were the ideal choice for hospital radio. Still, Tinker promised to feature them throughout the morning, 'If the squares upstairs don't pull my plug.' He followed 'Girlfriend in a Coma' with 'Heaven Knows I'm Miserable Now'.

This started me thinking about the 1980s. Hearing the name Dunderdale had already brought back some memories, but Morrissey's plaintive voice took me right back to my first year at college, September 1986.

# Everett Lafayette Van Freek

The first time I saw my new flatmate, Ringo, it was September 1986 and he was naked. Actually he was naked, tied to a telegraph pole and had a gladioli sticking out of his arse.

'Can I be of any assistance?' I asked.

'Are you a fan of the Smiths?' he replied.

This isn't the response you expect when you offer to help a naked guy in bondage. For a second I thought I might've stumbled upon a piece of street theatre.

'As a matter of fact, yes,' I answered, playing along.

'In that case, I accept your offer.'

I untied his legs, which had been bound to the pole with the belt from his trousers, and freed his hands, which had been knotted together with a rolled up T-shirt advertising *Hatful of Hollow*. I let him remove the gladioli himself. It wasn't actually up his arse, it was wedged between his legs but, whenever we told the story in years to come, we'd always say it was up his arse. If it's a toss-up between comedy and the facts it's always worth opting for the former.

'Bastards,' he said, pulling the flower away from him and tossing it into the gutter. His left eye was a little swollen and he had a smear of blood between his front teeth – other than that he didn't appear to be too physically damaged.

'What happened?'

'I was waylaid by a bunch of music critics,' he said, 'five of them, with crew-cuts and swastika tattoos.'

'Music critics?'

'Music critics,' he said, as he hopped around trying to force his leg into his straight-cut Wranglers. 'They took exception to my Smiths shirt. They said, "Isn't that the band who ponce around with hearing aids in their ears and flowers sticking out of their arses?" And I said, "Well, the lead singer, a gentleman by the name of Morrissey, wears a hearing aid as a gimmick and likes to have a flower protruding from his back pocket, but not actually out of his bottom-hole." And they seemed to take it funny.'

'You're not from around here, are you?'

He wasn't. Ringo was from Holland, the son of a French-Indian chemist and a Dutch-Welsh light opera singer. Shall I tell you why he was called Ringo? He was called Ringo because his full name was Everett Lafayette Van Freek.

'I'm looking for 47 Saddler's Row,' he told me.

'You're in luck, that's where I live.'

'You're the one advertising for a flatmate?'

'Heavy smoker and drinker preferred.'

'Those things will kill you.'

'So will walking around the streets of Walsall back-chatting skinheads.'

'Particularly if you're half Asian, I suspect. They taunted me with a few racist remarks.'

'It does tend to increase the risk factor.'

'Well, to tell the truth, I'm only a quarter Asian.'

'Then that's only half as risky.'

Actually, a large number of the area's residents were either Asian or Afro-Caribbean. Gangs of right-wingers would occasionally roam the outskirts looking for people to pick on. They were seldom drawn to the six-foot, eighteen-stone, bull-muscled, black martial arts enthusiasts who belonged to the karate club in Pansy's Walk. They preferred nine-stone, five-foot-seven, pipe-cleaner-thin Asian Smiths fans like Ringo.

'Where did they get the gladioli?' I asked.

'From the garden over the road,' he said, gesturing to a little garden that had clearly been stamped through and ripped at very recently. 'Strictly speaking, it should have been a daffodil of course.'

'Sorry?'

'They should have shoved a daffodil up my bottom if it was a genuine anti-Morrissey gesture. He wears a daffodil in his back pocket, not a gladioli.'

Everett Lafayette Van Freek is the only person I've met who'd complain that a bunch of skinheads had pushed the *wrong* kind of flower up his arse.

'When can you move in?' I asked.

Walsall was a culture shock to Ringo. He'd never seen anything quite like it before. Mind you, Walsall had never seen anything quite like Ringo before either. He was something of an oddity. Being of mixed race his skin was cafe au lait, and his features were delicate, rather feminine even, with high cheekbones. His accent was difficult to place. His parents – a father from Lille via Delhi and a mother from Amsterdam via Aberystwyth – didn't want to confuse him with a variety of tongues, so Ringo only spoke English and Dutch. In those days his pronunciation betrayed a slight Low Countries influence: 'Of courshe that ish true,' he would say. Also his grammar, though superior to that of most Walsall residents, occasionally featured the kind of odd and archaic expressions found among non-native speakers: 'Let us travel to the fish and chip mongers,' he would say. Sometimes he'd put this on for a joke and it wasn't always easy to tell if he was taking the piss. Certainly he had a good sense of humour. He was bright too; brighter than me anyway. He was also one of the few people since the 1970s I've heard use the expressions 'flaming Ada' and 'ace-a-mundo'. When quizzed, he claimed to have forgotten where he'd picked these up.

'So what's this flat of yours like?' asked Ringo, as I guided him towards *chez* McVane that day in September.

'Don't expect too much and you won't be disappointed,' I said.

'That's the line I use just before sexual intercourse.'

'And talking of sex . . .' I said, in what I hoped was a comically mysterious way.

'And talking of sex, what?' asked Ringo. 'Flaming Ada, you're not homosexual, are you?'

'No, I have a girlfriend: Monica. You'll be sharing with both of us.'

'Weird three-way ups and downs?' he asked, sounding a little nervous. ('*Upsh and downsh?*')

I wasn't sure what 'weird three-way ups and downs' involved, but I was certain we wouldn't be expecting it of Ringo. 'No, mate, relax: we're strictly hetero and monogamous. And we have two bedrooms. You'll have one to yourself.'

'Ace-a-mundo,' he said. 'I was hoping to be sharing with just one person, but it's not such a large deal. I'm an adaptable Dutch-Welsh-French-Indian.'

'Good to hear,' I said. 'However, that's not really what I meant by "speaking of sex".'

'Go on.'

'As well as being an adaptable Dutch-Welsh-French-Indian, are you also a broad-minded Dutch-Welsh-French-Indian?'

'You're a pornographer?'

'Nope.'

'You're a goat fetishist.'

'Well . . . no.'

'Flaming Ada, you don't sound very certain! If not goats, what? Another type of ungulate?'

'It's not me who's the fetishist.'

'Monica?'

'No, our neighbours.'

'Your neighbours are goat fuckers?'

The worrying thing is that I couldn't say no to that question with any conviction.

# The Glorious Twelfth

I'd tried to escape Walsall in my youth. I thought my brains would be my ticket out, and that did initially prove to be the case. Though I left school without qualifications I discovered that I had a high IQ. Encouraged by a puzzle I completed in the *Mirror*, I booked to take a Mensa test at Aston University. They found that with an IQ of 201 I was twice as brainy as the average person. In fact, I was statistically one of the most intelligent people who'd ever lived. Brainier, apparently, than Margaret Thatcher and Jimmy Savile. After a lifetime of believing I was mediocre I was astonished to find myself among the ranks of the freakishly gifted. I was thrilled; it was wonderful not to be average.

I sent a photocopy of my Mensa score to Bristol University and they accepted me onto a General Humanities degree without A Levels. I could barely spell but, given that in IQ terms I was one of the smartest arses in history, that didn't seem to matter.

I passed my first year, if not quite with flying colours, then with flying monochromes. I was set for a lower second-class degree at least. A breeze for someone with my ability. But things began to change when Mensa informed me of their mistake. It turned out that my IQ wasn't 201; it was 102. Someone doing a PhD in intelligence quantification had been given access to my file. He'd identified the error.

When he double-checked my score he found that my result had been written up backwards.

I wasn't a genius: I was average. Well, two points above average, but what's two points? A six-pack of Special Brew can put paid to two points of IQ in less than an hour.

As an apology they sent me a complimentary copy of a Mensa puzzles magazine autographed by Clive Sinclair. This wasn't much use to me because, having such an average IQ, I couldn't do the puzzles. It was on 12 August 1980 that I received the letter. The Glorious Twelfth. Like a grouse full of shot I began to plummet.

I didn't deserve to be at Bristol with all those brainy kids. When I returned that September for my second year, I was a different bloke. Where I'd previously been vocal and confident in seminars, now I was diffident and taciturn. Where previously I'd cut a swathe through the prescribed reading, now the texts seemed dense; meanings became elusive and obscure. My B-minus average became an E-minus average and, by the summer of 1981, I was back in Walsall. And Walsall seemed the appropriate place for me: I was average again, and where better to wallow in one's averageness than the town whose only claim to distinction is that it *sounds* like Warsaw.

My limitations were thrust upon me in the form of that number: 102; and my horizons were demarcated by those seven letters: WALSALL.

I burned my duffel coat. I gave up reading the *Guardian* and switched back to the *Mirror*. I gave up writing poems too, something I'd quite enjoyed when I thought I was a genius. I abandoned my flirtation with classical music and jazz and re-embraced pop. If ever I was around when the *South Bank Show* came on TV, I'd swear at Melvyn Bragg. For a while at least I became an anti-intellectual. I'd speak in a broad Black Country accent and, when anyone used a word with more than three syllables, I'd say, 'Yow wot?'

And I started to drink.

Or rather, I started to drink again. Prior to my fleeting life as a genius I'd spent long periods off my dingers. But it's odd that, when I thought I had something going for me, I'd eased up on the pop. Maybe I didn't want to risk my brain cells. After the Glorious Twelfth, though, I needed it again; the magic potion made me feel less disappointed with myself for being half the man I thought I was.

Finding work was a problem. Before the discovery of my apparent genius I'd been a saddlemaker – a skilled, well-paid job – but when I returned to Walsall it seemed that no saddlery companies were hiring. I was unemployed for months and I'd queue for my benefit along with the ever-increasing casualties of Thatcherism. When, eventually, I found work making fetish gear for sado-masochists I considered myself lucky. It kept me in lager. Plus I enjoyed it – my hand-tooled spanking paddles are the best in the business.

But I knew I needed something different.

By the time I met Ringo I'd decided to put self-doubt behind me and have another crack at higher education. Maybe I didn't have to spend my life stitching zips into gimp masks. I'd passed a year at Bristol University, after all. Yet my ambitions no longer stretched to such a prestigious university. I needed a college where I wouldn't feel out of my depth, one where someone of decidedly average ability might fit in. I was lucky to have the perfect institution right on my doorstep: the Walsall Academy for New Knowledge. I reasoned that even I could feel at home in the college that must have the most unfortunate acronym in the history of education; or, indeed, in the history of acronyms.

# Penny's Punishment Palace

'A brothel?' said Ringo, when we reached the flat. 'Flaming Ada.'

'You're more composed than I thought you'd be. Is it because you're Dutch? You're all broad minded about these things I hear.'

'Yes, the brothel I lived in in Holland was also a windmill.'

'Point taken. Is it going to be a problem?'

'I suppose I can see why you didn't mention it in the advert.' Our flat was in Caldmore (pronounced *Karma*): renowned as Walsall's red light area. Right back to the days when prostitutes used to greet you with 'Allo, dearie', you could find them in Caldmore. Though most walked the streets, a few worked from brothels like the one underneath our flat.

Our building looked like a bungalow with the bottom eighth of a tower block stuck on the top. It was actually three flats: the ground floor was a three-bedroom flat, the top two each had two bedrooms. Me and Monica had the top floor; Penny Stroker and her girls had the first and second. Penny, who I suppose you'd call the Madame, owned the entire building. Maggie Thatcher had a thing about people owning their own homes and in the 1980s councils flogged off houses and flats at a snip. By some miracle Penny had managed to purchase all three flats as a single lot for less than three grand. I'm not sure if Penny's form of private enterprise is what Maggie had in mind but, in her own way, she epitomized the spirit of Thatcher's philosophy.

Many of the local working girls wanted to be a part of Penny's business, despite the fact that she specialized in S&M. It was much safer in Penny's torture rooms than on the streets of Walsall. Girls who worked out of the brothel weren't allowed to street-walk. Clients weren't solicited on the streets but via recommendation, together with discreet adverts in specialist publications. Penny maintained separate addresses for the two lower flats because it meant that a girl could work from each flat throughout the day and night without breaking the law. She knew her rights did Penny, although she didn't always stick to the rules: sometimes five or six girls worked simultaneously, which wasn't legal at all.

From outside there was nothing to indicate that the building was a brothel. You had to be 'in the know'. Formally the lower flats were known as Flat 47A and Flat 47B; informally they were Penny's Punishment Palace. Not a great deal of 'regular' sex went on there. Penny's mainly catered for fetish clients and each flat was equipped with fantasy and discipline rooms containing every conceivable torture device from thumbscrews to Daniel O'Donnell albums. One room even had a trapeze, together with something called a rocking horse of shame.

'I make money by supplying the owner, Penny, with leather S&M goods,' I told Ringo.

'Interesting. You're a craftsman?'

'I like to think so. I make everything: discipline hoods, masks, collars, restraints, and every kind of whip you could desire.'

'How many kinds of whip is it possible to desire? Isn't a whip a whip?'

It was like asking Captain Ahab if a whale is just a whale. 'Oh no, no, no, God bless you.' I said. 'That's a common mistake made by people with no appreciation of fetish accessories.'

'That would be me.'

'Well, let me enlighten you,' I said. And I proceeded to enlighten him. I described the various categories and sub-categories of birches, cats, floggers, martinets and scourges. By the time I got to bullwhips I could sense he was beginning to wilt.

'Bullwhips are a real nasty bastard's whip,' I informed him, 'like the ones ringmasters use at the circus. They're single-stranded lashes, traditionally six foot in length (though I once made a ten-footer). Penny has stopped using them in her playrooms because of the damage they do to the light fittings. She prefers the shorter signal whip – about half the length of a bullwhip but, in the right hands, just as nasty.'

'You certainly know your whips,' said Ringo, with the tone of a man who has no butter for his cream crackers. Sadly for him, I was on a roll.

'For over-the-knee buttock thrashing,' I continued, 'punters prefer something even shorter than a signal.' And I listed the most common varieties of crops, quirts and tawses, possibly providing excessive information about their social and cultural history. I then went onto paddles. 'As a craftsman,' I said, 'I prefer paddles.'

'Paddles, you say.'

'Yep. The greater surface area gives me more scope for creativity. My trademark paddle has a Staffordshire knot patterned in silver studs at the business end and leaves a distinctive motif on the grateful recipient's arse.'

I was about to treat him to an account of the art of spanking-paddle production but the Dutchman, who was now laughing and pulling at his hair in mock exasperation, cut me short: 'And you say you make things *apart from whips and paddles*?' he panted.

'Ah, sorry, mate. Yes. I also make specialist items to order. This is where the real money lies. Punters put in requests through Penny and I do my best to satisfy their requirements. I've supplied everything from hessian-lined torture shorts to a spiked leather bishop's mitre. Now that I'm becoming a student, though, I won't have so much time to make money from leathercrafts; hence the need for a lodger.'

We walked in silence for a while as we turned out of Bath Street and into Newhall Street. I was conscious of having given him too much whip information. But I was nervous he wouldn't like the flat and my edginess had switched my gob to auto-twaddle. I hoped I hadn't scared him off.

'I suppose it's better to be in a flat above a brothel rather than in a flat below one,' said Ringo, at last.

'They don't cause any bother,' I said.

This was true. The S&M punters were very well behaved. There'd be the occasional rowdy drunk at weekends because this is when Penny's offered their vanilla (straight sex) services. Penny usually took care of any trouble herself with a few well-chosen words and, if necessary, a meat cleaver. Now and again she'd call her brother, Fierce Woody, who lived in a tower block near by. He was a twenty-stone power-lifting champion who, according to Penny, could have been world class if not for a recurring bilateral rupture. If Penny couldn't deal with the situation, Fierce Woody certainly could.

'Now and again,' I told Ringo, 'you get the odd kinky punter who likes to bark like a dog, or shout orders through a loudhailer but, as a rule, Penny's employees and her clients are quiet, decent neighbours.'

'Ace-a-mundo,' he said, uncertainly.

# Monica

I led Ringo into the hall of our building and past the ground-floor flat. Because the concrete stairs were uncarpeted and the plaster walls unpapered the place had the acoustics of Wormwood Scrubs. As we climbed to the first floor I was conscious of the resonant scrape of our footsteps. I had my fingers crossed that there wouldn't be any punters or prossers about because I thought they might undo my image of quiet, decent neighbours – if my whip lecture hadn't already convinced Ringo to try elsewhere.

Sadly, I wasn't in luck. On the first-floor landing we ran into one of Penny's girls. They like to give themselves fantasy names and this particular lady called herself Fanny Batter. She was dressed as Wonder Woman complete with golden tiara, metal wristbands and starry knickers. A coiled signal whip was tucked into her belt.

'Hi, Dave,' she said. 'Who's your friend?'

'Er . . . this is someone who might be moving into 47C.'

'Call me Ringo,' he said, a degree of awe clear in his voice.

Fanny winked a hello and, as she passed us, the air was suddenly thick with Charlie. Both of us turned to watch her descend the stairs. She was a big woman. The powerful muscles in her shoulders were only partially obscured by her long brown wig and her thick calves were almost splitting the seams of her plastic boots. You wouldn't want to be on the wrong end of her lash.

'Do you think her wristbands *really* deflect bullets?' asked Ringo.

He was unphased, it seemed, and I allowed myself a small sigh of relief. I took him up another flight of stairs, to the third floor and our flat. It was five thirty on a Friday afternoon and I was pretty sure Monica would be home.

She was another reason why I'd decided to have a second crack at education: because Monica was doing the same. She'd given up her office job and, like me, had enrolled on a full-time course at WANK. At twenty-three, she was a year younger than me, but still counted as a mature student. She was about to start a degree in Nursing Studies. Having taken A Level psychology, Monica knew all about IQ tests and had no time for them. She was always trying to ease me out of my depression about being average. Monica said that IQ tests only measure how good you are at IQ tests. They can't measure important things like creativity, for instance, or wit, or even general knowledge. I had a feeling she was right, but I was too dim to be sure.

Monica was unlike most Walsall women: she didn't have plasters on her heels; she didn't buy ankle chains from Elizabeth Duke at Argos; she didn't have nicotine stripes in her hair; and, despite being twenty-three years old, she didn't have a poster-sized, professional portrait of her four kids hanging on the chimney breast. And even if she *had* kids, she'd never name one Ferraro Roche.

Certainly, a combination of Monica and booze went some way towards making life in Walsall tolerable. By the time of Ringo's arrival, we'd been together eighteen months and cohabiting for a year.

'Monica, please meet Everett Lafayette Van Freek. He's come to look at the flat.'

'Call me Ringo,' said Ringo.

Monica, who'd been watching *Blockbusters*, stood and shook his hand.

'*Hatful of Hollow*,' she said, regarding Ringo's T-shirt, 'fantastic. I love the recording of "What Difference" they did for the Peel Sessions.'

Ringo beamed.

'Why don't you show Ringo around while I put the kettle on?' she said.

Given that we were standing in it, I decided to begin with the living room. It was the kind of room you could justifiably call large but cosy. It had two sofas positioned around a coffee table, an Amstrad music centre and a telly perched above a VCR the size of a family suitcase.

'Could I have a P please, Bob?' said one of the *Blockbusters* contestants.

Off the living room was a small dining area containing a round dining table with four chairs. Ringo took this in at a glance as I led him to his potential bedroom. This was a largish space with a three-quarter bed and a nice-sized wardrobe; it was also scrupulously neat, having been cleaned by Monica that very morning.

'Mmmmm,' said Ringo. It sounded like approval, but I couldn't be certain.

Next I made the mistake of showing him the master bedroom, which I shared with Monica. This was less tidy because it'd been my job to clean it and, as yet, I hadn't been arsed. By the time I remembered the state it was in I'd already ushered Ringo through the door.

'The other bedroom,' I said, trying to keep my tone chirpy. But it was like trying to be upbeat about cholera.

As well as being our bedroom, it also doubled as a study area and Monica and I had a desk each in separate corners. Monica's was reasonably tidy, but mine also functioned as a leathercraft work surface and was in a state.

It was topped by a thick plastic cutting board, five empty lager tins, and a bewildering array of tools. There were round knives for cutting leather, skirt-shaves for shaving it, punches for punching it and awls for bodging it. There were boxes of buckles, clips, rings, rhinestones, rivets, spikes and studs. There were six different types of glue from white latex to sealing paste. There was an oilstone, two mallets and a toffee hammer. In the corner of the desk was a Primus stove on which I heated my pyrography irons. Propped against the desk were over a dozen rolls of leather in all the favourite fetish colours, including black, white, red, pink and lavender, together with suede, pigskin and two full hides of bridle leather. Patterns and sketches for s&m equipment lay scattered around, while lengths of thread, twine, leather-lace and cord criss-crossed every surface. Beside my desk was a sewing machine with a half-stitched discipline hood hanging limply from the needle. The room reeked of animal skin.

'Er . . . Come and see the view from the living-room window,' I said, embarrassed.

Ringo followed me back into the main room and stood beside me at the window. The flat was on fairly high ground and a sizeable slice of Walsall stretched beneath us: from the spire of St Matthew's Church to the unsightly smear of Bath Street. The sun hadn't yet gone down, but prostitutes were already parading before the crumbling facades of the Victorian factories that lined the pavement. I stared at my hometown and racked my brains to remember why I'd invited Ringo to look at the view. Oh yes: it was a marginally less disturbing sight than our bedroom.

'It's not up to much I'm afraid,' I said.

'Yes, it should be demolished and the ground sprinkled with holy water,' said Ringo.

'Fuck me, just say if you don't want to live here,' I said, bristling, 'there are much worse flats in these parts, believe me!'

'Er, sorry, I was referring to the view not the flat. The flat's fine. Ace-a-mundo in fact.'

Monica returned from the kitchen with three teas on a tray. 'Did I mention that Monica is going to be studying at WANK too?' I said. 'She's taking a degree in Nursing Studies.'

Ringo grinned and his eyes widened. Had he any doubts about moving in I'm sure they were dispelled there and then, for one of the things I would learn about Ringo was that, as well as being a fanatical Smiths fan, he was also a galloping hypochondriac.

Ringo put the back of his hand to his forehead. 'Actually, Monica,' he said, 'I've been feeling a little giddeous. Also a tiny bit bilious in the belly area.'

'He's had a gladioli up his arse,' I said.

'Sit down and tell me all about it,' she told Ringo.

Quicker than you could say 'This Charming Man' he and his Smiths T-shirt were beside her on the settee.

I'd only exchanged a few words with Ringo, but I had a strong feeling that he and Monica would get along. He was the gossipy, sociable sort who knows what to say to make women laugh. That's something I'd been fairly good at myself. I'd trapped Monica with my patter in the days when she used to dress in trouser suits and carry her nightschool notes in a soft-leather briefcase. She'd been having a drink in the Pen and Wig with friends from her psychology class when I spotted her. She was auburn-haired and curvaceous. If she were a barmaid they'd call her buxom; if she were a painting they'd call her Ruben-esque; and if she were a model they'd call her unemployed. 'What's your favourite book?' I'd asked her, with my usual flair for originality. To my delight she'd answered with the title of *my* favourite: *Hollywood Babylon* by Kenneth Anger, and we'd spent the rest of the evening discussing the Fatty Arbuckle scandal, before moving onto other gossip-worthy celebrity shenanigans. We both knew our stuff: the type of firearm Jim Davidson had been arrested for possessing (an Argentinean officer's gun), and the film Joanna Lumley appeared nude in (*Games That Lovers Play*, 1970). What better basis for a relationship? Every time I popped a gag she'd put her hand over her eyes, shake her head and laugh. It was the kind of gesture that says: this guy's a tit, but he's funny. And it was exactly the gesture she was offering now in response to Ringo's cartoon account of his assault.

'And I said to the skinhead, I said: "I've no wish to be pernickety, my good fellow, but . . ."'

These days Monica's trouser suits had been replaced by woollen tights and DMs but she was still curvaceous: a healthy size 18, and happy with it. She was a bright, lovely, sexy woman and I hadn't shagged her properly in six months.

# Call Me Doctor

The next evening we had a meal to welcome Ringo into the flat. We invited Penny Stroker, our landlady, to meet him. Penny was a nice enough woman, but she lacked social graces. She burped thunderously at regular intervals, swore a great deal, picked her nose and, when she thought no one was looking, wiped it on the heel of her shoe. She also had an unhealthy habit of exploiting ethnic stereotypes for what she thought was comic effect. When I told her Ringo was a Dutch-Welsh-French-Indian, for instance, she said, 'I suppose for dinner we'll be eating curried leeks and snails' tits out of a fucking clog.' She'd never have guessed that she wasn't funny. Luckily Ringo wasn't the type to take offence and the two got along well. After five minutes she was calling him Clogs. She was very interested in the Dutch attitude to prostitution and brothels, and Ringo was able to tell her all about the way such things operate in Holland.

'The most famous brothel in Holland is Amsterdam's Yab Yums,' he told her. 'Many celebrities and VIPs seek pleasure there.'

'Well, Clogs, we don't get many fucking celebrities in Caldmore,' she said, 'but we do get some fuckers you wouldn't expect to see.'

'Like who?' I asked, glugging down the dregs of my second bottle of Blue Nun. I knew who she was going to mention because Monica and I had grilled her about such matters many times. It generally amounted to this: nobody remotely interesting.

'We get the bigwigs from the council down here all the fucking time,' she said, mentioning a few characters with a gossip-rating value of zero. 'One of our girls, Dusty, said that we had ***** in. He was a right fucking pig too, apparently. Him and his fucking rubber dolphin.'

'Anybody else?' Monica asked, trying not to yawn.

'Dionne Splendour, our new switch, told me something interesting last night as a matter of fact.'

'Erm, excuse me, what's a switch?' asked Ringo.

'Sorry, Clogs: a switch is a top *and* a bottom.'

'?'

'Sorry again: she's both a dom and a sub. In other words, she dishes it out *and* takes it as well. They're worth their weight in gold in my game, I can tell you. Anyway, you'll love this seeing that you're all going to WANK. One of their lecturers has started visiting us. He told Dionne he was a fucking literature man.'

Suddenly Monica and me were on the edge of our seats, and so was our new flatmate; he, like me, would be studying literature at WANK. 'What's his name?' he urged, eagerly.

'They rarely give their fucking names, Clogs. But he does like to be called doctor, she says. He's very insistent about that. "Call me doctor" he keeps saying. If he comes again, so to speak, I'll let you know.'

The only WANK lecturer that Ringo and I had both heard of was a Dr Daniel Dunderdale. As head of the School of English his name had been on the letters we received from the college. This correspondence, which Ringo and I had compared before dinner, simply confirmed our places on the English degree course and invited us to an induction day on Monday 8 September 1986.

'It wasn't Dr Daniel Dunderdale by any chance?' I asked.

'As I say, love, I don't know and, unless he wants to tell us, we won't ask. But I promise I'll tell Dionne to tip me the nod if the fucker turns up again.'

Thrilling stuff. And Monica and I were delighted to see that Ringo turned out to be as big a gossipmonger as any of us. This juicy information made his eyes sparkle like a dog at a bollock-licking festival. You could understand it: the prospect of a scandal associated with the School of English could make our first weeks at WANK a thousand times more interesting.

'This could even be worth first-class honours,' I told Ringo.

'*Ongelooflyk*,' he said.

'And what does that mean?'

'Ace-a-mundo,' said Ringo.


It was a nice evening and, as it wore on, Ringo looked more and more comfortable in our flat. It was as if he was beginning to fill a Dutch-French-Welsh-Indian-shaped hole that we previously hadn't noticed. I'd been concerned that he'd head for the hills as soon as the brothel was mentioned, but it looked like he had the requisite tolerance and/or daftness to cope. It had been harder to convince Monica to move in. It had taken me months to persuade her. Eventually I'd broken her spirit with my 'It's Where the Real People Dwell' speech.

'It's bohemian,' I'd told her, 'and, if you're going to be a student, it's exactly the kind of place you *should* live. Move somewhere alive, colourful, challenging, on the edge. Free your mind and learn something about yourself. Walk on the wild side, embrace the alternative, shun convention, don't be bor –'

'OK, OK, I'll move in,' she'd said, 'just shut the fuck up.'

And I don't think she regretted it. It had been good for

her to get away from her parents' semi. She seemed to enjoy the quirkiness of our situation too, and often bragged to her mates that she lived above a brothel – not that there was much to boast about as life above Penny's could be as tedious as anywhere else. But Monica was content, at least with *where* she lived. She wasn't always that happy with me these days.

'Anyone for another bottle of Blue Nun?' I asked Penny and Monica – there was no point asking Ringo because he'd already informed us he didn't drink. I tried not to hold it against him.

'Do you really need to open *another* bottle, Dave?' said Monica. 'Perhaps you should leave some for the rest of the wine-drinking world.'

I rose unsteadily to my feet. 'If they can't keep up that's their lookout,' I said.

Monica was one of those people who are always happy to have just *one* glass of wine. To me this is a freakish trait. After all, if you're not going to finish the job what's the point in starting? Isn't having one glass of wine a bit like having one twelfth of a blow job?

I uncorked another bottle. 'So,' I said to Penny, 'you say this WANK guy likes to be called doctor?'

# The Swallower & Co.

It was possible to have too much of the *Tinker Lawson Show*. When he introduced a series of tracks from the Dead Kennedys' *Plastic Surgery Disasters* I realized I'd had enough and I removed my headphones. Apparently Tinker's performance wouldn't finish until midday and I decided to tune in again later, assuming someone didn't yank him from the studio with a shepherd's crook before then.

Apart from Droppy Collins and myself there were four other patients in my bay of Vulture Ward. In the bed opposite was a guy who called himself Deekus and who kept ringing for the nurse and demanding painkillers. In his late twenties, Deekus was gaunt with a yellowish pallor and, after half a minute of listening to his whining, the thing I most wanted to do in the world was throttle him with his own drip-tube. He was the type who insists on telling his life story to anyone who makes the mistake of having fully functional ears. Like Droppy, he too was a regular: an alcoholic who kept falling off the wagon and aggravating something nasty in his guts. His autobiography was a narrative of woe that began with him drinking because he couldn't get a job and ended with him being unable to get a job because of his drinking. He was back in hospital this time because, after a two-week dry spell, he'd been forced to hit the bottle again when his sister's Labrador had a miscarriage. Woven into his tale of despair were constant criticisms of the NHS which had, apparently, failed him at every turn. Yet somehow he'd survived.

The bed next to Deekus was occupied by a gentleman who was seemingly too ill to speak or move. His name was Martin. I'm assuming Martin was too ill to move because he never moved, despite being talked at ceaselessly by Deekus. And I'm assuming he was too ill to speak because anyone who wasn't would be compelled to tell Deekus to: 'Shut the fuck up, you self-pitying twat.' Every few hours the nurses would change Martin's various drip-bags. He was on a special mat that massaged different parts of his body at different times of the day to stop him getting a deep vein thrombosis. A more humane hospital would also have provided him with earplugs.

Next to Martin was Gulliver. He was one of those people whose first question is invariably, 'What football team do you support?' When I told him that, although I'm a fan of football, I only tend to watch England games, he immediately filed me in the despicable 'part-timer' category. This, I'm told, is worse than not being a fan at all because, unlike non-fans, us part-timers insist on thinking we know something about the game, especially during European and World Cup tournaments. Gulliver was an obsessive West Bromwich Albion fan, a fact highlighted by the blue and white football strip he wore instead of pyjamas. He was in for an exploratory test of the camera-up-the-arse variety and was desperate to get this over with before the weekend because the Albion had a crucial game on which their hopes of promotion to the Premiership hung. Every time a nurse or a doctor passed his bed he'd enquire about the prospect of being discharged before the weekend. I was keeping my fingers crossed for him.

Opposite Gulliver was Donovan. He was in with

suspected kidney stones and had to piss into a bottle. The nurses would then take the bottle and sieve the urine for fragments of stone. He, like Gulliver, was in his forties and, as a knowledgeable Walsall fan, would converse endlessly with Gulliver about fixtures dating back to the 1970s.

So far Droppy, the swallower, was the only one who really gave me the jitters.

A guy who introduced himself as Nosferatu, but whose real name was Ryan, came to take a blood sample from me at about nine. He struggled to locate a vein.

'For someone who calls himself Nosferatu you're having a bit of trouble, aren't you?' I asked.

'Just be grateful that I'm a phlebotomist and not a doctor,' he said. 'Those idiots will rip your veins to shreds.'

'What's the difference?'

'I specialize in doing this so I get to practise it every day. The good news for you is I'm much better at it than they are.'

By this time he was on his sixth attempt.

'That's reassuring, Ryan,' I said, as my bodged and bruised vein finally relinquished a syringe full.

By the time he left I had four plasters on my arm, and I felt like a game of Kerplunk.

# Thieves Operate in this Hospital

At nine thirty it was time for my x-ray. As I was wheeled off the ward, the flyhole of my pyjamas kept riding open and it was a trial keeping it closed without looking like someone who enjoys being wheeled around with his hand on his prick (which, of course, I am). In the lift I was level with half a dozen crotches and arses. There's something uncomfortable about sitting when everyone else is standing.

Oddly, it reminded me of the time I was covering a Daniel O'Donnell concert for the *Reflector* and I remained seated during a standing ovation. Well, you know what a twat Daniel O'Donnell is? In the end, though, I felt so self-conscious that I stood up and clapped with everyone else. The only way I could justify giving Daniel O'Donnell a standing ovation, however, was to do it with irony. The vast quantity of lager I'd consumed before the show helped with this, as did the brandy I'd been sipping from my hip flask. I clapped my hands over-enthusiastically above my head and whooped and caterwauled with mock delight. Sadly, the crew who'd been filming the event for the *Daniel O'Donnell Live* video chose that moment to film a few crowd shots. Not only do I feature on the video as a fan apparently hysterical with love for the over-groomed Irish warbler, the bastards also used the still for the front of the video case. There I am wild-eyed and happy-clapping like a demented dervish. If I had a pound for every time a damp-gusseted old lady had approached me with the words, 'Excuse me, dear, haven't I seen you in a Daniel O'Donnell video?' I'd have fourteen pounds.

The porter left me in a queue outside the imaging department and I sat looking at the other sad Walsallites in need of attention. There were a couple of pensioners with skin transparent enough to read a paper through without the need of an x-ray. One was complaining to anyone who'd listen that a pendant bearing her name, Googie, had been swiped from her locker. If we had any valuables, she advised, we should nail them down. I wondered if that applied to her teeth because they too were missing. I felt sorry for her. Imagine ending up here: transparent and toothless in Walsall, gumming the story of your stolen name. 'Bit's bot beven bold,' she gummed, referring to the missing pendant. Which meant it was of value solely to someone called Googie and, let's face it, there can't be many. Only in Walsall would someone nick your name.

'It's a disgrace,' I said, expressing my solidarity with yet another crime-oppressed victim of my hometown.

'Babn't bi been bu bin ba Baniel Bo'Bonnell bideo?' gummed Googie.

That's fifteen pounds, I thought, glumly.

Next to Googie sat a large lady in leggings who was apparently in charge of a shaven-headed six-year-old with three studs in his left ear. His name was Armani-Dior. I knew this because every time he came over and gratuitously kicked the spokes of my wheelchair she would scream, 'Armani-Dior, fucking jack that in.' To which Armani-Dior would reply, 'Fuck off, yow fat fucker.'

In situations like this I find that it's often a good idea to feign sleep. I did so then, and pretended not to hear as Armani-Dior made a bogus 999 call on his mobile.

I must have succeeded in nodding off because, before I

knew it, it was ten thirty. Another set of grotesques had been installed in the waiting room and I was being wheeled into x-ray.

The x-rays themselves were quickly done and in two minutes I was wheeled out again. I then waited another half-hour for a porter to wheel me back to my ward. During this time I came close to a fight with a bloke who claimed he'd caught a cold in his kidneys.

'Is David McVane here?' said the porter.

'That's me,' I shouted, gratefully, as kidney-boy began to move towards me.

'Where am I taking you, Dave?'

'Vulture Ward, please.'

'Ah, you're going to the Lost Islands of Langerhans.'

'Sorry?'

'That's what people call the ward-bays in Vulture: the Lost Islands of Langerhans.'

'Any particular reason?'

'Probably; I don't know, though.'

We navigated our way around four or five trolley beds that lined the wall of the corridor. Each contained a patient, presumably waiting for a permanent bed to become free. I had the notion that they were secretly hoping someone would die. Themselves perhaps.

'Maybe they're not lost, maybe they were stolen,' I said, once we'd passed the infirmity slalom.

'Sorry?'

'The Islands of Langerhans. Maybe they were stolen.' I gestured to a large white and black sign on the wall. It said: THIEVES OPERATE IN THIS HOSPTIAL.

The porter chuckled. 'Let's hope they do a better job than the surgeons.'

When the porter deposited me back on the ward I decided to check on Tinker's progress. My rhino was beginning to stir again and I hoped the crackpot hospital jock might take my mind off it. He was playing the early Pulp number 'Death ii' when I joined him. He followed this with Garbage's 'The Trick is to Keep Breathing' and an obscure Lou Reed track, 'Harry's Circumcision'. He prefaced the latter with 'a big hello to everyone who'll be changing religion today'. Then, as promised, the Smiths: back-to-back he played 'Still Ill' and the frighteningly apposite, 'The Boy with the Thorn in His Side.'

I wasn't a boy, but I had a thorn.

# Enoch Lunt

'This is a book,' announced Dr Daniel Dunderdale, Head of English at the Walsall Academy for New Knowledge. He was holding a volume above his head and pointing to it as if we were partially sighted. 'A Bee Oh Oh Kay, book,' he said. 'You're going to be seeing a lot of these over the next three years.'

If you're thinking that this was his idea of a joke you'd only be half right. It *was* his idea of a joke – his sense of humour being hampered by a fondness for jokes that aren't funny. But he was also used to starting with the basics. You see the Walsall Academy for New Knowledge didn't attract the elite. He couldn't be certain the first-year under-graduates had seen many books. Unlike heads of English at bona fide universities he couldn't be sure his students knew what a metaphor was, or allegory, or assonance. In fact, he couldn't be 100 per cent certain they could take a shit without drowning themselves. This was the higher education establishment that students ended up at after the failure of every available A Level and/or following a botched NHS lobotomy.

It was the induction day for the class of 1986. Ringo and I were among the new cohort of students for the English BA course. Though I already had a year of higher education under my belt I was starting as a fresher and, like my new flatmate, I was full of anticipation. I was wearing a T-shirt that advertised the Housemartins' album, *London o Hull 4*; Ringo was wearing his Smiths' *Meat is Murder* shirt. He was also eating a packet of beef and onion crisps. At twenty Ringo was much closer to the age of the other students than me. I was only twenty-four but, among all the eighteen-year-olds, I was a trifle self-conscious in my status as mature student.

However, ability-wise, I had much more in common with the average WANK student than Ringo. Ringo was bright enough to be studying somewhere else. At school in Holland he'd been tipped for great things but had managed to cock up his final exams. This was owing to an illness that no Dutch doctor had been able to diagnose, but which Ringo referred to as 'diluvian skitter'. As a result of poor attendance he'd ended up with such pitiable qualifications that WANK had been one of only two colleges to offer him a place. The other was the University of Tampere deep in the heart of the Finnish Lake District. I believe he'd opted for WANK because of his morbid fear of frostbite.

The induction was in the Great Hall and the English staff team was lined up on the stage behind Dr Dunderdale, waiting to be introduced. At the time I was quite unaware of just what colossal gossip potential some of them would turn out to have.

One would be revealed as an impostor, not to mention a crazed fetishist.


It is said that WANK developed out of an institution founded by an eccentric Black Country industrialist, Enoch Lunt, in the nineteenth century. He believed it was possible for people – including the blighted working folk of Walsall – to improve themselves intellectually by following a simple programme of exercise, education and diet. Lunt picked up many of his ideas from Eastern mysticism and, his autobiography revealed, from his long philosophical conversations with his Auntie Susan. His pedagogical pontifications are collected in two privately published books, *Lunt: A Memoir* and *The Susan Dialogues*.

Lunt College went through various incarnations following Enoch's demise, but it remained an institution devoted to education. In the early 1970s there was talk of changing its name to something with a less embarrassing acronym but, despite many protracted meetings, the college executive couldn't come up with anything better. Later that decade WANK retained its name, and its distinct identity, despite being absorbed by one of the larger West Midlands polytechnics.

Surprisingly, WANK degrees are actually worth something. In the 1980s it became possible to get an excellent education in such minor colleges. The Tory government, convinced that higher education was plagued by repulsive lefties, set about bringing it to its knees. All over the country courses were axed and academics booted out of their jobs. Paradoxically, this had the effect of improving colleges such as WANK no end. Numerous gifted scholars found themselves fighting for employment in such institutions because there was nothing else on offer. In the 1970s all a lecturer at WANK needed was a box of chalk; in the 1980s posts were being sought by Oxbridge PhDs.

# One of them is a Sado-Masochist

On the day of our induction the question that pre-occupied both Ringo and me was: which one of our new lecturers had been spanking prossers in Penny's Punishment Palace?

I suspected our first suspect, Dr Daniel Dunderdale, least of all. From the little I'd seen of him so far, he seemed a nice bloke. In fact, he looked like a traditional academic, albeit a large, perpetually pissed-off one. That morning, for instance, he was wearing a corduroy jacket with chalk marks around the pocket. He sported a tie – I guess he had to because he was Head of School – but it was loose and knotted well beneath his unbuttoned collar. His baggy, dark green cords didn't really match the jacket at all, and his shoes, beige Hush Puppies, wouldn't match anything other than an identical pair of beige Hush Puppies. His lank fair hair wasn't exactly fashionable either; it looked like it'd been styled by a blind chimp with a Black & Decker. At best he could be described as dishevelled, at worst as a sack of shit. But he had a scholarly air; he gave the impression that he was a man who knew something, which is useful for a university lecturer.

'This is Dr Ebola Barker,' Dunderdale said, gesturing towards a woman in her late twenties. She had long, sleek black hair and the complexion of a not so recently deceased Goth. She was javelin thin, a fact thrown into painful relief by her decision to dress like Madonna: a black vest and a short black skirt above black tights. She had two giant wooden crucifixes around her neck, two large, dangly, crucifix earrings, and black lace gloves. She stood up from her chair when Dunderdale introduced her, waved a milk-white arm and revealed a shock of raven pit-hair. She looked as if she was making a statement, and that statement was: I'm stark, staring mad.

'Flaming Ada,' said Ringo, 'this lady needs some more dinners.'

I read in the subject guide that Ebola Barker taught a first-year course on French feminist theory titled, 'Post-structuralism and the Penis'.

She took the radio mike from Dunderdale. As she stood up, you could see slices of her alabaster legs through the deliberate tears in her tights. 'Hello,' she said, in a quiet voice, 'welcome. I look forward to sharing some ideas with you.'

A couple of the female students clapped.

I would later learn that Ebola's parents had been ultra-bohemian intellectuals who came across the word Ebola while backpacking around Africa in the 1950s. They seized upon it as the ideal name for their newly arrived daughter who they were transporting around in a yak-skin papoose. That the name would become synonymous with a deadly tropical disease suggests that, if you're desperate to avoid the mundane, it's wise to do a little research first.

A desperation to avoid the mundane was something Ebola inherited along with her name. The Madonna gear she wore for the induction, for instance, would never be seen again. I don't think I ever saw her in the same style outfit twice. One day she'd wear camouflage trousers, the next an Indian-print dress. One day she'd be bondage punk, the next executive power chick. She'd walk into the toilet dressed as a biker and emerge sporting a sari. She must've had a wardrobe the size of the NEC. The only thing that didn't change was her hair – long and straight like a fantasy witch's wig. It's difficult to say what effect she was seeking. I once heard her claim that her changing appearance was owing to a refusal to be 'contained by patriarchal definitions of femininity'. Ebola stared out at us, still holding the mike, and the room fell silent. Dunderdale waited for her to say some more but she didn't; she just blinked her eyes hard and frequently. This is something else I remember about Ebola. She was one of those people who blink too often, screwing their eyes up as tight as asterisks. I imagined her being tormented by some inner demon who spent his days stroking her optic nerve with a nettle.

Ebola continued blinking until Dunderdale cleared his throat loud enough to grab her attention. 'Anything else to add, Dr Barker?'

She shook her head and handed the mike back to him. He turned to the next academic in line. This woman looked to be in her early sixties. She was dressed in a knitted woollen twinset and was wearing a knitted woollen hat. As Dunderdale spoke she was knitting. 'Dr Winifred Wiggins is our early English specialist,' he announced.

In the subject guide I saw that she taught a course called, 'Restrictive and Non-restrictive Postmodification in the Medieval Love Lyric'.

'I was wondering,' said Ringo, when I pointed this out to him, 'if that's what you English call double Dutch?'

'Dr Wiggins, would you like to say a few words?' said Dunderdale.

Winifred Wiggins took her time. She counted the stitches along her needle twice before taking the mike.

'Studying Old English grammar is an art, not a science,' she said, then returned the mike to Dunderdale and continued knitting.

'Er, thank you, Winnie.' Dunderdale glanced at the next member of his department and seemed to wilt slightly. His tall frame stooped and his expression changed from pissed off and world-weary to merely pissed off. 'And now I'd like to introduce you to Dr Marmaduke Peabody.'

Dr Peabody didn't get out of his chair. He lifted his right arm half-heartedly and spoke a barely audible, 'Yeah. Hi.'

Marmaduke Peabody was a Cambridge double-first who'd just finished his PhD. He was clearly fucked off to find himself at WANK. Had he gained his doctorate five years earlier he could have expected a juicy lectureship at some prestigious redbrick university. There he'd have enjoyed numerous long sabbaticals on which to pursue his esoteric research. Whereas, at WANK, the college authorities barely knew how to spell sabbatical. Mrs Thatcher had certainly been bad news for Dr Peabody, which almost redeemed her in my eyes. His specialist subjects were working-class culture, and the African experience in art: two things about which he knew everything and nothing.

Even before his perfunctory wave it was clear he'd rather be sticking hatpins in his knackers than teaching at WANK. Throughout the proceedings he sat side-on to the students and kept yawning ostentatiously.

The subject guide said Peabody taught a course called, '*J'Accuse* Bill Cosby: the Negative Aspects of Positive Stereotyping in post-*Shaft* Popular Culture'.

'Can you imagine him at Penny's?' I asked Ringo.

'I think being here is torture enough for Dr Peabody,' he replied.

The next academic in this line-up was much more enthusiastic. He was already on his feet when Dunderdale turned to introduce him. He was wearing faded 501s and a Breton shirt. Standing about six foot two, he had blond hair and a strong, square jaw bristling with golden stubble.

'This is Dr Ruud Van Door,' said Dunderdale. 'He is our

American Literature man, visiting us from the University of Utrecht. He is only here for one term so you won't find him listed in the subject guide. However, I can tell you that one of his courses will be available to first-year students and that is, 'Never Too Tight to Write: Alcohol and the American Novel'.

'Ace-a-mundo,' said Ringo, jotting down the course title. 'That sounds right up my road.' I think he was drawn to the fact that Ruud was a fellow Dutchman.

'Hello everybody, it is nice to be here in Walsall.' Van Door had even less of a Dutch accent than Ringo and clearly hadn't been in Walsall very long; he lacked the jaded, cynical air of a local.

'Is he our man?' I asked.

'Doubtful,' Ringo replied. 'We Dutch seldom need to resort to brothels. The ones we have mainly cater for English tourists. Besides, do you know what you can catch from those places?' He went on to list a dozen or so infections, most of them in Latin.

Certainly it was difficult to imagine Van Door in a brothel. He looked a bit like Dolph Lundgren, star of the latest *Rocky* movie. Lundgren played the Russian baddy in the black shorts. Sylvester Stallone, of course, played Rocky: the American goody in the white shorts. I remember smuggling a bottle of vodka into the cinema beneath a T-shirt which read WIN ROCKY WIN. This is the kind of thing working-class men with average IQs do, in case you're wondering. We watch *Rocky* films and enjoy them – more so if we're wearing the T-shirt. I was hoping my studies at WANK would broaden my cultural horizons.

Dr Daniel Dunderdale continued down the line of staff introducing the remaining three one by one: Dr Steven Twist, a specialist in narrative poetics; Dr Barry Byetheway who taught Dickens and nineteenth-century literature; and, last but not least, Dr Prunella Fabb whose field was pornography and the novel. She looked a bit like Gabriella Sabatini, and Ringo feverishly noted down the title of her specialist course, 'Orgasm as Metaphor in Post-feminist Literature'.

We both agreed that Barry Byetheway was unlikely to be hanging around brothels. He was exceptionally well groomed for an academic, and gave the impression that he was a man of confidence and good sense. Steve Twist was a different proposition. He looked like the kind of chap who offers unsolicited flattery to farmyard animals. In short, a fat ugly loser. He wore a maroon tank top over a wide, round-collared shirt together with a pair of dark blue baggy jeans. From a distance they appeared to be Tesco's own brand. His longish, lank hair looked to have been pissed over by someone drunk on swine fat. Twist was one those plump, sweaty people who are anal and obsessive about something tedious. Trains, say, or beer-mats. Or narrative poetics.

'Ringo, my new Dutch chum,' I said, 'I think we have our boy.'

Later that afternoon we met Monica in the union bar. She was having a heated argument with a bunch of Business Studies types about the possibility of privatizing the Health Service. Thatcherites to a man, most wore suits and carried executive document cases, despite having an average age of nineteen. A couple sported George Michael haircuts complete with blond streaks. They couldn't see why they should pay National Insurance contributions and subscribe to private healthcare at the same time.

'You don't pay National Insurance contributions: you're fucking students,' said Monica. You know when Monica's getting mad because she starts swearing. Ringo and I had arrived just in time. Another two minutes and these young Conservatives would have witnessed the shortcomings of the NHS first-hand. There was thirteen stone behind Monica's punches.

'And you try getting private healthcare insurance if you're ill!' she shouted, as we tactfully guided her away. After a few snorts in her direction the Conservatives' talk turned to the investment opportunities afforded by the planned privatization of BP.

'Our brothel man is Dr Steven Twist, senior lecturer in narrative poetics,' I informed Monica. I knew a bit of meaty gossip would get her mind off the Tory tossers.

'How do you know?'

'He's fat and sweaty,' I said.

'Ah.'

'And ugly, and badly dressed,' I added.

'Well, that clinches it,' said Monica.

'I've told him he shouldn't buy into the conflation of morality and aesthetics perpetuated by the image-dominated pop culture industry,' said Ringo, who'd clearly been doing some advanced reading of our set texts.

'Yow wot?' I said.


We continued our discussion throughout the afternoon. While I sank lagers at a rate of five an hour, and the juke-box worked through Echo and the Bunnymen, Spear of Destiny and Billy Bragg, we considered how we might establish the identity of our man and use our knowledge to our advantage.

'We could make an arrangement with Dionne,' I said. 'Next time he shows up she could bang on the ceiling and we could burst in with a camera. Snap them in the act.'

'A capital idea,' said Ringo, trying out a phrase I think he'd heard David Niven use in *Casino Royale*. 'The photos would be quite a scoop for the student paper.' Ringo already had his eye on working for *Red Sox*, the WANK journal produced by the students' union.

'We'll only publish them if doesn't give us what we want,' I suggested, encouraged by Ringo's apparent enthusiasm.

'Which is what?'

'Top grades of course; get with the programme, Dutchboy. Photography might be risky though – Penny wouldn't like it, that's for sure.'

'Why don't you make a tape-recording, Dave?' said Monica, giving Ringo a sly nudge and wink. 'You could hide a cassette recorder in the room and make an incriminating record of his unsavoury demands.'

'Brilliant,' I said, 'and there'd be less chance of Penny finding out. A tape-recording isn't like a photograph; it's something that Dionne could take care of herself. We could give her a few quid to fix up a Dictaphone somewhere. No one would be any the wiser. Remember that Penny said he talks a lot; he likes to be called doctor.'

The booze was beginning to bring my IQ down. I'd been in double figures for a while and now I was just hovering between moron and cretin. And I was doing all the talking. 'You can get voice-activated Dictaphones that only record when there's something to record. All we'd need is some Blu-Tack and . . .'

I noticed the two of them staring at me with the kind of exaggerated, fixed smiles that imply you've snapped your cap. 'What?'

'You're serious, aren't you?'

'Aren't you?'

Monica shook her head. 'Er . . . no, Dave.'

'Ringo?'

Ringo chuckled. 'You have an ambitious imagination.'

'I think reckless is the word you're looking for,' said Monica.

'But just imagine if we could –'

Monica put her hand to her eyes and shook her head in her familiar gesture; her closed-lipped smile seemed to say:

this guy's a tit, and he's not always *that* funny. 'Dave,' she said, 'sober up, please.'

I just shrugged, deciding not to argue. I didn't want to spoil what till then had been a nice afternoon. But I wasn't sure where I was going wrong. They *were* good ideas. Weren't they?

# Kiss Me Softly, Amy Turtle

The session came to an end when Monica, after forcing two coffees down me, left for the library. As soon as she'd gone I was all for hitting the sauce again but Ringo persuaded me to call it a day and we split for home.

When we arrived at number 47, Penny collared us in the hall. 'Dave McVane, just the man,' she said. 'That fucking bollock-throttle you flogged us is killing one of our punters.'

Despite the coffee I wasn't completely sober. 'What?'

'That fucking thing with the wire noose that fits around bollock-bags,' she said, pulling me into the first-floor flat. Ringo followed. She led us directly into one of the torture rooms. I'd been in there many times in my role as fetish gear supplier, but it must've been an interesting introduction to the world of s&m for Ringo.

Of the five bedrooms at Penny's disposal three were dungeons, one was a general fantasy and vanilla room, and one a 'white room', used for medical scenes. The room we were in now was Penny's main dungeon. Well-equipped to the point of over-crowding, it contained a set of stocks, a whipping horse and a kennel. It also housed a full-size crucifix and a Saint Andrew's Cross, both of which had been made from railway sleepers. The walls were lined with torture implements hanging side by side like kitchen utensils; indeed, some of them *were* kitchen utensils. And there were whips of every variety, mostly made by me: cats, crops, paddles, tawses. These hung alongside fearsome coshes and truncheons that varied in length like organ pipes. Every type of cane was represented too: school master's canes with the U-shaped handles, straight-handled domestic canes, two-tongued, split-ended switches and, for the very naughty, ultra-thick malaccas.

'Kiss me softly, Amy Turtle!' screamed a naked pink gentleman. *'Kiss me softly, Amy Turtle!'* He was lying face down on a long trestle table with his arms and legs supported by two girls: Wanda-Jane and Fanny Batter. It took me a while to recognize them because Wanda was dressed as a traffic warden and Fanny as Maggie Thatcher.

One of the most important items in each of Penny's fantasy rooms was the poster-sized sign that bore the words:

ESCAPE PHRASES:
GENTLY, GENTLY, AMY TURTLE
KISS ME SOFTLY, AMY TURTLE

In fantasy role-play and S&M it's a good idea to have safe signals and safe phrases that participants know can terminate the scene.

You can't use ordinary words – 'Mercy!' or 'God no, not the video of William Shatner!' – because submissives like to employ conventional begging terms in their games. It's Penny's contention that it's best not to use short or mundane phrases because these can easily find their way into the elaborate scenarios her girls often construct with punters. A good escape phrase needs to be something incongruous and/or bizarre that won't be misinterpreted: 'Cover my toes in damson jam' perhaps; or, 'My doughnut's name is Geoff.' It's said that at one time the safe phrase at Penny's was the relatively apposite, 'Time for the cotton swabs, Mother.' This had been scrapped, though, because it occasionally became confusing during certain advanced infantalization scenarios. For a number of years Penny has had two safe phrases that she calls her Amy Turtles: 'Gently, gently, Amy Turtle' is used by submissives who want to continue their fun but with less force; 'Kiss me softly, Amy Turtle' is used by participants who want out of a scene – to go to the bathroom say, or, more usually, because they think they're about to die.

The origins of the phrase are connected to Penny being a fervent *Crossroads* fan and founder member of the unofficial Amy Turtle fan club. The character Amy Turtle, played by Ann George, was a gossipy cleaner at the Cross-roads Motel in the 1960s. Ann, a graduate of the Wooden Plank Academy of Dramatic Art, could have been replaced by a garden gnome, but diehard fans adored her. Penny's enthusiasm for the thespian skills of Ms George shows that she wasn't above indulging in her own form of masochism.

It isn't always possible to use escape phrases, of course. If a participant can't speak – because they are gagged, mummified or smothered – three sharp taps have the same meaning. Not all punters approved of the big show Penny made of her safe signals. For some, knowing there's a way out detracts from their pleasure. But Penny insisted on having them clearly advertised, not just for safety, but for ethical and legal reasons too. She felt that giving partici-pants a simple way of withdrawing consent was more likely to keep her on the right side of the law.

'Kiss me softly, Amy Turtle!' yelled the naked guy. '*Kiss me softly, Amy Turtle!*'

'We can't get it off him,' said Fanny, her pearls swinging and her blond wig slightly askew. Her matching powder-blue jacket and skirt barely contained her bulk. Though she'd kicked off her stilettos, she still stood an impressive six foot one.

The punter was wearing a device of my own construction called a bollock-boa. It had been a special order and I'd based the design on illustrations supplied by the punter himself, via Penny. Apparently his imagination was fired by a medieval torture device he'd seen in Hector McTaggart's *The Savage History of Man*. I'd interpreted his sketches pretty literally and constructed a very nasty object in the process. The bollock-boa consists of tethers attached to the wrists and ankles which are linked – via several knots and a roller-buckle mechanism – to a testicle noose. It forces the wearer, while lying face down, to keep their arms and legs bent backwards. If they relax, or their limbs slip, the scrotum gets throttled.

'We've tried cutting it off but it's no use,' said Wanda, 'the scissors just won't go through the straps!' I could see slices in the leather where they'd cut ineffectually at the surface, and I noticed the scissors themselves buckled and discarded on the floor.

'They won't cut because the leather tethers are plaited around a wire core,' I said, 'but it should just be a matter of pulling at this knot.' I inspected where the tethers and the testicle noose had been fixed together just above the punter's arse. Even in my intoxicated state I was conscious of the heat of his body – it was like approaching a radiator. His skin glistened with sweat and was scented with fragrance clearly identifiable as *eau de panic*.

'Your breath stinks of booze by the way,' said Fanny. 'Want a Tic-Tac?'

'Cheers, Fanny,' I said.

As she reached for her handbag she let the punter's arms drop slightly and the noose tightened.

'*Naaaaa*,' said the punter as he desperately tried to close the distance between his hands and his ankles. Only a twelve-year-old gymnast could have successfully achieved the position he strived for.

'Sorry, love,' said Fanny, and she clicked a couple of mints into my palm.

'You see, the problem you've got here is that you haven't used a slipped sheetbend,' I told her.

'Come again?'

'Slipped sheetbend: it's a type of knot that comes apart with a single pull – it tells you how to tie one in the instructions I gave you with the boa.'

'I never saw any instructions,' said Fanny.

'Nor me,' said Wanda, who then shouted into the living room to where Penny was manning the phone: 'Penny, Dave says there should've been instructions with this bollock-boa!'

'Pleeeeeaase,' said the punter, '*pleeeeeaase.*' His eyes were bulging and his teeth were bared; his skin, meanwhile, was stretched tightly over his face as if by G. force. In his bowed position he looked like a skydiver.

'I've not seen any fucking instructions!' Penny shouted.

'What you've done,' I told them, 'is used a water knot. That's the last type you want to use on a device like this.' I burped a cloud of minty lager fumes into the room. 'Sorry,' I said, wafting.

Penny, having finished on the phone, came trotting into the torture room. 'I thought you said that sheetbends are noose knots, like the one that goes around his bollocks.' Penny liked to learn the technical names for the various knots and ties bondage devices employed.

'No no no,' I said. 'A sheetbend is an easy-release knot; the one around his bollocks is a prussick knot.'

The punter whimpered.

'Right; now I remember,' said Penny. She examined the scrotum noose. 'It's just that I keep getting the prussick mixed up with the fisherman's loop.'

'They're exact opposites,' I said. 'If he had a fisherman's loop round his bollocks we wouldn't have a problem: the loop stays fixed no matter how hard you pull on it. In that respect it's similar to a bowline knot.'

'*Kiss me softly, Amy Turtle! Kiss me softly, Amy Turtle!*' wailed the punter. He was flinging his head from side to side, screaming over one shoulder and then the other. As he moved, beads of perspiration flew from his hair.

'OK, OK,' I said. I began manipulating the knot, trying to ease some slack into it. But it was no use: its twists and loops were locked tight.

'Wouldn't it be simpler if you rolled him on his side?' said Ringo.

'Good thinking,' I said, wondering why it hadn't occurred to me. It was much easier to keep the noose slack with the punter on his side – Wanda and Fanny still had to hold his arms and legs back, but it was less of a struggle.

I wouldn't go as far as to say the punter breathed a sigh of relief but his panicky gasps became less urgent. His testicles were bulbous and purple, though, like an over-inflated pig's bladder. They were so swollen the skin was practically transparent and lined with thin, snaking blue veins. The punter's cock seemed tragically miniscule in comparison: a button mushroom sitting on a Space Hopper.

Then I had an idea. I took out my Ronson and began to warm the knot with a flame. I figured that, if I heated it, the wire core would expand and loosen the knot. I worked the straps between my thumb and forefinger as I carefully applied the heat.

'Dave, look at this,' said Ringo, who'd been mooching around on a nearby tabletop. It was cluttered with items including dildos, butt plugs, poppers, cock-torture clamps and a half-eaten packet of Hobnobs. He was holding a book.

'What's that?'

'You're not going to believe it, it's *An Introduction to Literary Studies* by Pinkerton McBride.'

'Fuck me!'

'I wonder if it's the property of our WANK professor?'

'Who else could it be? Has it got a name in it?'

'Hang on, I'll check . . .' Ringo flipped to the flyleaf. 'Nope.'

'Dave, watch the flame,' said Fanny.

'*Naaaaaaaaaaaaaaaaaa,*' cried the punter.

The bollock-boa was on fire. Distracted, I'd let the lighter stray too close to the leather. The strapping had been greased with tallow to keep it supple and now the animal fat was cracking and popping with a fierce heat. The flame blazed large and orange around the knot and a stream of carbon-thick smoke spiralled to the ceiling. Unfortunately for the punter the wire was exposed in the loop around his bollocks. In a matter of seconds his scrotum was smoking with conducted heat and the sickening whiff of singeing skin combined with the pungent aroma of burning leather. Instinctively he went to grab his balls with his hands and the noose savagely cheese-wired his knackers. He came and went, as they say, simultaneously.

The good thing about accidents in S&M dungeons is that, when they happen, punters seldom complain. There'd been a few mishaps at Penny's but, as yet, none had landed her in trouble. There were whispers that the RSPCA *did* once threaten to take action when they heard that a gerbil had had a hypoxic fit up someone's arse. The doctor who removed the rodent reported the incident, but the punter was tight-lipped and they couldn't pin anything on Penny. Punters are always tight-lipped.

We managed to free the bollock-boa casualty before he regained consciousness and, when he eventually came round, he was so glad to be alive that he barely offered a murmur of complaint. He merely vomited and uttered something about Jesus. We helped him into a taxi with a towel around his balls and he was taken to hospital. The guy hadn't been castrated, but his scrotum was badly cut and he'd need stitches.

'Sorry, Penny,' I said, after a state of relative calm had been restored.

'Relax, Dave. No hard feelings,' she said. 'We should've charged the fucker a few extra quid for that carry-on.'

She made Ringo and me a cuppa and we chatted while she took calls. Naturally, we asked her about the Pinkerton McBride book.

'Fuck knows,' she said, poking at her left nostril with her little finger. 'I found it in the fantasy room a couple of days ago. I used the bag it came in to bury one of the arse-gerbils. Hudson's, I think.'

'So, it's a new book,' mused Ringo.

'Significant?' I asked him.

'Maybe . . .' he said, but then we were distracted by the entrance of Mercedes Crunch, emerging from the second dungeon with a man on a wrist-lead. Mercedes Crunch – or Mistress Crunch – was a genuine dominatrix, one of the few working for Penny. Most of Penny's girls were prostitutes who didn't mind doing weird stuff, but it would've been unwise to call Mercedes a prostitute – not unless you crave body modification of the most debilitating kind. Like many true doms, she didn't have actual *sex* with her clients: her sole role was to dominate and control them.

The man on the wrist-lead was having trouble crossing the room because he was wearing a hobble skirt. Also, he couldn't see where he was going because he had a toilet on his head. This contraption, known as a toilet box, is quite common in S&M. They're generally made of plastic or wood and they fit on a submissive's shoulders; the dom then positions herself on the box and delivers her load. Mercedes was taking her sub to the bathroom because Penny wouldn't allow water or hard sports in the dungeons.

Out of respect for the punter we killed our conversation as they passed through the living room. We didn't get a chance to resume it because, as soon as the bathroom door closed, the phone rang.

'Penny's,' said Penny, transferring a bogey from her little finger to the heel of her shoe. 'How can I help you?'

Penny always seemed to know instinctively when to be cagey with callers and when she could open up and list in full the Palace's delights. This time she was apparently conversing with an aficionado.

'We employ doms, submissives and switches,' she said, 'and our BDSM and fantasy services include abrasion, age play (including infantalization), animal training (we have cages and kennels), asphyxiation, bastinade, bondage, branding, candle play, cock and ball torture, corporal punishment (all schoolroom fantasies catered for), costumes and uniforms (with a special line in celebrities and dictators), crucifixion (nail-free only), electro-torture –' Penny placed her hand over the mouthpiece, tromboned a protracted belch into the air, then resumed '– enema, fisting, foot fetish, force-feeding, hard sports, humiliation, mummification, rack, rodent play (hamsters only for the time being), rubber (total coverage garments available), suspension, urethra play (including catheterization), and water sports of every variety. We have a white room for clinical scenes, but we no longer offer invasive surgical procedures. On Fridays and Saturdays we have vanilla specialists who offer full personal, O and A levels, CIM, facials and rimming.'

Penny stopped for a moment and a look of disgust clouded her face. 'No, sir, I don't think we have any girls who will perform *that* service.' And she put the phone down sharply, shuddering as if she'd swallowed a slug. Ringo and I were on the edge of our seats.

'Fucking hell,' I demanded. 'What did he ask for?'

'I can't bring myself to say,' said Penny, jamming her little finger knuckle-deep into her right nostril. 'Some of these freaks really are repulsive.'

Later, upstairs, Ringo and I reflected on events as the evening darkened and *EastEnders* cockneyed away in the background.

'I must say,' said Ringo, 'I didn't realize it would be quite *this* exciting living here.' He'd hidden it well, but I think he'd been a bit shaken by the scenes in Penny's. 'Her clients' desires certainly have me puzzled,' he added.

'When it comes to the Palace, Ringo, it's best not to try and understand them. It's like trying to fathom the point of Andrew Ridgely – you're onto a loser. But don't let today give you the wrong impression. It's not always so eventful here. This place is usually as fucking tedious as the rest of Walsall.' I took a listless drag on my fag and lazily fired a smoke ring at the lightshade. I was almost sober now and beginning to get bored.

Ringo nodded thoughtfully.

'Mind you,' I said, trying to cheer myself with scandal, 'things *do* seem to be improving. The book you found in Penny's puts even more jam in the "call me doctor" doughnut.'

'Doughnuts?'

'Forget it. *Do* you think it belongs to our WANK man?'

Ringo thought for a moment while, on the telly, Arthur Fowler and Pete Beale exchanged chirpy banter. 'It's just strange that the book was an elementary introduction – don't you think it's funny that an academic should buy a basic student text?'

'So does that rule out our "call me doctor"?' I asked, skilfully fish-mouthing another smoke ring.

'It needn't, but . . . I don't know, I suppose it could . . .'

'Well, be sure to stay on the case, Sherlock.'

'Do you mean Sherlock Holmes?'

'No, I mean Sherlock with the corkscrew cock,' I said, improvising.

'Who?'

Was he taking the piss? Either way, I couldn't be arsed to challenge him. I'd been hit, as I often am, by a sense of the pointlessness of life. It's not just driving past the Welcome to Walsall sign that does this. It often happens after I've been high with drink, as I was lunchtime, or adrenalin, as I was in Penny's. I come down hard, gripped by boredom and a crushing sense of futility. On such occasions my landscape becomes featureless in every direction. North, south, east, west, up and down: there's no heaven or hell, just more of the same bleakness. The solution? Open another can and kiss my paps goodbye.

'Time for a lager,' I said. 'The library doesn't shut till nine so I should be able to shift a six-pack before Monica gets home.'

'In an hour and a quarter?'

'Every man needs a challenge.'

'Fill your boots, my san!' cried Ringo.

I switched off *EastEnders* on my way to the fridge. It was for his own good.

# Pancreatitis

My rhino interrupted my appreciation of the *Tinker Lawson Show*. It started by nosing gently at my ribcage; now it was dashing its head against it like some heavy-metal rhino loopy on Twisted Sister. Trust me to be harbouring a bad-taste rhino. I was reluctant to buzz for the nurse, though, because I didn't want to be a whiner like Deekus. I was about to buckle when the registrar, Dr Fostus, reappeared.

'Well, Mr McVane, we have the results of your blood tests.'

'And did you find anything significant?' I asked, aware of Droppy Collins in the next bed straining to listen in.

'Mr McVane, your pain is undoubtedly caused by pancreatitis.'

I hadn't a clue what pancreatitis was, but I was oddly relieved to have my rhino labelled. I'd been fully reconciled to the thought that they wouldn't be able to find anything wrong with me. I imagined being subjected to all manner of dignity-sapping tests only to be discharged with the medical equivalent of: 'We're completely fucking clueless.' I'd heard that this is what very often happens with abdominal pains; they're notoriously difficult to diagnose. Doubly so, I would have thought, in Walsall's Wesley-in-Tame. You could walk into Casualty with a fluorescent pogo stick up your arse and they'd still ask, 'What seems to be the problem, sir?' So I was pleased that they'd diagnosed *my* little problem.

Unfortunately, however, it wasn't a little problem at all as I realized when Fostus began to explain pancreatitis and its potential consequences.

'I don't want to worry you,' said Dr Fostus, his voice sounding strangely like Boris Karloff's, 'but one in five people with severe pancreatitis don't recover from the condition.'

'By "don't recover" you mean they die?'

Fostus nodded, grimly.

'Is my pancreatitis severe?'

Fostus nodded, grimly again.

'OK, you've worried me,' I said.

'Well, I didn't want to.'

Yes you did, you bastard, I thought. He'd probably heard that I was a *Reflector* journalist and was seeking revenge for one of our derogatory stories; possibly our Sack the Wesley Quacks campaign. When will these people learn to take it on the chin?

'What is pancreatitis anyhow?' I asked.

Fostus answered slowly, enunciating his words in a clear and deliberate manner. 'Your pancreas,' he said, 'is a very important gland. It produces insulin, which regulates your blood sugar levels, and it produces enzymes that help your digestion. When it's working normally the pancreas secretes its enzymes into your stomach through a valve called the Sphincter of Oddy; when the pancreas is inflamed, as yours is, the flow of those enzymes is inhibited.'

Fostus's voice was monotone and ponderous, and his narrative peppered with the kind of superfluous detail that could only interest a real pancreas enthusiast. If he hadn't been discussing my personal pancreas, my personal Sphincter of Oddy, I would have fallen asleep with tedium. But he was, and I hung on his every word.

'And what happens when "the flow of those enzymes is inhibited"?'

'Then, Mr McVane, your pancreas begins to digest itself.'

'I'm guessing that's bad?'

Fostus nodded, even more grimly. 'I'm afraid so. You are very ill, Mr McVane. It surprises me, in fact, that you can converse with me as readily as you are; many people with severe pancreatitis become incoherent. Several go into shock.'

'Actually my pain is back, doctor,' I said, whining. That was something of an understatement. My heavy-metal rhino had become a faster-paced, thrash-metal rhino and was on the verge of developing into a pogoing, punk-rock rhino with a taste for displays of unspeakable gore.

The quack gave me another painkilling injection and then filled me in on what Wesley-in-Tame had in store for me by way of treatment.

'It is imperative that we rest your pancreas,' he said, 'which means that you can have nothing to eat and you will be drip-fed from now on. I will allow you thirty millilitres of water an hour to keep your mouth moist, but no more. We will monitor your blood sugars every four hours and we will also need to measure the amount of fluid you emit by means of a catheter.'

'A catheter? Do you mean to tell me you have to stick a tube up the end of my cock?'

'I'm afraid so.'

'You lying bastard,' I said.

'Pardon me?'

'You lying bastard. I don't need a catheter. It's just because I work for the *Walsall Reflector* and write those uncomplimentary articles about this bloody dump of a hospital. You're getting your own back, aren't you, you spineless sawbones?'

'Oh, that's you, is it?'

'I work for the public good,' I said.

'So do I, Mr McVane, and in this instance I'm working for *your* good. A catheter is essential and a catheter you shall have.'

I tried to faint, but reality wouldn't let me off the hook.

# Facts is Facts

Wesley-in-Tame Hospital got its name because it occupies a site close to where the founder of Methodism, John Wesley, had his head kicked in. A bunch of Walsall roughnecks had wanted to chuck him in the River Tame. It was the eighteenth century and John Wesley was spreading his Good News around the Black Country. He should have known better than to come to Walsall. The hospital's name is a misnomer, though, because he never in fact made it *into* the Tame. The roughnecks only threatened to throw him in if he didn't fuck off. The story goes that Wesley promptly agreed to do exactly that and, as a result, the Walsall thugs contented themselves with giving him a good kicking. That's what you get for preaching the doctrine of rectitude and sobriety in Walsall.

All this I'd learned when I'd glanced briefly at a history of Wesley-in-Tame for my *Reflector* articles. As I say, the hospital featured regularly in my Facts is Facts column. The people of Walsall loved to hear about its short-comings, and I'd supply them with all the biting criticism they desired. I'd been writing this column ever since I joined the *Reflector* in 1989. Even though I was no longer a reporter, having been 'promoted' to sub-editor, I continued to produce my weekly Facts is Facts. It was my chance to comment on some aspect of local news or Walsall life. But don't let the phrase 'Facts is Facts' fool you. The emphasis was on controversy and comedy. I'm pretty good at being controversial and comic, particularly when I'm off my paps.

Like most people who write comment columns I'm a mouthy twat, but unlike most, I refuse to toe any political line. Thus I can be leftwing, as in my piece about the community charge ('Why it's OK to Fleece Walsall Fat Cats'), and I can be rightwing, as in my pro-firearms piece ('Nothing Says Hello Like a Handgun'). I spoke out against poverty, but I hated benefit scroungers; I spoke out against racism, but was suspicious of the Welsh; I spoke out against pollution, but I'd piss in the sink; I spoke out against fox hunting, but I loathed vegetarians; I spoke out against sexism, but owned ninety-two porn films. And so on. In other words, I had no ideological axe to grind; I just enjoyed getting on people's tits as much as I enjoyed getting off my own.

You might be wondering why people read Facts is Facts, and the only reason I can think of is that Walsall folk are as dumb and antisocial as me. Mind you, after twelve or so years writing the column I should have lost just about every one of my readers. For instance, I'd probably alienated half my audience with my mock obituary celebrating Enoch Powell's death; then alienated the other half by saying, 'Let's hope Arthur Scargill's next.'

Most often I'd just go ahead and alienate everyone. I'd slag off Walsall people just for the sheer fun of it. Over the years I'd referred to them as: the white socks and leggings brigade; the trainers with suits brigade; the sovereign rings are great brigade; the extra lard please brigade; the furry dice brigade; the furry palms brigade; the poodle perm brigade; the bingo wings brigade; the slack bottom lip brigade; the my grandma's twenty-six brigade; the family tree's a stump brigade; my sister is my mom brigade; the crew-cuts for the kids brigade; the my metabolism's slow brigade; etc, etc, etc. Amazingly, Walsall folk just lap it up. For me it was great to vent my own obsessions, not to mention my love of sleaze and gossip. I'd fuelled numerous local rumours, conspiracies and scandals and insulted just about every resident of the town that I loved to hate. The geography teacher who was caught asking nineteen-year-old Pinky Skinner for directions at two a.m. in Caldmore (was he *really* lost?); the bird-watcher who fell off the gym roof at Queen Mary's High School for Girls (had he *really* spotted a rare Penduline Tit?); the Goscote dwarves love-for-sale shocker (weren't they *really* just small people misrepresenting themselves for novelty sex?); the karaoke king's Junior Asprin overdose (had he faked his own death for a record deal?). All of these I wildly exaggerated for effect, of course, but most had a basis in reality. Or at least some did.

Facts is Facts is where I started our Sack the Wesley Quacks campaign. This was my response to the fact that Wesley-in-Tame invariably came bottom of government hospital league tables, most significantly the one relating to patient mortality rates. Just a week before my admission *Reflector* readers called for an independent inquiry into the peculiarly high numbers of deaths at Wesley.

My last Facts is Facts piece opened:

It is harder to become a vet than a doctor, I'm told. Thank Christ. I would hate to think of my innocent pet gerbil, Pipsy, at the mercy of the incompetent croakers currently employed by the NHS.

I then went on for about five hundred words listing the many atrocities and gripes *Reflector* readers had recently brought to my attention. There's the patient who allegedly came round after an operation to find that a game of noughts and crosses had been played on his arse-cheek;

another who, after a post-surgery shit, spotted a double-headed Belgian franc in his faeces. And I ended the column with:

And so I implore the good folk of the Borough to write to the Medical Council and demand a formal inquiry. My name is Dave Ichabod McVane and, whatever they tell you, FACTS IS FACTS.

I always closed with that sentence. My column, indeed all of my journalism, could best be described as badly written bollocks, but it's generally penned when I'm shitfaced. And, as I say, I've never relied too heavily on the facts either. Facts generally turn out to be tedious and have a habit of anchoring your story in the mundane. I was equally dismissive of that related term, 'truth'. One person's truth is another person's offensive bilge. Thus I took pride in generating both adoration and vitriol in equal measure, often from the same person. A reader might call me the champion of the ordinary man one week and accuse me of hysterical, ill-informed shite-spurting the next. I loved that: I knew then that I was treading that admirable line between offensive and offensive. This was my gift to my fellow townsfolk. Why? Because they didn't deserve any better. They were gullible, bigoted, boring and, above all, average. My column was an insult to the intelligence its readers didn't have.

# Thank you, Cyndi

From the corner of my eye I noticed Droppy Collins set down his copy of the *Black Country Bugle*. He turned onto his side so that he was facing me, head propped on the heel of his hand. This ominous posture suggested that he might want a conversation. I tried to remember what my mother told me about not murdering people.

'Pancreatitis, eh?' said Droppy. 'That's very nasty, yow know.'

'Do tell,' I said. As you'll appreciate, I was feeling a little irritable. I was beginning to sense I needed a drink – not so much the taste of one, that would have made me vomit. Rather, I needed the hit of one, the kick of one, the slobbering juicy kiss of one. A double brandy would perform fellatio on my brain stem.

'Yow'll 'ave to 'ave a catheter, yow know that, doh yow? That'll smart.'

'They've informed me of that particular requirement, Droppy, yes.'

'They'll come and stick a paracetamol suppository up yower arse fust, though.'

'Christ!'

'Yow'll be glad on it, doh worry, wack, it'll tek away some of the pain. Not all, though.'

'Cheers, Droppy.'

'They'll want to do some mower tests too. Yow'll 'ave an

ultrasound scan to see if yow've got gallstones. Am yow a pisshead?'

'Pardon?' I said, but our conversation was interrupted when a petite nurse, who looked about fourteen years old, arrived and pulled the curtains around my bed. Her name was Cyndi and she was a second-year student. She asked me to lower my pyjama bottoms and to roll onto my side. I obeyed and she inserted a paracetamol suppository up my arse.

'Thank you, Cyndi,' I said, as my eyes watered and my arse-cheeks quivered with embarrassment. It didn't sound quite right somehow. Are you supposed to thank somebody for shoving a plastic capsule up your log-chute? Perhaps if you're a client of my old landlady, Penny Stroker.

Droppy had been taken to x-ray by the time Cyndi re-opened the curtains. Now Deekus was standing at the end of my bed.

'Are you Dave *Ichabod* McVane who writes Facts is Facts for the *Walsall Reflector*?' he asked.

'Er, yes. That's me,' I replied, though I wasn't really in the mood for a conversation, not with a suppository dissolving in my jacksy.

'It's naffing brilliant, mate. Can I shake your hand?'

I took his limp, clammy hand. 'You read it every week?'

'I never miss it,' he said. 'It's about time somebody had the guts to tell it like it is. The state of education, the council, the roads and the naffing good for naff-all NHS.'

'We all like to have a moan. It's just that I get paid for it.'

'Take this place,' Deekus said, driven by the force of his indignation. 'I came in as a glue-sniffer when I was sixteen and I've been back eighteen, no, tell a lie, nineteen times. If they earned their naffing salaries I wouldn't be such a naffing regular, now would I?'

'I suppose some problems are difficult to –'

'And they naffing hate me,' he continued, 'the nurses, the

doctors, all of them. They slam my food down in front of me, they give me the tightest pair of support socks they can find –'

'I think they're supposed to be tight because –'

'The tea is always luke naffing warm and they're constantly moaning at me because I drink too much. How much tax do you think I pay when I buy a pint of ale? It's their wages I'm funding, and they've got the naffing brassneck to ask me to stop. The cheeky fuckers.'

'Well, I imagine there's a medical reason for –'

'And another thing –'

Deekus was cut short by the quack who'd come to fit my catheter. Thank Christ. I never thought I'd be glad of the arrival of someone who was about to stick a rubber pipe up the end of my prick, but a conversation with Deekus can drive you to perverse distractions.

'You're here with my catheter, Dr Fostus!' I shouted, with misplaced enthusiasm.

# Snooker Cue up the Bell-end

'Yaaaaaa,' I said, yelping. '*Yaaaa, haaaaa. Yaaaaaa, haaaa.*'

'I'm sorry, Mr McVane, but it has to go in a little further,' said Fostus.

'Yaaaaa,' I said, '*yaaaaa, haaaaaa.*'

I don't know if you've ever had a snooker cue jammed up your bell-end? If so, then you'll have an idea of what I was going through. Fostus began by squirting a lubricant into my urethra. This, allegedly, had anaesthetic properties, though the rubber tube he inserted may just as well have been wrapped in sandpaper. When the pipe entered my bladder a geyser of urine arced out and plastered Fostus's fringe to his forehead. To his credit, he didn't flinch.

'*Yaaaaa, haaaaaa,*' I said.

'That should do it; now we just have to inflate the bulb that will keep the catheter in your bladder.'

'YAAAAAA, HAAAAAAA,' I said.

When they opened the curtains around my bed most of the ward was looking at me: some with sympathy; some with amusement; some with know-it-all understanding. Droppy, who was now back from x-ray, and Deekus, fell squarely into the latter category.

Deekus padded over to my bed again, pulling his drip-stand along at his side.

'The paracetamol suppository is naff-all use is it, Dave? They could get a better anaesthetic but they don't bother. It's all down to money: they spend so much on paying the staff, there's none left for essentials.'

'It didn't hurt that much,' I lied.

'I've had eighteen catheters fitted over the years. No, tell a lie, nineteen. Now they don't bother catheterizing me because they couldn't give a toss what happens to me.'

I could, I thought: I hope you die a painful death, a malignant twaddle-merchant yapping in *your* ear.

He looked at my white board. 'I see Dunderdale is your consultant. Dear oh dear.'

'Is that a problem?'

'Haven't you heard the stories?'

'Stories?'

'Complaints.'

'What complaints?'

'Don't get me started.'

'All right then,' I said, hoping he'd take the hint.

He didn't. 'Pancreatitis, is it?' he asked, purely because my answer would give him an opportunity to talk some more about himself. Not that he needed one.

'Yes,' I admitted, with a sigh.

'My pancreas has gone,' he said, 'or most of it has. The Wesley butchers have diced it to the size of a budgie's dick. Now I'm diabetic on top of everything else, and every time I have a drink I end up here.'

'Have you thought about not drinking?' I asked, wondering if budgies actually had dicks.

Deekus looked at me as if I'd suggested he post his genitals to Geriatrics. Clearly my suggestion didn't merit a reply; he turned and padded away without another word. He changed the TV channel to catch the end of that morning's episode of *Trisha*.

'I love this,' Deekus told the ever-prostrate Martin. 'It

deals with real issues, and the presenter does a decent job for a black girl. It's nice to see one of them working for someone other than the NHS.' He then proceeded to complain about every aspect of the show.

Deekus depressed me. It's strange that in all the years I'd been writing Facts is Facts, I'd rarely encountered my readers face to face. The idea that I was fuelling the puerile whinging of twats such as Deekus troubled me. I know alcoholism is supposed to be an illness but the annoying thing about Deekus and his ilk – and I'd met plenty of them over the years – is that they refuse to take any responsibility for their predicament and haven't got the wit to imagine any other way of leading their blighted lives. If you can't, or won't, dig yourself out of your hole, fine. But don't blame other people for your own trip to Wankerdom or drag them along with you. The twat: it's people like him who've driven me to drink.

'He's a wanker,' said Droppy, as if reading my thoughts. 'He's in and out o' this place mower often than I am.'

'And what are you in for, Droppy?' I asked. 'You never got round to telling me.' For the first time I noticed that he had raised white lines of flesh running horizontally and diagonally up the length of his forearms. They looked like the scars of self-imposed wounds.

'I'm a swallower, wack.'

'You've told me that much. But what exactly *is* a swallower?'

Droppy sniggered and reached under his pillow. He pulled out a saw blade from a Swiss Army knife and held it up to show me. 'I shat this out this morning,' he said, beaming with pride. 'Not bad, eh. It day 'urt a bit, wack.'

'Jesus. You swallowed it?'

'I day cowing inject it.'

'*Why* did you swallow it?'

Droppy shrugged. 'They say I got Munchausen's

Syndrome. I crave attention apparently. Mostly I swallow things for bets, though. I can swallow anything: razors, knives and forks. They woh give me cutlery in 'ere just in case I scoff it down. I've spent half me life in 'ospitals, wack. And in nut-houses too, o' course.'

Droppy went on to relate some of the things he'd swallowed. The list was harrowing and included everything from a light bulb to a squirrel's head.

'So you've been on this ward before?' I asked.

'Langerhans? Oh arr. Loads. There's nowt I doh know about this place.'

'Why do they call it Langerhans?' I asked, certain that if anyone could tell me Droppy Collins could.

'Because they get so many people with yower problem, wack,' he said.

'Pancreatitis?'

'Arr. If yow bugger yower pancreas up yow lose yower Islands of Langerhans. They get mower cases on it 'ere than anywhere else in Britain, I 'ear.'

It struck me that Droppy sounded quite well informed, medically speaking. I'd run into this phenomenon numerous times, particularly in the mail I received at the *Reflector*, and with those I'd interviewed in my days as a reporter. Many people have a fascination with medical matters and enjoy the feel of medical terminology on their lips – a fascination fuelled by TV programmes such as *Casualty* and *Holby City*. I suppose in Walsall it goes hand in hand with a perpetual awareness of mortality and decay. Certainly, there's an unhealthy obsession with infirmity here. You can hear more about diseases of the respiratory system in a Walsall bus queue than in a year at Harvard Medical School. The people in that bus queue might not have the good sense to leave Walsall or cut down on the Superkings, but they know how to spell emphysema. It's illness itself they're keen on, however; they know nothing, say, about the Health Service in the broader sense (except that they think it's crap). They couldn't tell you the name of the current Minister for Health, but they know what a myocardial infarction is.

'What's a myocardial infarction, Droppy?' I asked, deciding as I often do to test my theory.

'That's an 'eart attack, wack,' answered Droppy, correctly.

Before I had a chance to quiz him further Dr Fostus came striding up to Droppy's bed carrying a sheaf of x-rays. He was boiling with fury. Droppy began to slide sheepishly beneath the bedclothes.

'Mr Collins,' he said, snatching at the curtains and dragging them furiously around the bed, 'you've some explaining to do.'

His violent tugs at the curtains failed to close them fully and from my own bed I could see Fostus holding up an x-ray in front of Droppy.

'Well,' Fostus hissed in a fierce whisper, 'what's this?'

From my vantage-point I could plainly see the x-ray and the outline of Droppy's stomach, pale against a dark background. In the centre was a single word, written in fancy lettering. That word was, *Googie*.

Droppy had shat out his Swiss Army saw blade, but it seemed unlikely that he'd be discharged anytime soon.

I reached for Tinker Lawson. Amazingly, he hadn't been shut down, asked to leave or, for that matter, arrested. I tuned in just in time to hear the last thirty seconds of the Happy Flowers' psychotic classic, 'They Cleaned My Cut Out With a Wire Brush'. Tinker then went on to dedicate 'Suffer Little Children' by the Smiths to 'everyone in Paediatrics'. How thoughtful.

# Germaine Greer's Anus

Most students on the English degree at WANK chose four courses for each term, but I only had to pick three because I had advanced standing thanks to my year at Bristol.

I chose Ruud Van Door's 'Never Too Tight to Write', which was all about heavy-drinking American writers, and I picked Ebola Barker's 'Poststructuralism and the Penis', which addressed what Ebola termed 'phallocentrism in pre-postmodern literature'. I also chose Dr Steven Twist's course on narrative poetics, just in case he *did* turn out to be our S&M boy. Ringo picked the same, together with Prunella Fabb's course on orgasms in literature. Apart from his or her options, everyone had to do Dunderdale's critical studies foundation course on 'Learning to Evaluate'.

Predictably, by far the least interesting course was Twist's. In my mind it went a long way towards confirming his status as a perverted sadist. The first session was a lecture on Aristotle's ideas on the mechanics of tragedy. This was so boring that I actually preferred listening to Ringo who, throughout the lecture, whispered a detailed account of a 'haemorrhoidal tribulation' he'd developed since arriving in Walsall.

'It probably has to do with the gladioli incident,' he said. 'After being shamed in that region I'm having to strain on the lavatory.'

Ebola Barker's course was entertaining. In the first session she told us that she wanted to 'deconstruct the preconceived ideas about feminism and feminists' that we would have 'inevitably internalized as the passive subjects of patriarchy'. This effort to 'deconstruct' took a variety of forms. Firstly she showed us a photograph of Germaine Greer's anus. We knew it was Germaine Greer's anus because the photo also had her face on it; not to mention her vagina.

'I bet you didn't know feminists did this kind of thing, did you?'

The queasy and wan expressions of my fellow students confirmed that we didn't. Ebola explained that it was a protest photo published in *OZ* in the 1960s. She went on to show us a slide of a fat, ugly feminist whose name I can't remember, followed by one of a beautiful feminist whose name was Gloria Steinem.

'But,' said Ebola, blinking furiously, 'if I asked you which one of these women looked like a feminist you'd say the first one, right?'

There were murmurs of semi-agreement from the class.

'Of course you would, and you all know why, don't you?'

More murmurs of semi-agreement.

One of the things that made me nervous in Ebola's lectures, apart from the fact that I never knew what the fuck was going on, was her tendency to ask students direct questions. She'd suddenly turn on you, demand your opinion and then, I suspect, delight in watching you squirm as your mind blood-hounded its recesses for a twaddle-free response. It was a mistake to confuse her frailty with timidity. She could be aggressive, ferocious even, and she enjoyed her power. Out of the sixty-odd students who attended Ebola's first lecture, naturally she singled me out.

'You,' she said, at that stage unaware of my name, 'the older student in the Banks's "Built for the Job" sweatshirt.

I'd like your opinion on this: Why is it that men *and women* seem intent on containing and reducing a plethora of distinct positions, ideas and people by constructing simplistic, negative stereotypes? What reason would you give for these *mis*conceptions, these *mis*representations, this *mis*leading *mis*information. Come on, don't be afraid to have an opinion.'

I think that was the last time I ever sat at the front of a lecture theatre. I could feel the eyes of my younger colleagues grilling the back of my head, waiting for something intelligent from the 'older' student. I hate speaking in front of a crowd; whenever I try I can always hear a squeak of failure in my voice. But Ebola wasn't going to let me off the hook; she stared on, torturing me with each merciless snap of her eyelids. My mouth felt the way it does the morning after a skinful: parched and inarticulate. But I had to come up with something. To this day I find it hard to accept that I answered her question with the words: 'Does "plethora" mean a lot?'

Ebola's eyes asterisked in disbelief.

Serves you right for coming to teach in Walsall, I thought.

There was a rumour that some years earlier Ebola's enthusiasm for outrageous teaching climaxed with her doing a striptease in front of her entire class. Amazed? Allegedly, to the music of Scott Joplin, she removed everything but for a bikini made of gummed-together pornographic photos. I never met anyone who actually saw it, and no one ever had the guts to ask Ebola if it was true, but it was an established part of campus mythology by the time I began studying at WANK. People discussed it the way they discuss the fabled Marianne Faithfull–Mars bar incident. Having met Ebola, and seen her teach, I'd say that it *was* a credible myth. She was certainly eccentric, provocative and keen to challenge convention. She was also fervently committed to her subject. Often, during her lectures, her frantic blinking would squeeze tears from her eyes. I was never sure if they were tears of passion or despair, but they always impressed me.

But, of my optional courses, Ruud Van Door's was the best. As well as Ringo and me, only five other people were taking it. It was an evening class lasting from six till nine, which was a good time in my book because it meant that all the sessions could take place in the union bar. At the first Ruud put two quid in the jukebox and keyed in tracks for the whole night. One was 'The End' and, to accompany this, Van Door gave a spontaneous talk about how the lyrics revealed Jim Morrison's self-destructive impulse.

'An impulse fuelled,' Ruud told us, 'by the Romantic myth of self-destruction that American artists, Morrison included, inherited from European culture.'

'Did Morrison drink himself to death?' I asked.

'It was drugs with him, mostly. But he identified heavily with artists who famously drank themselves into an early grave; Dylan Thomas, for instance.'

'Is there any evidence that alcohol can have a *positive* effect on writers?' I wanted to know.

'The standard answer to that question is no, and it's true that drinking often undermines a writer's talent. Scott Fitzgerald's work declined on booze, as did William Faulkner's. But that isn't always the case. Charles Bukowski, for instance, claims that he can only write well when he's pissed.'

'Why does Charles Bukowski love booze so much?' asked Ringo, who for health reasons only drank fruit juice.

'When he was young he lived a miserable life on Skid Row in LA,' answered Van Door. 'He was ugly and lacked in self-confidence. LA isn't the place to be poor and ugly. I suppose booze helps make life bearable for people with low self-esteem who live in limited, oppressive environ-ments.'

'Like Walsall?' I quipped.

'Well, not quite *that* bad,' Van Door admitted.

Everyone laughed.

It was the best seminar I'd had since the Glorious Twelfth. I made lots of germane, intelligent points, feeling much more confident and comfortable in a bar than in a classroom. I was in awe of Van Door too. He was a great teacher. He had an easy-going manner and he spoke about writers as if they were real people. He laced his talks with biographical anecdotes about his heroes, bringing them to life. His seminar felt like a course on literary gossip: right up my rue, as was the heavy Charles Bukowski bias. Van Door loved to talk about the American writer's wild life: his fist fights, his women, his decision to stop off at a bar on the way home from hospital despite having been warned that a single drink could kill him. I was fascinated. And another good thing about Van Door's class is that it was easy to understand. Devoid of literary theory, it was manageable even for me. It was tragic he'd only be teaching us for a single term.

# Woooosh, Slack

When Van Door's class ended at nine I was aflame with two principal desires: the first was to read everything that Charles Bukowski had ever written, the second was to get off my dingers.

I achieved the second with some ease and, by eleven, Ringo was having to help me up the stairs to our flat. As we were passing the second floor of Penny's, 47B, we heard something that turned our already pleasant night into a positively gripping one.

*Woooosh, slack, woooosh, slack*. It sounded like one of the many hand-tooled spanking implements I'd made for Penny was being employed either on or by one of her patrons.

Ringo listened, wide-eyed. 'Someone is having their arse clouted?'

'I reckon so, mate,' I said, stifling a burp. 'Someone is, indeed, having their arse clouted.' It wasn't that uncommon a noise. The ex-council flat doors were made of plywood and cardboard and had the soundproofing qualities of fishnet. Also, given the acoustics, sound waves bounced around the stairs and landing like Frisbeed cymbals. I was about to carry on up, when Ringo grabbed my arm.

'Someone is speaking,' he said, 'listen.'

I strained to hear but, at first, could only make out the spanking noise: *woooosh, slack; woooosh, slack*. It was as regular as the ticking of a clock, and louder than usual. At first I thought that someone was using a slapper. This is a type of paddle that has an extra tongue of leather at the top in order to increase the volume of the slapping noise. I'd made several over the years, including one double-cheek version. But this didn't have the distinctive 'popping' sound of a slapper. Nor was it a crapper – a cross between a crop and a slapper. These are loud, too, but have a much higher pitch. No. It sounded distinctly like one of my Staffordshires – being used pitilessly by the sound of it.

Ringo pulled me over to the door and I heard that, indeed, someone was talking.

'Yes, doctor, again, doctor.'

*Wooosh, slack; wooosh, slack.*

'It must be one of Miss Stroker's girls,' said Ringo.

'Obviously,' I said, the intoxicating effects of the half-crate of beer I'd drunk lifting somewhat.

'She's with "call me doctor"!'

'Hurt my arse, doctor' – *wooosh, slack; woooosh, slack* – 'punish me the way I need to be punished, doctor.'

*Woooosh slack; woooosh, slack.*

Whenever I overheard the girls in sessions like this they almost always sounded ridiculously corny. Despite the theatrical stylization, as actresses they were only slightly more adept than Ann George. However, *this* scene seemed different. The girl's voice was shaky and it sounded as if her pain was genuine. Hers weren't the usual bored and half-hearted 'ouches'; these squeals had substance and were punctuated with involuntary gasps. It was like listening to someone doing a screen test for *Carry on Spanking* while standing in a bucket of wasps. I knew the girls were discouraged from using the escape phrases – house policy being that the customer is always right – but on this occasion I felt that an Amy Turtle couldn't be far away.

'It's him all right,' I said. 'We've got to stick around to see who it is.' Though I'd no evidence to speak of, I'd convinced myself that Twist was our man. The thought of him, plump, clammy and wobbling with delight while spanking Dionne, cranked my sobriety level several notches higher. Another few drinks would have gone down a treat.

Ringo agreed that we should try to unmask the pervert, so our immediate problem was where to conceal ourselves. We looked around the landing for a hiding place. It was cluttered with stuff: pot plants, which Penny had placed there in an effort to brighten the place up; piles of rubbish waiting to be taken down to the bins. First we attempted to arrange a stack of large cardboard boxes into suitable cover, but failed. One of the boxes had contained a flat-pack torture rack, the other an aluminium humiliation cage – at least this is what Ringo claimed: the writing on the boxes was in Dutch and he translated it.We then tried to hide behind a couple of gigantic cheeseplants only to find three two-gallon bottles of meths already concealed behind them. I think Penny used the stuff for sterilizing invasive torture tools: bollock-skewers and the like. I briefly considered taking a swig from one of them but thought better of it; I wasn't quite *that* drunk (or that sober).

Eventually we were forced to accept the total absence of suitable hiding places on the second-floor landing.

'Outside,' I said, urging Ringo back down the stairs. 'We'll hide outside and catch him when he leaves.'

And so we combed the street for hiding places. I made several attempts to climb a tree but only succeeded in scuffing my ox-blood Dr Martens. Apart from the tree, the street was completely open. None of the terraced houses on the opposite side of the road had convenient walls to hide behind. For once, there weren't even any parked cars around. There really didn't seem to be anywhere from which to conduct a surreptitious observation. How do private dicks do this kind of thing?

'Why hide?' asked Ringo. 'Can't we just confront the rascal in his shame?' I think the word 'rascal' had entered his vocabulary from a recent viewing of Basil Rathbone in *The Hound of the Baskervilles*.

'It'd be best to keep our knowledge a secret till we know what to do with it,' I said.

'Yes, but how?'

At that point a couple of streetwalkers turned into the road. One was wearing a snorkel parka with thigh-length patent leather boots; the other sported a chainmail bikini and an anorak. Their sartorial inspiration seemed to be a combination of *The Happy Hooker* and *Angling Today*. I guess the weather had something to do with it. It was a chilly, clear night and the jaundiced Walsall moon glared down like a lizard's eye.

'*Psssst*,' I said, not sure how to hail a prostitute.

'Are you looking for business, mate?' asked the one in chainmail.

'We need to see who comes out of Penny's without being seen,' I said. 'We'll give you a couple of quid if you hide us.'

'How?'

'Er . . . with your bodies?'

'Freaky,' said bikini girl, without any enthusiasm.

After a bit of haggling they agreed to stand with us. We thought they could embrace us, and thus conceal us when our quarry appeared. Our plan was to push our faces down into their necks and make like lovers canoodling as soon as the front door opened. It was my plan: you can tell this because it was fundamentally flawed.

These two girls were unlike the ones who worked for Penny. They found their punters on the street, mainly among the kerb-crawling motorists who circle the district in second gear till they spot a girl they fancy. It was a risky business for the girls. Penny told me that she'd never met a streetwalker who hadn't been seriously assaulted. Beaten up; raped. The fact that their trade is illegal makes life a hundred times more dangerous for them. At least that's what Ringo had told me. If a prostitute is hassled in Amsterdam they throw a panic button that has the Dutch equivalent of Fierce Woody stamping on the offender's windpipe quicker than you could say, 'No, please, not my windpipe, Mr Van Woody.'

It was a while before anyone emerged and the girls were soon moaning about losing money. They were in the process of telling us our two quid's worth was up when, finally, we heard movement from the main door to the flats. I grabbed the one in the anorak and chainmail undies.

'OK, we're in business,' I whispered.

My girl took this as a cue to seize my arse and pull me towards her. Ringo's made a similar advance.

This better *had* be one of our lecturers, I remember thinking, as I buried my head in the prostitute's three-tier, Bonnie Tyler style mullet.

It was indeed.

# The Fake

When I saw Ebola Barker walking out of Penny's Punishment Palace that night I nearly choked on my prostitute's mullet. Ebola was wearing a business suit with a slightly out-of-vogue jacket. On her twig-like frame the padded shoulders appeared ridiculous. She looked like a kite.

'Flaming Ada!' I heard Ringo splutter. The exclamation seemed to float across the street and flick Ebola's earlobe.

She stopped and stared over at Ringo. Though I pushed my face deeper into the lacquered layers of Miss Chainmail's coiffeur, I sensed that she recognized us. I could feel myself turning crimson with shame, despite the fact that technically I hadn't done anything wrong. Technicalities mean nothing in such a situation. I decided not to acknowledge her; instead I chose to close my eyes and hope she went away. I bet you're surprised I managed to score 102 on my IQ test, aren't you?

Ebola didn't go away. She crossed the road and approached us. I kept my head buried despite the fact that, with every breath, the stink of Miss Chainmail's lacquer threatened to introduce the contents of my gut to the cruel Walsall night.

'Hello, gentlemen,' she said. 'You meet all sorts in these parts.'

Ringo and I buried our heads even deeper. My girl was

chewing gum and I could hear her masticating loudly in my ear; Ringo's was smoking a fag over his left shoulder. Their palpable feline contempt reminded me of why I've never fancied shagging a prostitute.

I could feel Ebola staring at us and I didn't dare look up and catch her eye. I could almost hear her lashes batting at us in the dark. Mercilessness again.

'Haven't you two got anything to say for yourselves?'

My lady-of-the-night muttered 'for fuck's sake' under her breath but, thankfully, she kept her end of the deal and stayed with me. So did Ringo's. I had a feeling we'd owe them at least another quid each after this. Though they didn't say as much, I had the impression that we disgusted them. It was as if this pretend snog had been the most repulsive thing they'd been asked to do all night.

Eventually, Ebola began to walk away. Thank God.

Ringo and I took the stairs four at a time. We burst into 47C and gave Monica a breathless account of what had happened.

'Ebola Barker, lecturer in English at the Walsall Academy for New Knowledge, is a lesbian sadist,' I panted.

'You both whiff of cheap perfume,' said Monica, who was curled in an armchair reading one of her nursing books: *Cardiopulmonary Resuscitation: A Bluffer's Guide.* 'And, for your information,' she continued, 'Ebola isn't a lesbian sadist; she was here because she's researching a book.'

'Brilliant,' I said, 'what a stroke of genius. If I was an academic who'd been caught red-handed in a brothel, that's the excuse I'd give.'

'But you wouldn't bother interviewing me for an hour and a half about the psychological implications of being a woman who lives in a flat above an s&m brothel, would you?'

'I might,' I said, 'if I wanted to be completely convincing.' I was clutching at straws.

'Dave,' said Monica, becoming a little impatient, 'sober up.'

'Sorry.'

'Besides,' she said, setting down her book, 'I have a little gossip for *you*. I bumped into Dionne Splendour in the hall earlier and she told me that your lecturer is a fake.'

'Eh?'

'An impostor. He told Dionne that he fabricated his CV to get his job. He hasn't got a doctorate – he hasn't even got a degree. She says he's always bragging about it when they're together.'

'Fuck me. Did she tell you his name?'

'No, no name. She says if he comes again she'll ask him.'

This information cheered me and Ringo up on the spot.

'I knew it!' he said. 'Remember what I said about the book we found in the dungeon: who would need an introduction more than an impostor?'

'You're a genius,' I told him. 'My God: what does it say about higher education in this country when people without qualifications can bluff their way into such posts?'

'Do any of your lecturers *strike* you as impostors?' asked Monica.

'I suppose it rules Twist out,' I said. 'Only someone with a doctorate could be as tedious as that tosser. And, let's face it, he's such a social outcast – perfect PhD material surely.'

'Yes, he seems very informed about his subject,' said Ringo.

'Is there anyone who doesn't?' asked Monica.

We both thought for a moment.

'Prunella Fabb's good on literary theory, but her general reading isn't as wide as it could be,' said Ringo.

'Er . . . she's a woman.'

'I'm just saying.'

'Actually, there's a rumour that my medical ethics lecturer is shagging Prunella Fabb,' said Monica.

'The one who lost his prosthetic ear in the refectory?' I queried.

'No, no: that was Dr Plunkett, the gay one; it's a guy called Darius Smiles who teaches medical ethics. My friend says she saw him and Fabb entering the adult bookshop in Stafford Street.'

'That's interesting,' I said, 'because I've heard Fabb is shagging Weldon Kilter, the War Studies research student.'

'I've heard she's a lesbian,' said Ringo. 'Someone told me she was having passion with that big lady who works on the door at the Giddy Kitten in town.'

'Are you saying Fabb comes here, butched up, for s&m spanking sessions?' I asked, always keen to entertain the outlandish.

'What is "butched up"?' Ringo wanted to know.

And we went on in this way fuelled, at least in my case, by a six-pack. It was great; after our humiliating encounter with Ebola the evening was redeemed. The air buzzed with scandal. After examining the 'call me doctor' intrigue from every conceivable angle we went on, as we often did, to mull over some of our favourite celebrity sleaze stories.

Ringo had been impressed with one tabloid story about an ageing disc jockey who was suspected of necrophilia ('Veteran Jock's Kinky Crypt Capers'). A frequently debated favourite of Monica's concerned an ex-children's TV presenter who'd been caught with a dominatrix. Monica wondered why the tabloid accounts tended to make reference to the gentleman's 'black and blue peter', even though the guy in question never actually presented *Blue Peter*. Ringo told her that this was because 'comedy always takes precedence over reality'.

This insight seemed to set Monica musing about the issue of gossip itself.

'Where would we be without gossip?' she asked, to no one in particular.

'Bored log-less,' I said, taking a long pull on my lager and crushing the empty can in my palm, a gesture as irresistible as popping bubble wrap.

'Do you think it says something about *our* lives that all we talk about is other people?' she said.

'What else is there,' I asked, burping, 'apart from the obvious?' I raised my crumpled can.

'Politics? Philosophy?'

'Politics *is* gossip,' said Ringo. 'More so these days than ever.'

'What about philosophy?'

'I hear that Michel Foucault was an s&m freak,' said Ringo.

'Who's she?' I asked.

They both laughed as if I'd cracked a joke.

'For me,' said Monica, 'I think gossip provides a great way of bonding with people.'

'Apart from with the people you're bad-mouthing,' I said.

'Monica's right,' said Ringo, 'it's the perfect social . . . grease?'

'Lubricant,' said Monica.

'Lubricant, yes; and an ideal means of consolidating relationships.'

'That's true,' said Monica, 'but sometimes I feel guilty about how much I enjoy salacious gossip.'

'I don't think you should,' said Ringo. 'I love it too. For me it's because I feel comforted by the fact that other people, with their frailties and peccadilloes, are as human as I am.'

'Yep,' I said, warming to the debate, 'I like scandal and gossip because it kills me to think that anyone's having a better life than me. I hate the weasel-minded rich fuckers who seem to have it all; I hate the self-satisfied beautiful people and the know-it-all brainy people; most of all, I hate the goody-fucking-two-shoeses: the holier-than-thou shithouses who think they're better than me. What I want to hear is that everyone else is a miserable, self-centred useless cunt too. Personally, I can't wait for the bad news about Cliff Richard.'

Ringo laughed uneasily and Monica gave me a thin smile.

'I was just agreeing with Ringo,' I added, wondering what I'd said wrong.

'You can just nod next time, mate,' he said.

Monica laughed.

I shrugged and opened another can.

# The Death of the Author

I don't imagine that the best way to endear yourself to a radical feminist – even an avant garde feminist intent on deconstructing feminist stereotypes – is to be seen cavorting with a half-naked prostitute outside a brothel. Needless to say, our next 'Poststructuralism and the Penis' class was a tense affair. Ringo and I sat sheepishly at the back, terrified that Ebola would make an exhibition of us.

When she entered the lecture theatre she was wearing a pair of leather trousers so snug her skinny legs resembled a pair of riding crops. We eased ourselves down in our chairs and she didn't seem to notice us. She began as she always did, by frowning, blinking, frowning again, and then by saying, 'I'd like to begin.' The room had been a clamour of chatter, titters and scraping chairs but, with these words, it snapped into silence.

This week's lecture was to be an introduction to the theory of a mad Frenchman called Roland Barthes. It's difficult to understand, but Ebola did her best to articulate it in the simplest terms. She lost me after a minute and a half. I'd been off my knockers the night before and that morning it was all I could do to shave without slicing my lips off. Every now and then my image of Ebola would multiply by two. Certainly there were two of her when I first realized she was speaking to me. I chose one of the liquorice-lace figures and said 'Pardon?' to it.

'No text is an island. What is your understanding of that concept, Mr McVane?'

There was a terrible silence as Ebola blinked at me expectantly. She'd walked to the back of the lecture theatre and now stood only a few feet away. As I met her eyes she blinked some more. I tried not to blink too much myself in case she thought I was taking the piss. 'No text is an island,' she repeated. 'What do you think that statement implies?'

Mercilessness again.

I had no idea how to answer her question because, hungover as I was, I thought she was saying, 'No text is an *Ire*land.' What the fuck *could* that mean? There was nothing for it but to have a crack at it, though.

'Erm, does it mean,' I spluttered, my voice sounding weak and high-pitched, 'does it mean that, erm, it's not overly possible to capture an Ireland with, erm, through, erm, the vehicle of linguistic narrative?'

Ebola blinked three times as she exclaimed, '*What?*'

I could feel myself blushing amid the snorting and tittering of my fellow students.

'What I'm, erm, asking is, erm, does it mean that the conveying of the *trueness* of Ireland can never be absolutist and that, consequentially, all that we can ever approximate to, or indeed approximate at, is the approximate?'

Ebola looked like a woman who'd just seen a leprechaun take a shit in a shot glass.

'What,' she asked after a second or two of open-mouthed silence, 'do you mean when you say island?'

'The country Daniel O'Donnell sings about?'

Ebola's eyes clenched in disbelief.

She went on to explain that 'No text is an *is*land' means that no narrative can have meaning independent of other narratives and, more importantly, independent of readers. This appeared obvious to me, which made me wonder if I properly understood it.

'It means,' Ebola said, her voice quiet but charged with profundity, 'it means that authors don't create meaning and authors don't control it. It's impossible to be original and it's impossible to be understood.' She spoke slowly, with her eyes clenched tight, as if reading her words from the back of her lids. As she finished, there was a pause in which all that could be heard was the occasional cleared throat and shuffle of paper.

When Ebola opened her eyes they were watery, wide and blazing with purpose. She had more to say. She lifted her index finger to ensure the room stayed quiet. All around pens hovered above notepads. As slender as a conductor's baton, her finger held everyone's attention.

'Because,' she said, her expression as grave as if she'd been announcing the end of the world, 'because *we too* are texts, because our very minds are built from the signifying systems we inherit, we can never be original either; we can never be in control. No man or woman is an island. We are trapped by language, ladies and gentlemen. And because we are trapped by language we are trapped by ambiguity, trapped by ideology, and trapped by banality.' She blinked on the final word and tears sparked from her lashes. Nearby, a young woman stifled a sob.

Jesus. I'd always understood the phrase 'no man is an island' as having something to do with our emotional and spiritual need for God and fellow man: in other words, sentimental claptrap. But in Ebola's context it implied some kind of cage that enslaved our minds. She sounded pretty sure of herself and, though I wasn't really certain in what sense *I* was a text, if Ebola said I was then I was willing to accept her analysis. It didn't trouble me the way it seemed to trouble her, but perhaps I'd have been more worried if I were more intelligent. Maybe I was better off dim?

Ebola took some deep breaths, blinked her tears into her

sleeve, and said, 'Thank you for your attention.' The lecture theatre boomed with applause – something I never saw happen with any other academic – and Ebola, clearly touched, allowed herself a small smile.

As the students filed out, Ringo and I were trapped at the back of the queue out of the lecture theatre and Ebola collared us. By now she'd fully composed herself.

'It was rather rude of you to ignore me the other night, gentlemen.'

I instantly began to gibber an explanation as to why she'd caught us with a couple of prossers. She listened with her arms folded and her left eyebrow raised, semi-amused by my suffering.

'You see, Dr Barker, it's . . . well I'm not even sure if I should say anything –'

'For pity's sake, get on with it!' she said.

'Erm . . . Erm . . .' I said. I felt like a previously uncatalogued life form on day release from a swamp. Ringo got me off the hook.

'We've been told that one of your colleagues seeks distraction at Penny's,' he said.

Ebola raised an eyebrow at Ringo's diction and, obviously intrigued, pressed us for more. 'Do you have any idea who it could be?'

'We think it's a man,' I said.

Ebola managed to roll her eyes before they succumbed to three rapid blinks of frustration. I thought she'd be impressed that I hadn't automatically ruled a woman out of the equation, but no. You could tell she knew I wasn't A-grade material.

'At first we thought it might be Steven Twist,' I said.

'Why?'

'Because he's f – He just looks the part,' I said. Even as I spoke I knew I sounded like a dim-witted wanker. Am I always such a tit or is it just when I try to explain something more complicated than what I'd like to drink?

Ebola rolled her eyes again. 'Hopefully, after you've finished my course, you'll learn not to make assumptions based on stereotypes. They are a means of reduction and oppression.'

'I understand,' I said. As dumb as I may be it was obvious to me that Ebola was almost pathologically intent on avoiding being deemed a stereotype herself. Thus, though she called herself a feminist, she was unlike any feminist I've seen before or since. I had the impression that she was less interested in feminism than in avoiding being ordinary or pigeonholed or, for want of a better word, normal.

'I want you to forget about the person who visits Penny's,' she said.

This sounded like an order and, despite being in awe of Ebola, I bristled slightly. It also struck me as a pretty odd request. 'Any particular reason?' I asked.

'Yes: s&m brothels like the one in your building exploit women. I don't approve of them but, nevertheless, I believe people have the right to a private life free of interference. Certainly they have the right to explore the limits of their sexuality without encroachment from either the law, outdated puritans or snoops.'

Was the bitch calling me a snoop?

'I tried to interview some of the girls last night but they wouldn't talk to me,' Ebola continued. 'Eventually someone called Penny Stroker came to the door and threatened to "kick my fucking cunt round my fucking neck".'

'That sounds like Penny,' I said. 'Why are you interested in s&m brothels anyway, Dr Barker?'

'I'm working on a book about –'

'I disagree,' said Ringo, cutting her off. He'd been pondering Ebola's earlier point. 'I disagree that brothels necessarily exploit women. There is always that danger, of course, but I believe in the legalization of prostitution because in an atmosphere of tolerance criminal exploitation is less likely.'

Trust Everett Lafayette Van Freek to start arguing the toss. I was expecting Ebola to plant a set of her varnished black toenails in his groin, but she didn't. She nodded and, perching herself on the back of a chair, started discussing the issues surrounding prostitution with him. Both of them agreed that it should be legalized, but they differed on the various social mechanisms that might be employed to protect the women who worked as prostitutes. They were both informed and articulate, and way over my head. After ten minutes of listening without contributing anything to the discussion, I left.

I glanced back as I exited the lecture theatre. They looked an odd pair: Ebola, scarcely the weight of Barbie's thong, and Ringo, the slim and diminutive Dutch boy. Physically, they barely registered on the world. But they seemed to have more substance than me, despite my six-foot frame and incipient beer belly.

I heard the tinkle of Ebola's laughter and, as I closed the door behind me, I was surprised to see her rocking, helpless with mirth. It was a pleasant sight and sound. She looked less angry, less intense, less cruel. The only other time she'd appeared so relaxed and at one with herself was the time I'd seen her sneeze.

Now I too went in search of relaxation and where better to find it than in the union bar? I entered to the sound of the Stranglers' 'Golden Brown' and spent the afternoon drinking seven and a half pints of lager and reading one and a half poems by Charles Bukowski.

# The Death of Maureen

Later that day Monica and I had an argument. It wasn't because I came home pissed – I almost always did. It was because I came home pissed and killed Maureen, the goldfish I'd purchased for her three months before. I was trying to remove a strand of Pot Noodle from its bowl; the noodle having been thrown from my fork during my drunken attempts to eat a belated lunch. Actually it was during my drunken attempts to *stir* my belated lunch. Maureen's bowl was smashed and she perished, probably beneath the ornamental miniature shipwreck we'd bought for her to swim around. I tiptoed gingerly through the glass shards and tried to revive Maureen by dropping her into a saucepan of water and poking her with my finger. She just bobbed, buoyant but lifeless like a scary slice of carrot.

It wouldn't have been so bad if this was the first of Monica's fish I'd killed. Sadly, it was the eighteenth. I'd killed the other seventeen, all of them tropical, in one go. Arseholed naturally. I'd tripped over the power cable that supplied current to the aquarium's heater. The wires shorted in the unit and electrocuted all the fish. Apparently, this wouldn't have happened with a quality aquarium, but I'd picked ours up cheap from a bloke down the Red Lion. As the tank crackled and fizzed, I put my hand into the smoking water in an attempt to scoop some of the fish to safety. It's one of those daft things you do when you're off your dingers, like loosening the knot on a bollock-boa with your Ronson. Monica charged into the kitchen to find me semi-conscious on the lino, covered in water, broken glass and dead tropical fish. As soon as she established that I wasn't dead she gave me a bollocking. Maureen had been a conciliatory gesture on my part: my way of saying sorry. Now I felt terrible.

'Maybe you could try leaving a pub sober once in your life,' said Monica, as I discreetly slipped Maureen into a Christian Aid envelope and deposited her in the pedal bin.

'Sorry, Mon,' I said.

'This is a disgusting state to get yourself into on a weekday lunchtime,' she said.

'Sorry, Mon.'

I knew she was right, but I couldn't think of anything else to say. I just sat and hung my head, despicable in my status as Dave McVane, the drunken goldfish killer. I was relieved when Ringo came home brimming with good cheer and interesting news.

'Your flatmate has had knowledge of a woman this very afternoon,' he said, beaming.

'You haven't spent the afternoon in Penny's Punishment Palace?' I teased, thinking: he can't mean Ebola Barker.

'Go on, Ringo,' said Monica, 'tell us.'

He grinned at us.

'You can't mean Ebola Barker?' I asked, realizing that this is exactly who he did mean.

'Dr Barker has had sexual advantage of me, yes,' he said.

'Jesus, she *is* radical,' I said.

'Is it entirely ethical?' Monica wanted to know.

'She says so. She says we're both adults and if she wants to fuck my brains out she can. I'm quoting Dr Barker there. She is a woman who takes what she wants, and she wants me. I think I'm in love.'

'Isn't she a bit old for you?' asked Monica.

'She says she doesn't mind pursuing what she calls a "generationally differential relationship".'

'Well, that's great,' said Monica, though I had a feeling she wasn't particularly pleased. Why? Normally she'd be loving this! Mind you, I'd noticed that she'd become a little protective of Ringo lately.

'She was a bit aggressive, though,' he confided, waggishly. 'She's a lady of domination. My knees feel as if their hats are on backwards.'

'Caps,' I said, forcing myself not to ask exactly how his knees might have suffered.

'I was joking,' he said. 'Do we have a suitable unction, Monica?'

'Try some Tiger Balm.'

Later, when Monica had gone to bed, I asked Ringo what it had been like with Ebola.

'You don't mean sexually?' he queried, seeming slightly shocked. He was smearing Tiger Balm into his knees and had his trousers rolled halfway up his thighs.

'Of course not!' I lied. 'I mean as a person, away from the classroom.'

He became thoughtful and took a long, contemplative sniff of his balm-smeared hands.

'You know her nervous blink?' he said at last.

I nodded.

'Every time she blinks it's as if she's taking another bite out of the world. She has hungry eyes.'

'Is that good?'

'I don't know . . . Maybe not. I think she devours too quickly; she strips the flesh and then moves on, bored.'

'Fucking hell, you make her sound like a plague of locusts!'

'I don't really want to go into detail about the sex,' he said, 'but she worried me a bit.' He paused and, cupping his Tiger-Balmed palms over his nose again, took another long, appreciative sniff. I was aching for more and he knew it.

'In what way?' I said at last.

'She needed to be in control too much.'

'Christ, did she make you do anything weird?' To my surprise I had a question mark throbbing in my loins. I hardly ever had erections these days.

'Depends what you mean by weird . . .'

Ringo's the kind of person whose sentences often end in three little dots. They make you want to reach into his throat and pull the information out from whatever mischievous part of him was responsible for these infuriating half-narratives. Sometimes it was only after he'd made you literally beg, that the information was forthcoming. On this occasion, however, I had the impression that he wouldn't be satisfying my pathetic, all-too-human need for completeness. He was a more circumspect gossipmonger when the gossip featured himself. I could see, though, that a real unease about Ebola lay beneath his post-coital exhilaration.

'You said she's a dominatrix, did she order you about?' I prompted.

'She did, but she's not as cruel as she'd like to be.'

'Fuck me! How cruel would she *like* to be?'

But he didn't reply, he just sat there with his trousers rolled up and his knees shining. He grinned. Had he a knotted hanky on his head he would have looked like a British sunbather of the 1950s. He wasn't going to tell me any more. It was partly because he was too nice a bloke and partly, I think, because he cared for Ebola. Something about her had affected him.

# What about Harold Shipman?

I must have nodded off because when I woke it was to the closing bars of the Smiths track 'Rubber Ring' which, Tinker Lawson told us, 'was dedicated to anyone due to have their haemorrhoids cauterized today'. Tinker was just introducing the Pistols' controversial classic 'Bodies' when the porter arrived to take me for my ultrasound scan, just as Droppy had predicted.

The ultrasound was to check if I had any gallstones. I was transported in a wheelchair again, though to a different place this time – a tiny room that would have made a modest walk-in wardrobe. It was dominated by a narrow bed, like a pasting table, and a machine about the size of a home computer. The latter had a sticker on the side: the image of a bird with a massive beak above the words 'Keep Your Pecker Up'.

I had some trouble getting onto the pasting table with my catheter urine-bag swinging at my side. Moving when you've got a catheter is a bit like moving with a knitting needle piercing your genitals.

An ultrasound scan is the one they give pregnant women and, the size my stomach had inflated, I could have been eight months gone. Once I was on the table they covered my belly in cold, clear jelly and slid a sensor over it. The sound-image was shown on a monitor as a smear of meaningless shapes. Usually, I suppose, these meaningless shapes reveal someone's cherished foetus but, in my case, they revealed a total absence of gallstones.

I was wheeled back to the Lost Islands of Langerhans in time to see Droppy eating his lunch. His knife and fork were both chained to wooden blocks the size of a Swiss roll. The kitchen staff at Wesley were taking no chances with their cutlery. He was having some trouble slicing his lamb chop, but was persevering. Also on his tray was a sachet of Fibre Gel. Presumably roughage would help Googie retrieve her pendant sooner.

I'd been back from my scan little more than five minutes when Fostus appeared. He shot Droppy a savage look as he passed his bed, but then turned his attention to me.

'Do you drink, Mr McVane?'

'Doesn't everyone?'

'Alcohol.'

'Yes, I am partial to the odd tincture.'

'Do you drink excessively, Mr McVane?'

'One man's excessively is another man's scarcely. Besides, I'm a journalist,' I said.

'What does your being a journalist have to do with it?'

'Drinking excessively is a contractual obligation,' I quipped. I was being a smart-arse again and Fostus, like Frigata, didn't need the hassle. He gave me a pained look.

'So, you do drink a lot?' he asked, with a sigh.

'We've already discussed my beer gut. Sorry, my liquid grain storage facility.' Fostus remained straightfaced – not even a flicker of a smile. This man was to humour what Amy Turtle was to the dramatic arts. I thought doctors were full of banter and wisecracks. So much for *M*A*S*H*.

'The reason I ask is that the main cause of pancreatitis, apart from gallstones, is alcohol abuse. It is the one we see most often around here.'

'Among the bays they call the Lost Islands of Langerhans?'

He nodded, as grim-faced as ever. 'We have many alcoholics who, because they can't stop drinking, develop chronic pancreatitis. This is a very nasty condition. We often have to remove part of the pancreas, including cells called the Islets – or Islands – of Langerhans. The cells are named after the man who discovered them, a German I believe. They produce insulin and, without them, patients become diabetic. They have a reduced life expectancy and they're in constant pain. If they survive the surgery.'

I swallowed. 'Will that happen to me?'

'Your ultrasound scan shows that your pancreas is massively inflamed. It's possible you might have some necrosis.'

'That doesn't sound at all good.'

'It is very serious, I'm sorry to say. It means that some of the pancreatic tissue may have been destroyed. I'll have to speak to Mr Dunderdale about it, but he'll probably recommend a CAT scan which will give us a better idea of any damage.'

'You're lying, you bastard,' I said. 'All this is because I'm Dave Ichabod McVane: you're trying to put the shits up me; teach me a lesson.'

'What?' he said. Then he thought for a second. 'Mr McVane,' he continued, in a level, excruciatingly measured voice, 'you're correct to think that I don't approve of your ill-informed and inflammatory column, but I am a professional. I have taken an oath that I intend to uphold, and were you the devil incarnate it would make no difference to my commitment to you as a patient. And that goes for all the doctors here.'

'What about Harold Shipman?' I shouted, as Fostus walked away.

'He doesn't work here,' he answered, without looking back at me.

'No, but what about him?' I yelled, as the doctor turned out of the bay and out of the Lost Islands of Langerhans.

# Drinkers, and People Who Drink

After Fostus had gone I lay with my eyes shut, listening to the monotonous whirring of my drip machine. I'd been given another painkilling injection: pethidine; so, despite my outburst, it didn't take long for a feeling of floaty calmness to return. Droppy was still struggling with his chained-up cutlery and Deekus was watching the BBC News at One. There was a report about the Chancellor, Gordon Brown's, decision to increase National Insurance contributions in order to help boost NHS funds. Deekus hooted his approval, which might have had something to do with the fact that he didn't pay any National Insurance himself. He expressed his scepticism about whether the cash would make any difference, though: it was his view that NHS staff were likely to 'piss the money up the wall'. Pissing money up the wall was certainly an activity he knew plenty about. Mind you, so did I.

I know all about pissing money up the wall because I'm a drinker.

You might think you know what a drinker is but, just in case you don't, let me tell you. A drinker is massively different from someone who drinks. You can tell them apart when the evening begins. Someone who drinks, for instance, will begin drinking when the drinking starts; a drinker will begin drinking *before* it starts. When meeting some friends for a drink, I'll stop off for a drink on the way. Why? Because my friends don't drink as much as me; besides, it's nice to have a buzz on by the time you meet up.

You can also tell drinkers apart when the evening ends. Someone who drinks, for instance, may be completely oblivious to the fact that there's only five minutes to go before closing time; a drinker never will be. A drinker will have his ears cocked for the first bell, and he'll dread the sound of the second. The second is the serious bell because it's the one that means you have to get out. After the first, a drinker will know exactly how long there is to go before the second; he'll know precisely how many chasers he can fit in between last orders and booting-out time. I could usually fit in two between 'Time gentlemen, please' and 'Time gentlemen, *please*.' Then I could get another one down in the occasionally narrow gap between 'Time gentlemen, PLEASE' and 'Haven't you lot got any homes to go to?' By the time the staff were telling us that 'the gaffer's on the phone to the police', I'd be tipping what was left of my short into the dregs of my pint to make it look as if I'd downed it. When the police arrived I'd down it, and leave. Why I made such a big deal out of staying in the pub I don't know: I always had a fridge full of lager at home to fall back on.

One of the reasons I'd taken a job at the *Reflector* was because I thought a career as a journalist wouldn't interfere too much with my penchant for getting off my dingers. You know what they say about journalists being piss-heads? Well, that used to be the case when I started. When I worked on the entertainments' page in my early years, for instance, I hardly ever saw a film or a play sober. In fact, I hardly ever saw a film or a play. Given that all films and plays premiere somewhere other than in Walsall there was always an existing review that I could plagiarize. As work-related activities go, getting paid to watch films or plays is a good one; but getting paid to get shitfaced is even better.

Thus, while everyone else was in the theatre I'd be in the bar.

Restaurant reviews were also something I'd put myself forward for. I'd always have a fish starter and a red meat main course because this gave me an excuse to order a bottle of white wine *and* a bottle of red. In Walsall, of course, fish comes in batter and red meat in pastry, but at least wine takes your mind off the taste. The two bottles would sit nicely on the two or three lagers I'd have by way of an aperitif. Naturally, I could seldom remember what the food was like when I came to write up my experience but this problem was easily solved by stringing together a few impressive phrases from *MasterChef* or, for a dumbed-down account, *Junior MasterChef*.

*Walsall Reflector* workers need to drink. The unrelenting tedium of the job would kill you otherwise, even on the entertainments' page (which, as the name implies, was by far the most entertaining). For instance, the best you can hope for in terms of excitement are interviews with those minor celebrities who turn up for sad end-of-career gigs at Walsall Town Hall. *Opportunity Knocks* runners-up from the mid-1970s with thinning perms and white slip-on shoes. That or ex-*Crossroads* no-hopers struggling to eke out a living doing voice-overs for dog biscuit commercials. Whenever they appear in Panto the phrase 'from TV's *Crossroads*' appears beneath their name. Interview them sober and their pitiful desperation will make you crave oblivion.

I never had the chance to report on anything interesting. The great scandals of the 1990s passed me by. The stories that might've provided stimulus enough to distract me from the hop and grape were all happening somewhere else. Where was I when *EastEnders*' lovely Gillian Taylforth was blowing her boyfriend on the M1? Where was I when gap-toothed Tory David Mellor was having his toe sucked? Where was I during Squidgygate? I know where I *should've* been. I should've been rummaging through Jonathan King's dustbin or scanning Gary Glitter's hard drive. But I wasn't. I was reviewing the comedy of Chippy Tickles at the Pleck Working Men's Club, or commenting on the quality of the pickled eggs in Bernie's Banjo Shack. I don't know about other drunks' excuses, but that's mine.

Times have changed, though. Sadly it's becoming harder and harder for a self-respecting pisshead to maintain a career in newspapers (other than by selling them on street corners). These days journalism is full of eager young Media Studies graduates who have private gym subscriptions and who eat something called hummus. They frown on pissheads. They don't even drink Diet Coke because they're worried about its caffeine content. Instead they consume mineral water but, if feeling reckless, might risk a J2O. Newsrooms used to smell of fag smoke and sweat; now there's no smoking and all armpits are scrupulously deodorized.

This new breed of journalist has ruined the job. They're fuckers. (I'm on a roll now, so please indulge me.) They are fuckers, not only because they don't drink, but for a plethora of other reasons. They are fuckers because they use the *Reflector* as a stopping-off point on their way to bigger and better papers. They are fuckers because they remind me of *Blue Peter* presenters. Mainly they are fuckers because they make me look bad. When I arrive at my desk in the morning they eye me with disapproval. While they are polishing their copy or double-checking their references I, who as their sub-editor should be doing these jobs, am combing www.hangoverguide.com. They spend their time in the office pestering Newsdesk for promising stories and eagerly phoning contacts; they are optimistic and, as such, take an interest in press releases from National Newswire and Reuters, in the vain hope that international affairs might have some bearing on Walsall life. While they're doing this, I'm worrying about whether I could make to it the bog in time if I need to be sick, or if, as is occasionally the case, I'll have to use the wastepaper bin. Which they don't like at all.

The new breed just refuse to agree with me. They refuse to laugh at my jokes; they refuse to see the funny side when I drop my guts in the office; they refuse to bring me cheap fags from their mini-breaks overseas, even though they don't smoke; they refuse to see that Ronan Keating is a wanker; worst of all, they refuse to romanticize me the way I, when I was their age, romanticized Ernest Hemingway, Jeffrey Bernard and, above all, Charles Bukowski. Why can't these people admire a drunken writer?

I was busy contemplating how little I have in common with these fuckers when Deekus approached me.

'It's too much booze then, is it, Dave?'

'All the evidence seems to point to that.'

'You don't have to tell me about it, mate; if they can't think of anything else they'll blame it on the naffing booze. Look at me: I'd only drink, what? Forty or fifty pints a week; maybe a bottle or two of whisky to settle my stomach. That's nothing. They don't live in the real world that's their trouble . . .'

Deekus continued talking but I replaced my headphones and tried to ignore his jaundiced spectre. I know it's rude, but it would have been even less polite to throttle him.

Tinker Lawson was telling his listeners that his show should have finished ten minutes ago but he'd locked himself in the studio and 'the bastards' were going to have to drag him out. He played 'E-Coli' and 'Blood on the Floor' by Throbbing Gristle and then, positively benign by comparison, the Smiths' late classic, 'Death at One's Elbow'.

# There, There

At WANK, our one compulsory course, Dunderdale's 'Learning to Evaluate', was unpopular with many students. I think this was because they considered Dunderdale to be a moaning old fart, even though he was only in his thirties. It was also unpopular with Dunderdale's young and trendy colleagues. From what I could gather, this was because its purpose was to teach students how to determine good books from crap books, an activity which they considered subjective, ideologically loaded and, hence, to be avoided. I enjoyed it, though, and next to Ruud Van Door's course, it was my favourite that first term. I liked it because I liked Dunderdale. He was an old(ish) cynic who enjoyed looking down his nose at things; I was a young(ish) cynic who enjoyed doing the same. Where Dunderdale loved slagging off popular fiction and the people who read and write it, I loved slagging off Walsall and the people who live there. I enjoyed being miserable about Walsall the way I think he enjoyed being miserable about the critical acumen of the average reader. Though I didn't have his brains, his breeding or his education, I identified with him a good deal. We both loved to moan. But, unlike me, he believed in something.

I recall something that he said in his very first class: 'Whatever the trendy postmodernists tell you, there is right and there is wrong, and there is greatness and there is mediocrity, both in life and in art.' He loved to talk about the truth and he held it in high esteem. 'There is truth,' he would say, striking an impressive pose at the lectern, 'there is truth, there is truth, there is truth. Always strive for it; never try to avoid it.' It was dramatic stuff and I lapped it up, even though many of his anti-relativist arguments went straight over my head.

Ringo and I were attending one of Dunderdale's classes on the morning we heard the news.

It was the seventh week of term, a few days after Ringo had slept with Ebola Barker. Dunderdale usually began his lecture by tearing up a copy of a Danielle Steele novel but this morning he entered the room empty-handed. He looked more stooped and weary than usual. His eyes were red as if he'd been crying.

'Ladies and gentlemen,' he said, 'I have some terrible, terrible news. I have just been informed that one of our members of staff has died. Dr Ebola Barker passed away over the weekend. I have no more details at present but, as a mark of respect, this and all of today's lectures will be cancelled.'

Ringo gazed into space for a long while, unblinking. I put my hand on his shoulder to ask if he was OK but he didn't respond. I squeezed his shoulder and gave it a little shake. As I did so a tear pearled in his eye, as if my squeeze had forced it out. It was followed by more quiet, restrained tears which gradually became more pronounced until he was sobbing freely. I've always tried to avoid public displays of emotion and so I was bit embarrassed. I combed my lexicon of sympathy phrases and drew blank after blank.

'There there,' I found myself saying at last. It's not that I'm uncaring; it's just that banality has me in its shackles. If I'd tried a hundred times I couldn't have come up with anything more appropriate or comforting.

'There's something funny about her dying like this,' he

spluttered, as his body shuddered with grief. 'There's something funny about it.'

'What? What are you talking about? What do you know about it?'

I took Ringo over to the union bar, luckily bumping into Monica on the way. She readily agreed to skip her class ('Dressing Geriatric Bed Sores: Theories and Paradigms'), in order to help me console our flatmate. She was infinitely better at this kind of thing than me; I'd long envied her unselfconscious ability to embrace people.

Though normally teetotal, Ringo allowed himself a medicinal brandy. I ordered a double for myself and, while out of sight of the others at the bar, I downed an extra one. I needed it. The news of Ebola's death had shaken me too and I had a funny taste in my mouth, as if I'd been sucking metal.

'Drink this, mate,' I said, 'you've had a shock.'

He'd been weeping into Monica's shoulder, but a couple of sips of the brandy steadied him.

'Ringo, mate,' I asked, as gently as I could, 'what did you mean when you said there's something funny about Ebola's death?'

'Oh, I don't know . . . Maybe I was over-reacting. It's just that when we were together I talked to her again about the "call me doctor" business.'

'And what about it?' asked Monica, who had also been left ashen-faced and shaky by the news.

'She said that a member of the English Department isn't who they seem. She said if I only knew the truth about them all my illusions would be shattered.'

'Christ,' I said, 'who the fuck was she talking about?'

'She wouldn't tell me. But if she knew who was visiting Penny's, perhaps she also knew what Dionne Splendour knows: that he's a fake.'

'Is it possible that someone was responsible for Ebola's death?'

'Oh, I don't know,' he said, suddenly calming down considerably. 'I'm sorry to be so dramatic; I'm just upset.'

'There there, mate,' I said. 'There there.'

# The Scream

The police were waiting for us when we arrived back at the flat at about four o'clock. They wanted to question Ringo down at the station. Apparently someone had seen him and Ebola together and had given the police his name.

Ringo didn't get home until seven. I'd been sleeping off the double brandies on the settee and his return woke me. Monica made us all a coffee and Ringo, still jittery, filled us in on what had happened.

'It was an overdose,' he said. 'Barbiturates, apparently, combined with alcohol.'

'Christ, why was she taking barbiturates?'

'The police found a lot of slimming tablets in the house. They make it hard for you to get to sleep,' he said, looking at Monica, our resident medical consultant, for confirmation.

'That's right,' she said, 'some slimming tablets are amphetamine-based.'

'So, do the police think it was suicide or an accident?'

'They don't know. They're waiting for more post-mortem reports on her body.' Ringo's voice faltered and he struggled to continue. Monica told him to take some deep breaths.

'But they've ruled out foul play of any kind?' I asked, when he'd composed himself.

'They didn't say anything about that, no.' Ringo had a

peculiar look on his face: slightly puzzled, slightly frightened.

'What is it, mate?' I asked him.

'I, I can't . . . I don't know what to make of it,' he said.

'Tell us,' said Monica.

'Ebola had been beating someone's bare bottom with a leather paddle. They found hairs and skin on a spanking paddle. They wanted to know if I'd been her pleasure slave.'

I wondered where the phrase 'pleasure slave' came from. It was another example of Ringo's odd speech which, in those days, was often slightly off-key. In other circumstances I'd have laughed out loud at it but, that day, the gravity of its implications gave me a gobful of glue.

'Ringo,' I said, having to force my tongue away from my palate before I could enunciate the words, 'the paddle wasn't by any chance decorated with a Staffordshire knot made out of silver studs?'

Ringo nodded.

'That's a Penny's Punishment Palace paddle,' I said, though everyone in the room knew it perfectly well, 'one that I made for her dungeon.'

'How did Ebola get hold of one of those?' asked Monica.

'Maybe she picked it up when she was round here the other week,' Ringo offered.

'How, though?' I said. 'There were none in this flat and she didn't get into the Palace: Penny warned her off, remember. You can't get them retail. It must've been from a punter.'

I suggested that we continue this discussion in the pub, where we could really get our teeth into it, but Ringo and Monica declined. I left alone.

When I returned from the Red Lion at midnight the flat was in darkness and I went straight to bed. I fell asleep immediately but, as is often the way after a skinful, I pinged bolt awake again an hour later. The street outside was quiet except for the occasional motorist slowing down, stopping, opening and closing a door, and then swiftly departing. Above Monica's breathing I could hear Ringo in the living room. He was listening to my Amstrad with the headphones on. I guess Ebola was on his mind. Despite the headphones, I could faintly make out Morrissey's voice – fretful, resigned to despair and social inadequacy – floating through the night. Ringo was playing the *Hatful of Hollow* album: 'This Night Has Opened My Eyes', 'You've Got Everything Now'; he was torturing himself. In the pub nineteen games of pool had taken my mind off Ebola, but now my thoughts returned to her.

I was a little concerned that I wasn't as upset about Ebola's death as I should be. I was sorry, yes, but I couldn't help believing that my feelings should be more profound. Monica often bemoaned what she called my 'lack of emotional depth', though I'd argue that she was wrong, that my feelings were as deep as the next man's. And, now that I'd had a few beers, surely I'd be able to tap into the well of sentimentality that often seems to lie beneath my cynicism – but I couldn't.

As far as I was concerned Ebola was dead and that was it. I hadn't really liked her and I couldn't help it. As pissed and potentially treacle-eyed as I was I couldn't weep for her.

I think Ringo switched to Aztec Camera for a while before I heard him retire. I lay awake for quite a bit longer watching the clock radio move through the one thirties and forties. Eventually I began the descent into sleep. I must've been on the verge of unconsciousness when I was startled by a long, agonized scream from the flat below. I couldn't tell if it was a male or female scream, but it climbed into me through every pore of my skin to leave my nerves wailing in fright.

'Jesus freaking H.,' I gasped, my heart racing and a pulse thumping in each eardrum. Monica, though, didn't stir and, as my heartbeat gradually slowed, I was forced to listen to the numb silence alone.

Harrowing noises from Penny's weren't uncommon, but I seldom heard screams like that one. I lay awake for hours more and, as sobriety slowly returned, I struggled in vain to recoat my flayed nerves with something resembling a skin of calm.

# The Diversions
# of the Devil's Juice

Ultimately, the verdict was accidental death. Ringo told the cops about Ebola's sadistic and possibly fraudulent colleague – whoever he might be – and about where the paddle they'd found must've come from. However, either their questioning led them nowhere, or they didn't feel this line of inquiry worthy of pursuit. I suppose they just wrote her off as a kinky neurotic who'd overdone the booze and barbs. But her death disturbed me and devastated Ringo. For him, Ebola was a bright, inspirational person. Though I agreed she was bright, I thought she was a bit cracked. Her struggles to find herself were obvious and a little sad. It's difficult not to be suspicious of a woman who publicly strips down to undies made of gummed-together porn. I know it's only a rumour but the very fact that such a rumour flourished tells you something about her, surely. Let's face it, it's the behaviour of someone who's trying far too hard. Ebola's death was a strange business, though, and a difficult one to assess: not even Ringo had known her that well. We would find out the truth eventually. But not till sixteen years later.

Life returned to normal pretty quickly at WANK. One consequence of Ebola's demise was that Winifred Wiggins took over the last few weeks of her 'Poststructuralism and the Penis' course. Winnie was hampered by a complete lack of knowledge of poststructuralism, and a complete refusal to utter the word penis in public. She insisted on calling it 'Postmodernism and the P' (pronounced *pee*), which sounded a hundred times more offensive. Nor did she appreciate my waggish suggestion that the name of the course be changed to 'Postructuralism and the Pocket Rocket'. Luckily for her, and us, one of Winnie's more informed and less prudish colleagues helped her with the marking.

We submitted our first essays just before Christmas. I picked up D grades for almost everything; Ringo scored As. I was happy just to be afloat, though, because, despite attending lectures and visiting the library regularly, I almost never studied with a clear head. By now, thanks to Ruud Van Door, the hard-drinking Charles Bukowski had become my hero. I'd read everything of his I could get my hands on, even sending off to America for obscure books with titles like *Confessions of a Man Insane Enough to Live with Beasts* and *Poems Written Before Jumping out of an 8 Story Window*. As a fellow drunk living in a soul-sapping crap-hole his words spoke directly to me. What I also liked about Bukowski was that he hated posers as much as I did. And he hated academics. It wouldn't surprise him that someone could bullshit his or her way into a college post. Academics are all bullshitters to him. My essay on Charles Bukowski was the only piece I scored a decent grade for all term. Ruud Van Door gave me a B+ for an essay entitled 'The Diversions of the Devil's Juice: Alcohol and Redemption in the Poetry of Charles Bukowski'.

Monica reckoned that I used Charles Bukowski's example as a justification for my own excesses. She was probably right. But I reasoned that if Bukowski could write three dozen books while off his tits, then I could knock out a few essays. Besides, I found booze and Bukowski complemented the cynical side of my nature extremely well; consequently this had become nicely honed during my first term at WANK.

Apart from offering unwanted insights into my status as a tit, Monica was as tolerant as could be expected. She'd nag me about my repulsive farts, my tendency to fall asleep with my face in a chicken dansak, and my deficient erections, but she did her best not to consign me to a park bench. I suppose it didn't hurt that she was doing well at college. She, like Ringo, received straight As for every piece of work. And it was useful having Ringo around because he'd take Monica off my hands, not to mention distract her from my inadequacies as a boyfriend. They'd go to the cinema; I'd go to the pub. They'd go to a concert; I'd go to the pub. While they were gulping down *Platoon*, *Hannah and Her Sisters* and The Fall, I'd be doing hilarious beer-mat tricks for the pensioners in the lounge bar of the Red Lion.

In the week before Christmas we discovered the identity of the WANK impostor and S&M man. Monica was having an end-of-term curry with the other students on her course, and Ringo and I had been out on our own. We returned home from the pub and, on the way upstairs, bumped into Penny Stroker.

'Hey, Dave, hey Clogs,' she said, 'how're they swinging?' She then lowered her voice to a whisper. 'Listen, lads, remember a while back I told you one of your teachers was paddling his way through our girls?'

We remembered.

'Well, I found out his name.'

'Go on,' I said.

'Hang on,' said Penny, 'it gets more interesting. He told Dionne that he isn't even fucking qualified to be a lecturer; says he just invented his qualifications.'

'Really?' I didn't want to let on to Penny that we already knew; it might have landed Dionne in trouble. It was one thing for Penny to blab; another one entirely for her girls.

'Fucking really. He's a nasty piece of work too, lads. If you could see the state of Dionne's arse after that fucker's finished with it it would turn your stomach.'

'Name, Penny; can you give us his name?'

Penny fired a long and resonant burp into her fist, and then gave us his name.

# Don't Get Me Started

I removed my headphones again as Tinker introduced 'We Must Bleed' by the Germs: listening to those American punks requires a different sort of illness to the one that ailed me. Deekus was trying to muscle in on a football discussion Gulliver and Donovan were having. It was his opinion that big business had ruined the game for the working man, and that it is David, rather than Victoria, Beckham who 'takes it up the arse'. I opened one eye and noticed Droppy sitting in my visitor's chair, staring at me. I just about managed to suppress a yelp.

'Er . . . hello, Droppy,' I said.

'No gallstones, then, wack?'

'No, Droppy.'

'It's probably the ale, then.'

'Apparently so.'

'I've sin it a thousand times in this place.'

'Really?' I said, with a sigh.

'Oh arr, wack, arr. They'll wanna tek a CAT scan I suppose, to see if yower pancreas has really lost the plot.'

'Dr Fostus said he'd ask Dunderdale about –'

'Yow've no chance of seeing Dunderdale, wack.'

'Do you think you could perhaps leave me alone please, Droppy?'

'Doh worry, wack, if it's knackered they can 'ave a goo at 'acking the knackered bit away. Mind you, wack, it's one o' the wust operations I've sin. And I've sin a few. Yow'll be in 'ere for three month at least, if it guz well.'

Deekus was suddenly standing at Droppy's side. 'He's right, you know; just ask me if you want telling what it's like having your pancreas messed with. Nasty, very nasty. You'd think they'd be shit-hot at it here seeing how many they do, but oh no. They lose a lot of patients during that operation. I only pulled through by the skin of my teeth. If it'd been up to these bastards I'd be a goner. I don't want to worry you, Dave, but Dunderdale's the worst of a bad bunch. Naffing hell, he should be in jail.'

'He's right, yow know, wack,' said Droppy. 'If yow ask me he doh know what he's doing.'

'I'm sure you don't get to be a consultant surgeon without knowing something, Droppy. Now do you think the two of you could let me get a bit of rest?'

'Of course, mate,' said Deekus, 'but it's true. Dunderdale's the biggest joker in the pack. He's only been here a month and he's had loads of complaints already. Take it from me; there's nothing goes on around here that I don't know about. He's a naffing liability. I think he drinks. Mind you, everybody else does on the Lost Islands of Langerhans.'

'True. Very true,' said Droppy.

I was saved by Annette, the auxiliary, come to do my observations. The moment she arrived Deekus and Droppy scurried away. 'Don't take any notice of those two, dear,' she said. 'They're as stupid as a boat full of stupid.'

'I don't. I'm sure Mr Dunderdale is a fine surgeon and as sober as a judge; or, for that matter, a surgeon.'

'It's not my place to say,' she said.

'And what does that mean exactly?'

'It doesn't mean anything except that it's not my place to say.'

I was suddenly angry. If she'd said it with a 'I'm only

sending you up' twinkle in her eye I wouldn't have minded. But she didn't. She said it as if there might really be something amiss with my surgeon: a gentleman who may well have to tinker with my vitals.

'It *is* your place to say, though, isn't it?' I said. 'All you're doing by saying "it's not my place to say" is putting the shits up me. And surely it's not your place to put the shits up me. Or is it? Is that what you're trying to do? Is it because I write for the *Reflector*? Is it because I'm Dave *Ichabod* McVane? It *is*, isn't it?'

'Don't be silly, Mr McVane,' she said. 'Calm down.'

She didn't say it with any conviction, though, and I began to wonder if this was because she was trying to frighten me or because Dunderdale *really was* dangerous. Or both.

Annette took my blood pressure and temperature in silence as I quietly seethed. She put a little peg, a pulse-oximeter, on my finger to measure the oxygen level in my blood. She took a blood-sugar measurement too. The latter involves bodging a hole through the skin with a device not dissimilar to a staple gun, smearing the resulting bubble of blood onto a paper slide, and then popping this into a machine which displays your sugar level immediately; on this occasion: 6.5.

'Is that OK?' I asked.

'Fine, Mr McVane, fine.'

'My Islands of Langerhans are doing their job, I take it?'

'For now.'

'Meaning?'

'Nothing.'

'Do you mind not being so mysterious, nurse?' I said, flaring up again. 'Unlike the rest of the patients here I'm in a position to make my treatment at this hospital very public indeed.' This sounded a bit self-important and, since the *Reflector* only had a circulation of 20,000, it was largely untrue. Still, it seemed to hack Annette off.

'Listen, Mr McVane,' she said, 'I see people with your problem every day. The reason I said "for now" is because, though we might discharge patients with a warning not to risk drinking any more, they always do. They always come back, and back, and back, for as long as it takes them to finish themselves off. You might have normal blood-sugar levels now; let's see how you're faring in a year's time.'

'Please don't compare me to these people,' I said, feeling a bit of a cunt for referring to my fellow patients as 'these people'. Who did I mean, anyway? Deekus? Yes, I suppose. I might over-indulge but I was nothing like the Deekuses of this world. At least I hoped not.

Annette gave my catheter tube a bit of an unnecessary tug as she checked my urine level and then she left. The second she'd gone Deekus squeaked his way back to the side of my bed.

'I wouldn't let that bitch talk to me like that. You've got rights, you know.'

I rolled over and shut my eyes, but Deekus continued to talk at my back; his voice nipping at the space between my shoulder blades.

'You've got enough naffing problems, mate, without that shit-shovelling slag giving you grief. You'd think they'd be grateful to have employment, wouldn't you? There are people crying out for jobs like hers – white people too . . .'

On and on he went. If I hadn't got a five-pound bag of piss strapped to my dick I'd have dropped the fucker. It was only when he mentioned the name Dunderdale again that I took any notice of what he was wittering on about.

'And as for that twat Dunderdale; he's an arrogant bastard, when he can be bothered to put in an appearance, of course. He's too busy poncing about acting the big *I am* to worry about his patients. Not that he's got many left he's such an incompetent bastard. And woe betide you if you should make the mistake of calling him Dr Dunderdale;

oh Christ no. "It's *Mr* Dunderdale to you, Deekus," he'll say. "You don't call a consultant doctor." Anyone else would let it go but not him.'

I turned to face him at last. 'Deekus,' I said, 'how old is Dunderdale, would you say?'

'I don't know, mate, difficult to tell. He's got one of those posh, upper-class faces. Privilege you see, they don't age like the working classes.'

'Take a guess.'

'Mid-fifties I suppose.'

'And what does he look like?'

'Blond bloke, biggish, a bit stooped. Drinker's nose. Nasty naffer when you rub him the wrong way. Then you can look out because he'll –'

'You don't know his Christian name by any chance,' I said, cutting Deekus off before he got on a roll.

'Not unless it's mister,' he said, tittering at his own joke. 'One of them naffing nurses will probably know. They all stick together, particularly if you try and sue them. Oh yes, they close ranks straight away then. If you knew how many times I've had a watertight case against this place and my solicitor has said, "Deekus, they all stick together when they're being sued, mate, you'll never win." It's a clique, the Health Service, oh yes, don't get me started on the times I've . . .'

My mind began to drift away again and his voice droned on. I replaced my headphones – knowing that Deekus was totally incapable of recognizing ordinary social cues.

Tinker Lawson had by this time reached an almost hysterical climax. He was screaming obscenities at the hospital authorities who were hammering on the studio door. Tinker was claiming to be a good friend of Chris Evans, and saying that he'd been a fool to think the 'wankers at Wesley-in-Tame would ever appreciate a quality performer'.

He then played a Marilyn Manson number called 'May Cause Discoloration of the Urine or Faeces'. To my delight he followed this with two more Smiths classics, 'Pretty Girls Make Graves' and 'Cemetery Gates'.

# Pervo!

When Penny told us which of our lecturers had been visiting her Palace we found it difficult to believe. As Ringo and I walked up to 47C our legs were wonky with the weight of the scandal we carried.

'Do you think she's got it right?' I asked Ringo. 'Surely she's made a mistake?'

'His name wasn't top of my list,' said Ringo.

'But . . .'

'But . . .'

'Blimey.'

'Flaming Ada.'

'This is news.'

'Could it be bigger?'

'Prince Philip?'

'Dennis Thatcher?'

'Harry Secombe? Cliff Richard? Basil Brush?'

'Who?'

'Never mind, never mind,' I said. 'No, it couldn't be bigger. We've got plenty of fodder for the gossip-trough here, that's for fucking sure.'

'Ace-a-mundo,' said Ringo.

I could see the excitement brimming in him too. We were going to relish interpreting the consequences of this titbit. Except that it was more than a titbit; it was a twelve-course banquet. We would gorge ourselves.

I reached for my smokes, but noticed I was low. They'd be essential for the protracted gossip session that lay ahead, so I decided to nip to the offie for forty B&H.

I legged it there and back because it had begun to rain; an icy, squally shower. And on my return to our building I bumped into him. He was just descending the steps from the house, on his way out of Penny's.

'Mr Dunderdale,' I said, deliberately calling him mister; if he hadn't earned a PhD I wasn't going to credit him with one.

He pretended not to see me at first. His collar was up and he had his hand cupped over his nose in an effort to shield his face. I wasn't going to let him sneak away, though. This was far too good an opportunity to miss. I grabbed him by the sleeve of his raincoat.

'Mr Dunderdale,' I repeated.

He turned to look at me. 'David McVane? What are *you* doing here?'

'I live here, Mr Dunderdale. What are you doing here?'

He blanched when I told him I lived in the building. I could see the panic in his face: the look of a man who knows you have his nads in your pocket. He must've realized that it was useless to lie about *his* reason for being there. He wilted; I suppose I should have felt sorry for him.

'Have you anything you'd like to say, Mr Dunderdale?' I asked. I had the impression I sounded like a *News of the World* journalist and this, for reasons best known to my subconscious, gave me a bit of a thrill.

'I don't suppose there's any chance of you forgetting you've seen me?' he asked, desperation clear in his voice.

What a surprise, he wanted me to lie. I was ready with my smart-arse answer: 'Wasn't it you who said we should never avoid the truth, Mr Dunderdale? Wasn't it you who said that our very lives depend on us finding the truth and championing it?'

'In this instance,' he said, 'the truth is that to be true to myself I have to live a lie.'

'Yow wot?'

'Never mind. I'm just asking you to give me a chance. Imploring you, actually.'

'Sorry, Mr Dunderdale.'

'My wife will . . . I don't know what my wife will do.'

'Sorry, Mr Dunderdale. From what I hear you're a piece of scum.'

'What?'

'You're a sadist; a pervert. And worse, you're a liar.'

He seemed to ponder this for a minute and then replied, 'I'm not sure if this is the time or place to discuss morality. But, for what it's worth, I don't believe I'm a "piece of scum". I don't deserve what will doubtless happen to me if people get to hear of my . . . my . . . little weakness.'

'Sorry, Mr Dunderdale,' I repeated, enjoying the kick of power my knowledge had suddenly given me.

'Very well, then. I don't suppose there's anything else to say. Except this: could you please do me the courtesy of using my correct title; it's *Doctor* Dunderdale to you.'

'I'm not one of your hired girls, *Mr* Dunderdale. I'm not going to credit you with qualifications you haven't got.'

'What?'

'To think I respected you; I looked up to you.'

He stared hard at me for a moment and then shrugged. 'Oh, what's the point?' he said. 'It's all over now. First Ebola and now this.' And with that he began to walk away.

'Wait a minute,' I shouted. I ran after him, driven by my need for an explanation – and did he just mention Ebola? I grabbed again at his sleeve and he turned. As he did so his raincoat swung open to reveal a pair of pink leather torture shorts. The top half of Dunderdale's body was naked apart from a matching pink leather harness that tightly criss-crossed his pallid chest. At its centre, where the straps met, was a thick metal ring to which a lead could be attached by means of a bulldog clip. Generally speaking, S&M attire is cheaply and poorly constructed but both these items, I can assure you, had the patina of professional craftsmanship: I'd made them. I remember it took me hours to fix thin strips of leather around each buckle and ring attachment on the harness so the stitches didn't show. I'd had to borrow the state-of-the-art skiving machine at Garner & Barnett's leather factory to render the strips condom-thin; tight and unobtrusive. You don't get such attention to cosmetic detail with the cheap stuff.

'Those shorts must be chaffing,' I said, referring to their hessian lining.

The shock of seeing Dunderdale in this attire was considerable to say the least. Though he was a big fellow, he looked pathetic. Where the leather shorts ended, his milk-white legs began. They were substantial but flabby and his blue-veined skin cringed against the cold, with the fine hairs above his goosebumps standing to attention like iron filings in the presence of a magnet. On his feet his brown socks and suede Hush Puppies were tragically incongruous.

'Just leave me alone,' he yelled, pulling his coat around him. 'You've caught me out, isn't that enough?' There were tears in his eyes.

There'd be tears in mine too had I been wearing his knickers. The hessian was of a particularly coarse variety that I'd blagged off a guy I know in the saddlery trade – they use it as foundation material for saddle seats because it's grainy and you can glue things to it easily. I'd had a dilemma whether to fix the lining to the leather with latex glue, or just to let it hang freely within the trouser. I'd opted for the latter because I feared the latex could stiffen and distort the shape of the garment.

'I'd have thought you'd have taken those off for the walk home,' I said.

He turned away from me again saying, more to himself than to me, 'Mistress Dionne makes me wear them.'

For an instant I glimpsed his fantasy character. Mistress Dionne indeed! Ringo would lap that up! It seemed that Dunderdale, like his mistress, was a switch. I'd heard this was quite unusual in punters, but then 'unusual' was clearly a term that suited our Head of School.

I'd have happily continued mocking Dunderdale but he began to walk away, with an understandably awkward, bow-legged gait. I considered shouting 'pervert' after him but the word seemed trite. My brain cantered through its lexicon for an alternative and, genius that I am, I came up with one.

'*Pervo!*' I shouted.

Dunderdale didn't look back.

I thought I'd seen it all in my time living above a brothel. I'd long since stopped being scandalized by human beings' pathetic, tireless search for stimulation. I'd heard screams from punters with their bollocks on fire, I'd seen grown men dressed as Shirley Temple. I, personally, had made things out of leather that would've put the Marquis de Sade off his baguette. But, because I'd never known any punters personally, I'd never thought of them as real people. I hadn't considered what Penny's clients did in their 'normal' lives. In fact, I'd never thought of them as having lives. They have, though, and now it was in my power to ruin Mr Dunderdale's.

# Staffordshire Knot

'You'll never guess who I just met at the door,' I said to Ringo when, breathless, I reached our flat. He was sitting on the settee rubbing Tiger Balm into his knees. His conviction that his session with Ebola had been a catalyst for some mysterious, debilitating shin and kneecap disorder meant that these days the flat reeked perpetually of Tiger Balm.

'Who?'

'Dunderdale!'

His eyes widened. 'Where is he now?'

'I just left him walking towards town.'

'Right,' he said, rolling his jeans down and grabbing his jacket.

'Where are you going?'

'I've a few things I want to say to him!' Ringo left the flat, taking the stairs like Carl Lewis. So much for his dodgy knees.

I thought I'd better follow him, just to make sure he didn't get into any trouble. I caught up with him on the second-floor landing where he'd halted his descent. He was listening at the door of 47B.

The sound of spanking was again coming from the room: *woooosh, slack; woooosh, slack*. Dionne's voice was, again, clearly audible: 'Hurt me, doctor, hurt me. I deserve worse, doctor, beat me some more.'

'The bastard's still at it!' Ringo said. 'He's come back for more!'

'Maybe my catching him has thrown him into dom-mode?' I said. I had no knowledge of the psychology of an S&M 'switch', but it sounded plausible. He hadn't hung around: no more than five minutes had elapsed since our encounter.

Before I could stop him, Ringo was banging at the door.

'It's Ringo from *Red Sox*, would you like to comment on your presence in a brothel?' he shouted. He was bluffing, of course; he knew he wouldn't be allowed to write about the staff's sexual shenanigans.

He banged on the door some more. I could see that he'd make a great journalist.

I was in the process of pulling him away when the door opened and Dionne Splendour confronted us. She was holding a giant bath towel around her naked body. The towel was splattered with a plethora of repulsive stains. You could have written a review of it for *Postmodern Art Quarterly*.

'What the fuck's going on?' Her face was flushed and her hair was a knotted mess.

'Have you got *Dr* Daniel Dunderdale in there?' Ringo demanded.

She glanced nervously over her shoulder. 'So what if I have?' she hissed in a panicky whisper.

'Tell him I'd like a quote for the student paper.'

'Look, clear off, Clogs, or I'll call Penny and she'll give you a pasting; either her or Woody.'

'Just tell him I came to England for an education, but not this kind of education!'

'He's got other things on his mind right now . . .' She glanced over her shoulder and seemed about to say something else, but thought better of it. Instead she jerked her thumb in the direction of the street and mouthed 'just fuck off' at us. As she turned to re-enter the flat the towel swung away from her rear and I noticed Staffordshire-knot flagellation marks on her buttocks. The marks weren't of the pink, playful variety; they were raised welts with spots of dark blood beading at their peaks. I should've known the man who caused them was dangerous. I should've kicked down the door and made a citizen's arrest there and then. Instead I turned to Ringo and said, 'Flaming Ada!'

Ringo and I couldn't wait for Monica's return: both of us were thrilled with our pot of gossip gold. In the right circumstances a good scandal, or even a half-decent salacious rumour, can tie a knot of excitement in the pit of my stomach. The anticipation of passing it on gives me a feeling akin to the anticipation of sex. A feeling which is much more compatible with booze.

That evening I could barely contain myself. As I chatted to Ringo I sipped, smoked and listened out for Monica's key in the lock.

'We know, we know,' I blurted, a millisecond after Monica had walked through the door. 'The academic who visits Penny's, we know who it is!'

'Daniel Dunderdale,' said Monica.

It was like a premature ejaculation: I'd wanted to build up to it and the bitch had stolen my crescendo. 'How the fuck do you know?' I asked, vexed almost to distraction.

'I met Dionne just before I went out. She was due to see him tonight, apparently, and she wasn't looking forward to it. She says he's a bit of an animal; she finds him scary.'

'He certainly scares me,' I said. And I told her about the welts on Dionne's arse.

'Jesus. He's your Head of School, isn't he?'

'Oh yes.'

'Then this really *is* news.'

'It's the news of the fucking century, Monica!'

'Isn't Dunderdale one of your favourite lecturers?'

'He seems to know what he's talking about, yes,' I admitted. 'It's hard to believe he's not for real. Perhaps Dionne got it wrong about him having faked his CV.'

'She seemed pretty certain,' said Monica. 'She was 100 per cent, in fact. He likes to be called doctor because he isn't a real one. He even bragged about it. Said he had everybody at WANK fooled. I expected him to be some lowly junior lecturer or something; but the *Head of School* . . .'

'Maybe Dunderdale was lying about being a fake?'

'What would be the point of that?' asked Ringo.

'Did I tell you he mentioned Ebola Barker?' I said. I couldn't answer his question, but still needed to fuel the flames of the scandal. '"First Ebola and now this," he said. What do you think of that?'

Monica thought for a moment. 'Are you saying there's a link between them other than a professional one?'

'Maybe.'

'It's interesting, certainly,' said Ringo. 'Ebola was on his mind; maybe there *is* a connection between them.'

'And the paddle!' I said, getting excited again. 'Don't forget about the paddle – that links Ebola to Penny's, which means they're *both* connected to Penny's.'

'Come on, Dave,' said Monica, 'you've made dozens of those.'

'Yes, but all of them went either to Penny or her clients; and Dunderdale's clearly a spank fetishist.'

'You don't know for sure that the paddle links Ebola either to Penny's or to Dunderdale.'

I hated it when Monica wanted to put a lid on my imagination. It contravenes the scandalmonger's code. 'I don't not know it!' I said.

'Sober up, Dave.'

'Sorry. It's true, though.'

What a story! As committed Tory haters we'd recently

been cockahoop over the news that Jeffrey Archer had paid a prostitute to keep her mouth shut. The smug twat was nabbed forking out two grand of hush money to the 'massive-nippled' prosser Monica Coghlan. How sweet life had suddenly become. We'd tittered over and savoured that scandal for many long hours. But Dunderdale's shenanigans, being so much closer to home, topped even Jeffrey Archer's duplicitous knobbing.

I particularly looked forward to watching Ringo break the news at our first lecture after Christmas. I'd leave the tale to him because he was much better at storytelling than me. He was born to it. He could bide his time; he'd feed our fellow students information drop by drop, pacing and structuring his narrative with a delicacy and relish that would give Steven Twist fodder for a hundred lectures. 'And you'll never guess what else . . .' he'd say, pausing in his monologue for a tantalizing and deliciously tortuous moment while he reknotted his laces or popped a pointless paracetamol. He would hint darkly at a possible connection between Dunderdale and Ebola. Had he done her in because she discovered he was a fraud? Had he done her in because she'd seen him at Penny's and threatened to blab? Had she topped herself because he wanted to end their affair? Ringo would hint darkly at just about everything. Wasn't Dunderdale sighted on the grassy knoll in November 1963? Wasn't there some speculation that Dunderdale was Libyan? Hadn't Dunderdale been seen leading Shergar onto a spaceship? The lack of real evidence for any of these speculations is neither here nor there. All good storytellers and all eager listeners know that when there's a whiff of intrigue, facts are as irrelevant as they've always seemed to be in the life of Jeffrey Archer.

It would take us years to find out the truth about Dunderdale, but at least something out of the ordinary had happened in Walsall.

# Dunderdale, You Bastard

Naturally we wouldn't be content merely to gossip about Dunderdale with students. Monica, Ringo and I were all agreed that we should go to the Dean with what we knew. It wasn't just because Dunderdale was a frequenter of brothels, of course. Firstly, the idea that he'd invented his qualifications meant there was a principle at stake. Secondly, it was possible that he really *might* be mixed up in Ebola's death. There was obviously a sinister dimension to Dunderdale; who knew what he was capable of? If we told the story to the Dean, then he'd know the proper way to proceed. We would tell him about the brothel; we would tell him about Dionne; we would tell him about Dunderdale's tears when he announced Ebola's death; we would tell him everything.

On the evening of our discovery we talked till past midnight. We must have debated every aspect of the Dunderdale intrigue. What motivated men like him? What drew them to places like Penny's? *Was* there a connection between him and Ebola? What was the precise nature of their relationship? Was it sexual? What does it say about real academics if it's possible to be a convincing fake? On and on.

After my third or fourth description of Dunderdale's bizarre attire, however, the conversation turned to my former occupation: fetish leathercraft. Ringo, who'd never studied my handiwork up close, insisted I show him some. All I had handy were a few items that had been returned for repair. I showed him a particularly fine leather discipline hood with a ten-inch rhino horn dildo fixed to the top. The horn had become dislodged and I'd resecured it with glue and leather lacing. I also had an electric blue, stretch-leather scrotum pouch and a Viking helmet knob-cap, both of which had seams that had needed re-stitching. The scrotum pouch was an s&m device from Penny's and the knob-cap I'd made as a special order for a male stripper called Thor. The former had a leather drawstring across the top that, like the bollock-boa, could be tightened to induce testicular torment. This had snapped and needed replacing. Ringo ran his eyes over the goods and asked questions about the detail of their construction. He'd evidently forgotten how boring I can be on this subject, so I reminded him.

It had been quite a night and, although talking about leathercrafts took my mind off events a little, I was still very excitable. I'd downed numerous large brandies as the three of us conversed and, by the time Monica and Ringo retired, at about three a.m., I was off my dingers. Monica got quite annoyed with me and insisted I kip on the settee. I was used to this.

I tried to settle down but was still far too pumped up to sleep. I decided to smoke a joint to help calm me down. I had a sizeable chunk of Moroccan red hidden in a cassette box (Lloyd Cole and the Commotions, *Rattlesnakes*). With immense difficulty, I rolled myself a two-skin joint. When, finally, I'd succeeded in making something potentially smokable it resembled a map of the Thames, but I was determined to fire up.

I lit up and took a couple of long bangs. It was strong stuff – Monica and I had smoked a considerable quantity of it while watching *Live Aid* the year before. We'd laughed for an hour and a half over Brian May's poodle perm. I hadn't touched it since. I can leave pot lying around for months without it demanding my attention. Like Marmite or kippers, and unlike drink, it's one of those things I have to fancy rather than something I have to have.

I sucked hard, watching the end flare orange in the dark. I felt the distinctive pot-tingle descend on me, like slipping on a woolly hat. It's strange that, up till then, as enjoyable and entertaining as I found the Dunderdale business, I hadn't fully considered the funny side of it. And it *was* funny: hessian-lined trolleys, for Christ sake! I'd mocked him in the street but I hadn't laughed out loud at him. How did I manage to control myself? My God, he'd looked pathetic in his torture shorts and harness. The respect I'd had for him as my lecturer melted away as the raw human being was exposed: pale, trembling and nauseatingly average. But it was funny; it *was* hilarious. And now, as I smoked, the pot revealed that humorous dimension in all its glory.

I began to titter.

With my appetite for levity whetted by the image of Dunderdale in his s&m get-up, I sought further comic stimulus. Surrounded as I was by fetish leathergear, I didn't have to look far. I lined the three items up on the coffee table: scrotum pouch, knob-cap and rhino-horn helmet. They weren't the most bizarre things I'd ever made, or the nastiest, but they looked ridiculous. It occurred to me that as yet I hadn't checked the efficacy of the repair jobs I'd done on them. I was struck by a sudden impulse to do just that. I suppose it's just one of those daft things you do when you're pissed: like killing fish or torching someone's bollocks.

The best way to check a seam, I've always found, is to wear the item that needs checking. I'd done it many times before – though never when quite as pissed as I was now. With my jeans round my knees, I donned the scrotum pouch, and the knob-cap. Both looked fine. I pulled on the rhino-horn helmet and wobbled the phallus around a little. Caught up in the moment, I decided to strip for full comic effect. I kicked off my 501s and removed my Breton shirt. My discipline hood had zip-up eyeholes and, with these open, I posed in front of our lounge mirror. I looked like a plonker. How could people possibly find this kind of gear sexually arousing? Funny, yes. But arousing? Perhaps, like Ebola, they might in their struggle to avoid the mundane. People will do anything to free themselves from that particular snare. Like coyotes, they'll gnaw their own legs off if they have to.

With my fingers interlocked at the back of my head I began circling my hips hoola-hoop style. The tassled ends of the scrotum-pouch drawstrings swung. I tried to make each one swing in a different direction: clockwise and anti. My attempts made me giddy and I gave up and started thrusting my pelvis at the mirror. My Viking-hatted knob swung up to reveal an electric blue scrotum. My genitals felt snug and oddly desensitized. The leather was thinned calfskin: as soft and malleable as cloth. It cupped impressively and, I must admit, erotically. Perhaps this malarkey had more appeal than I'd given it credit for.

Then I heard what sounded like a bumping noise coming from the landing.

I stood, uncertain, then decided to investigate. I remember standing at the top of the stairs, joint in one hand and a large tumbler of brandy in the other, debating whether or not I should attempt to walk down them. I was aware of very little except that I was shitfaced. I had a vision of myself bouncing down all three flights, limp as a crapulous crash dummy, if I wasn't careful. Also, I was conscious that my attire might seem a trifle outlandish even for the landing of a brothel. The bumping sound seemed to get louder, though, and I thought I heard a woman talking loudly. Did I hear someone speak the name Dunderdale? It sounded like 'Dunderdale, you bastard', or maybe it was just 'you bastard', or maybe it was nothing at all. I was off my knockers so it was impossible to be sure. I remember taking another long drag on the spliff and then, for some reason, deciding that a bolt of brandy was the best way to calm the dope sting in my throat. I was dimly aware of how stupid I was being; I distinctly remember thinking, this is really stupid, and then taking another drag and another swig. As has often been the case in my life, I was helpless in the face of intoxication's seductive lunacy.

I fell down the stairs.

It's surprising how easy falling is when you're shitfaced. You don't panic. Gravity is as seductive as lunacy. You let it take you, like a sneeze or an orgasm. It's as simple as laughing. For my part, I enjoyed the ride. I came to rest on the second-floor landing and lay there, bucking with laughter, my rhino horn swinging.

I remained in that state for what seemed like an hour and a half in pot-time but which was probably no more than ten seconds in reality. I crawled around the landing in the pitch-blackness trying to relocate the stairs. My head hit something and sent it tumbling; my arse hit something else. Eventually I felt the first step and began to crawl up. There was a brief glow of light as a door opened and I became conscious of someone near by. I prayed my leather hood would stop anyone from recognizing me. Then someone spoke again; actually they shouted: 'Dunderdale, you bastard.' I'm sure that's what they said: 'Dunderdale, you bastard,' followed by, 'No, please no.' Some discipline hoods have perforations by the ears so you can hear yourself being insulted, but mine didn't and everything was muffled. But I certainly wasn't going to take it off. Instead I took some deep breaths and tried to steady myself for the ascent to my flat. As I climbed I was conscious of the weight of my rhino-horn helmet and the heavy sway of its dildo. I could picture myself in my mind. It was as if I was standing beside myself observing the spectacle I'd become. I was reminded of Timothy Lea, randy hero of those 1970s *Confessions* novels. Apart from the *Skinhead* series they were the only things I read as a kid. As a result I used to go around saying 'It was so good I almost creamed my jeans' and 'I don't know what came over me' – making out like I was Robin Asquith, star of the film version of *Confessions of a Window Cleaner*. I'd tried to reread one a few months earlier, to try out Dunderdale's theories about crap fiction, but had found it impossible. It was full of clichés and I wasn't convinced by any of the situations. But now here I was *in* one. Ebola had been right: no matter what you do, it's bloody hard work to be original.

I must have been halfway up the stairs when I started tittering again and was then, again, convulsed with laughter. I slid back down, bouncing my chin off at least three steps. I hit the landing with a crunch and was knocked clean out. Unconsciousness didn't come instantly: awareness breezed out of me like a steady exhalation after a luxurious yawn.

I could no longer picture myself, or anything else for that matter.

All was blackness for what may well have been a long time. At some stage, however, I must have re-entered consciousness and decided to have another go at climbing the stairs as the next thing I remember I was back in the flat, on the sofa. And Monica was punching me in the face.

# Riding Crop Rainstorm

Why was Monica punching me in the face and pulling on my rhino horn?

'Wake up, you stupid wanker,' she said, 'the fucking house is on fire.'

I blinked to bring her into focus through the zippered eyeholes of my hood. Her nightshirt read: *Groggy and Irritable*.

I could feel the sting of smoke in my eyes. I could hear glass shattering and a powerful roar from downstairs. Out of one squinted eye I spied Ringo wearing an Ajax football top and a pair of shell-suit bottoms. He picked up my Amstrad, which I believe still had U2's *The Unforgettable Fire* on the turntable, and tossed it through the window.

Unzipping the mouth of my hood I attempted to say, 'What are you doing, you stupid Dutch tosser?' I only succeeded in uttering an incoherent splutter before falling into a helpless coughing fit that concluded with me honking my nads up. It was such a copious, prolonged vomit that I recall having the absurd thought that it might put the fire out. I remember selfishly swinging my head around to clear the puke residue from my mask – never once had it occurred to me to take the fucking thing off! Some vomit flecks peppered Monica and she screamed louder at this than she had at the fire. I think I was in the middle of trying to apologize when I passed out again. I can't recall exactly if I floated or sank out of consciousness; either way I was a drowning man.

When I awoke I was descending a ladder over a fireman's shoulder. I knew I still had the helmet on because the outsized horn was bobbing in front of my eyes. At the bottom of the ladder, I was flipped onto a stretcher and then wheeled backwards into an ambulance, but not before flashgun pops betrayed the presence of several amused photojournalists. That week the *Walsall Reflector* ran the headline, DRUNKEN PERVERT SAVED FROM BURNING BROTHEL, beneath a photo of yours truly wearing an electric blue scrotum pouch with tassled drawstrings, and a Viking helmet knob-cap. I wish I'd still been wearing the dildo helmet too, but a fireman had just pulled it, smoking, from my head. If only he'd revealed Robin Asquith's cheeky cherub face and not my own scorched visage of shame.

In those days Walsall had three hospitals. I was taken to the General on the Wednesbury Road to be treated for smoke inhalation and shock. Monica and Ringo were admitted too, but released after a few hours. I was in a much worse mess than them partly because, in my drunken state, I'd inhaled so many noxious fumes. My nostrils were ringed with thick black carbon deposits for days afterwards. Also, I had a line of marks around my mouth and eyes where the heat from the discipline hood's zips had burnt my flesh. The marks gave me a cartoon-like, startled expression. It occurred to me that, if this *had* happened to Robin Asquith in *Confessions* then this was the expression that he'd have had. But it had happened, as the *Walsall Reflector* so kindly pointed out, to David McVane. And it wasn't remotely funny.

In fact, for days later it hurt whenever I laughed because the burns from the zips crossed the creases of my laugh lines. One became infected and left me with a scar that, from whichever angle I view it, takes on the shape of a Staffordshire knot. Every time I look in a mirror the shiny cicatrix is there, pearl-white, mocking me.

The blaze completely gutted the building and we were homeless. A couple of oxyacetylene canisters that Penny's girls used for extreme blowtorch torment had exploded. It's rumoured that, in the immediate aftermath of the explosion, riding crops and nipple clamps had rained all over Caldmore. But 47 Saddler's Row was so badly damaged it was impossible to say what exactly had started the fire.

Penny Stroker and Dionne Splendour kept a low profile after the event and refused to be interviewed by *Walsall Reflector* journalists. Indeed, we never saw them again. We heard they'd told the fire brigade that a candle Dionne had been using for wax torture might somehow have been left burning. The fire brigade seemed to believe it, but I didn't. I was right not to.

# Dunderdale Takes a Dive

'I think Dunderdale tried to kill us,' I told Monica and Ringo as, ten days after the fire, the three of us sipped coffee in Sam & Ella's cafe. We'd all moved into the college halls of residence for the time being: because it was the Christmas holidays they were empty.

'Dunderdale tried to kill us! What evidence do you have for that?' asked Monica.

It was the first time I'd broached the subject. I told them about my experiences on the stairs. The noises; the possibility that someone had uttered his name. Even to me it sounded insubstantial.

'Someone shouted, "Dunderdale, you bastard, no." I'm sure of it.'

'How sure?' asked Monica.

'Pretty sure.'

'You've no idea what's happening when you're arse-holed,' said Monica.

Even Ringo was sceptical. 'Flaming Ada, Dunderdale would've been long gone by that time.'

'Maybe he came back?' I ventured.

'Why?' asked Monica.

'So he could set fire to the fucking building!' I bawled. I needed a drink.

Monica didn't reply: she never does when I raise my voice.

'You know me,' Ringo said, 'I'll always go for a conspiracy if there's a whiff of one, but where's your proof? And Monica's right: your memory's not that splendid when you're pissed as a flute.'

'Newt,' I said. 'The expression is "pissed as a newt".'

'I know.' He grinned. The bastard was always taking the piss these days. Plus, he was siding with Monica all the time.

I was annoyed because I could tell that they didn't have any faith in what I said or in my perspective on anything. They never seemed to lately. I had a notion that, as far as they were concerned, I was just a brain-addled pisshead. And when your best mate and your girlfriend think that, then you know you've got a problem. Or you should do.

We all sat in silence. I wondered how long before the pubs opened. My semi-melted Swatch said 10.30 a.m. Half an hour to go.

I insisted that Ringo and Monica should come with me to see the Dean on the first day back after the Christmas break. It was the second week of January 1987. They only agreed after I promised not to mention my theory that Dunderdale had started the fire at Penny's. Before we'd even arranged an appointment to see him, however, we learned that Dunderdale wouldn't be returning to his post at WANK that term.

The Dean's secretary informed us of the situation. 'I'm afraid we've had some bad news about Dr Dunderdale,' she said, a little tearfully.

'Resigned, has he?' I said. 'Well, that's not going to stop us exposing him!'

'Dave,' said Monica, 'let's hear what she's got to say.'

He hadn't merely resigned; it was more dramatic than that.

Through her tears the secretary gave me a wilting look.

'We had a call from his wife this morning,' she said. 'Dr Dunderdale is missing, presumed dead. He was seen jumping off a bridge into the River Tame three days ago.'

Despite this shocking news I was still all for going to the Dean with our information, but Monica and Ringo were reluctant. That lunchtime on the first day of term we argued fiercely about it in the union bar.

'If he's committed suicide, what's the point?' asked Monica.

'It's the action of a guilty man,' I said, taking a long pull on my barley wine. 'The truth needs to come out so that he can be shamed.'

'Shamed the way you've been shamed?' said Monica, referring to the photos of me on the night of the fire. 'Are you sure you're not just looking for revenge, Dave?'

'Absolutely, 100 per cent, not. And I resent the accusation,' I said.

'What's the point in shaming Dunderdale?' asked Ringo. 'You can't be shamed if you're dead. It will hurt his wife, not him.'

Ringo was siding with Monica again. Did he think she was right or was he trying to get into her knickers?

'How do we know he's dead? Jumping into the River Tame is hardly like jumping into the fucking Orinoco! The pollution might kill you but that's about it. And as for his wife, she has to be a psycho too. She must've known he was a fake; a sadistic impostor living a lie.'

'Not necessarily,' said Monica. 'Either way, can you imagine how distressed she'll be at the moment?'

'We can't keep it to ourselves,' I said. 'He was a pervert and a liar!'

'OK, put it this way, if Jeffrey Archer had died last year would you want *his* story exposed knowing that it would do nothing other than distress his wife?'

The bitch knew I had an inexplicable soft spot for Mary Archer. 'You win,' I said. 'We'll leave it.' With that I went to get a round in: orange juice for Monica, tomato juice for Ringo, two bottles of barley wine in a pint glass for me.

They were making me seem like an unreasonable nutter again. I was particularly angry with Ringo who, previously, had wanted Dunderdale's nads on a platter. This was the scandal of the decade. How could we let it end here? If he wanted to be a journalist he'd need to be a bit more ruthless in his pursuit of scoops like this. So what if Dunderdale had left behind a grieving wife?

'Let's not forget that the man was a brutal spank fetishist,' I said, when I returned to our table.

'I thought you said you were going to fucking leave it!' hissed Monica.

'There's no law against having unusual sexual preferences,' said Ringo. 'Why else would they have invented Sugar Puffs and Brylcreem?'

'He was a fraud,' I said, immune to his attempt to inject levity into the proceedings. 'He wasn't a real PhD. He was impersonating an academic. There *is* a law against that, I'm sure. Don't we owe it to the college to tell them their Head of English wasn't even qualified?'

'They probably wouldn't be bothered,' said Ringo. 'He did the job well, that's all they'd care about. Besides he's almost certainly dead and –'

'OK, leave it, leave it,' I said, a little too loudly.

There was a moment of silence until the opening bars of the Smiths' 'How Soon is Now?' began thumping from the jukebox. The three of us listened to the whole song without speaking. When it faded I said, 'Arson is a very serious business!'

My flatmates groaned.

'Well, isn't it? And what about Ebola? There was something going on between those two that needs investigating.'

Monica was exasperated: 'What exactly, Dave? It's all in your head.'

'Don't you dare say that!' I shouted. 'Ringo thinks there's a connection too, don't you, Ringo?'

Ringo shifted uncomfortably in his seat. 'We were just speculating about that, weren't we? There's nothing concrete to connect them.'

'The spanking paddle? The fact that he mentioned her name when I confronted him?'

Ringo shrugged. Clearly I wasn't convincing him. 'Hang on,' he said, 'maybe you're looking to turn Dunderdale into a monster because you feel guilty about his suicide. You blame yourself.'

'Now you really are talking shite,' I said.

'You shouldn't blame yourself,' said Ringo.

'I don't. I blame Dunderdale for being a tosser, end of story.'

'There's no need to beat yourself up over it,' he added.

'I'm not.'

'Are you sure?'

'Fucking *yes*!'

'OK, OK, don't have a go at Ringo,' said Monica. 'Anyway, knowing you as I do, Dave McVane, you just want to inflate all this into a juicy scandal to stop yourself getting bored. Isn't that it?'

'You and Ringo like a good scandal as much as I do,' I wailed.

But, even as I spoke, I wondered if the pleasure it gave them was of quite the same order as the pleasure it gave me. Was Monica right? Was I looking to inflate the Dunderdale business just to fend off the bleakness? Just for the entertainment value it offered?

'I have a lecture to go to,' said Monica and she drained her drink and stood to leave.

'Us too. Come on, Dave,' said Ringo.

I was fuming. They'd made me feel petty and paranoid. 'I'm all right here,' I said, 'you go.'

So they left me in the bar sinking barley wines. And that's where I seemed to stay, metaphorically at least, for my entire academic career.

Life fell into a routine rapidly after that extraordinarily dramatic first term. Indeed, nothing, and I mean *nothing*, noteworthy happened at WANK for the rest of my three-year course. My time there left me cynical and demoralized. Dunderdale turned out to be a suicidal clown and the next best lecturer, Ruud Van Door, returned to Holland. Ebola Barker – who was weird but at least colourful – was dead. We were left with the likes of Winnie Wiggins, Steven Twist and Marmaduke fucking Peabody. Thanks to Van Door I tended to assess academics in relation to their opinion of Charles Bukowski and, when it came to the English department at WANK, the responses were predictable. Barry Byetheway and Steven Twist had never heard of him, Peabody yawned in my face, and Winnie asked me if he was a Latvian philologist. The only unexpected response came from Prunella Fabb who informed me that she'd once met someone who'd given him a blow job.

In the second year things went even further downhill when a replacement for Dunderdale was found in the shape of Marcus Tavistock, a managerial type who decided that the School of English should become more vocationally orientated. He had the staff teaching courses called 'English 1', 'English 2' and 'English 3', but which could have had titles like 'Sound Bite Construction for Creative Entrepreneurs' and 'Blurb Writing for the Global Market'. I took courses in journalism because they were the only vaguely interesting options. Besides, it's what Bukowski had studied in his brief time at Los Angeles City College.

I must admit I did develop a romantic idea of myself as a

boozy journalist drinking strong liquor between dispatches from the front line. I had an image of myself filing stories of injustice and horror from, say, a pay phone in the lobby of a Phnom Penh brothel. I'd be wearing a linen suit. I'd be free of Walsall and, as a chronicler of global affairs, I'd have a glamorous excuse for my cynicism and my hard drinking, not merely the excuse of being bored, average and terminally unfulfilled.

# Part Two

# Monica and Ringo

I was privileged to hear Tinker Lawson's final moments as a hospital shock jock. He was just introducing a second Marilyn Manson number, 'Scabs, Guns and Peanut Butter', when the door of the studio gave way.

'They're going to replace me with some arse-licker who'll feed you the lie of escapist pop trash,' he shouted. Then there were sounds of a struggle, muffled swearing and breaking vinyl, and Tinker was deposed by 'Cheeky Charlie Eccles: the Pensioner's Chum'. He began with a song by Daniel O'Donnell that had me snatching the headphones from my ears as urgently as if they'd suddenly metamorphosed into a pair of copulating vipers.

I'd sent text messages to tell Monica and Ringo of my admittance to Wesley-in-Tame. It's forbidden to use your mobile on the ward, so I'd done my texting secretly under the bedclothes.

> in hospital!
> cum c me.
> am dying.
> visiting hrs 2-4. 6-8.

Theirs were the numbers I used most on my Nokia, along with Gino's Dial a Pizza. Ringo would have been expecting me at work that morning because, as the editor of the *Walsall Reflector*, he was my boss. He'd grown accustomed to my late arrivals, of course, as I spent so much of my time hungover. We hadn't had to use the 'David *Ichabod* McVane is unwell' line yet but, inevitably, that day was now here.

Monica was used to getting text messages from me. Although we were no longer an item, she was still my gossip-buddy. And sixteen years on, our celebrity scandal topics still featured Jeffrey Archer, though these days they were supplemented by Michael Barrymore and *Big Brother*. In the summer of 2000, 90 per cent of our texts had been about Nasty Nick. You'd think there'd be more to life, wouldn't you? There is to Monica's.

Ringo arrived first, at about ten past three.

'Where the fuck have you been, you tosser?' I said. This is no way to speak to your boss, I know, but ours was that kind of relationship.

Ringo didn't answer because the second he arrived his mobile went off. The ring tone was 'Vicar in a Tutu', a novelty he'd downloaded from the Internet. My own phone played 'Roll Out the Barrel'. He immediately switched the caller to his answer service and began glancing around him, nervous as a rabbit on Roger a Rabbit Day. As a hypochondriac, he didn't like being in hospital. He kept shooting worried looks about the ward and I could tell he was reluctant to inhale.

'Flaming Ada,' he said, 'you look like death on a stick. Is that a bag of piss?'

I told him everything I knew about pancreatitis, and everything I'd been through with the catheter. As I spoke his hand moved from his stomach to his cock and back again six times. He'd heard of pancreatitis, of course, just as he'd heard of all the other conditions it's possible to die from.

'It's a pissed-up bastard's disease, isn't it?' he queried.

'More or less.'

Like me, Ringo had secured his job on the *Reflector* the year we graduated: 1989. It was a happy coincidence that there'd been two trainee reporters' posts going at the same time. In those days journalists tended not to be graduates; they did courses like the NCTJ (National Council for Training of Journalists) qualification. But the *Reflector* took us despite our minimal professional training. Ringo had more experience than me. In his second and third years at WANK he did himself some good by editing *Red Sox*. Then he did himself even more good by graduating with first-class honours. Unlike me, the Dutch-Welsh-French-Indian was the most literate reporter the Walsall paper had ever seen. In three years Ringo worked his way up to news editor and demonstrated that his skill at structuring news stories wasn't restricted to gossip sessions with his fellow students. His ability to resist the allure of more glamorous, national papers paid off when the *Reflector*'s owners, Allied Midland News, wanted to appoint a new editor. That was five years ago and in that time he'd acquitted himself well.

Unlike me, who was now three stone heavier and bald, Ringo had hardly changed physically since his student days. At thirty-six, he was still trim and energetic. Where my eyes were generally bees-winged and bloodshot, his were as clear and alert as a gazelle's. His speech had altered somewhat, however. It was still littered with *Flaming Ada*s and *Ace-a-mundo*s, but he seldom lapsed from standard English. The quirky diction had gone, as had his slight Dutch accent. You could tell he'd had an education, and his understanding of the English language – which was a second language to him, of course – was far, far superior to mine. He could have had his pick of jobs. When asked why he'd chosen to stay in Walsall he'd reply that it was because he was a masochist. This wasn't true: I'd lived above Penny's long enough to know what masochism involved. My theory is that it had something to do with him being Dutch. He had a Dutchman's tolerance and a Dutchman's love of the absurd. Being an outsider, he found eccentricity and humour where most people saw stupidity and squalor. He loved to tell people he lived in the ugliest town in England. And when he learned that traditional Black Country costume includes clogs, his fondness for his adopted hometown was confirmed.

Monica arrived about ten minutes after Ringo. She kissed me on the cheek and him on the lips. They'd been married now for seven years. I'd been Ringo's best man.

'Christ, you look ill,' she said.

'I don't feel too bad,' I lied.

Actually, though I wasn't in too much pain, I felt weak and light-headed. It was a bit like a combination of flu and a bad hangover. As is the case with flu and hangovers, I was unsure whether my speech was fully coherent. I had to keep checking it for bollocks.

I repeated my story to Monica, watching Ringo's hands shuttle between cock and stomach once more. As Senior Lecturer in Health Studies at the University of Central England, she knew more about the implications of my illness than her husband. She'd picked up a first, too, and went from WANK to Wolverhampton University to do an MSc in Clinical Studies. Following that she researched a PhD on the relationship between alcoholism and occupation, and she could now call herself Doctor Van Freek. Her thesis demonstrated that, though teachers and journalists used to be the biggest pissheads, these days they've been overtaken by healthcare workers. Which doesn't bode well for me, does it?

'I've warned you, haven't I?' she said. 'How many times have I told you to cut down on your drinking?'

'I was always too drunk to pay any attention, Mon.'

She covered her eyes with her hand and shook her head. It was the kind of gesture that seemed to say, 'He's still a tit, but I'd rather he was alive.'

'You bloody fool,' she said. When she dropped her hand I could see that her eyes were wet with incipient tears. Monica is one of the few people who can shed tears over a tosser like me. I've often wondered why she continues to care and, frankly, I'm not sure. Mind you, we get along better now we're no longer an item. Whereas before she'd get angry with me for being 'a stupid drunken twat' now she's chill. My boozing is easier for her to live with now she knows I'm never going to be the father of her children. These days, the things we have in common – tittle-tattle and scandalmongering – can thrive between us unimpeded.

'It's worse than you think,' I said. 'My consultant is called Mr Dunderdale.' This was an attempt to divert attention from my imminent death. Having Monica weeping over my corpse-to-be wasn't the tonic I was after and I'd been looking forward to telling them my consultant's name. He was someone we hadn't discussed for years.

Looking back, it's remarkable how quickly Dunderdale seemed to melt from our lives in the new year of 1987. He was rapidly superseded by fresh intrigues, all of which seem rather petty now. There was a rumour that Marmaduke Peabody was a member of the National Front, for instance; and another that Prunella Fabb had a sister who'd shot dead the lead singer of a band called the Goosed Buttocks. Neither was substantiated. As our degrees progressed, our favourite national scandals included Frank Bough and his fondness for fetish pursuits ('Uncle Frank and his Red Camisole'), and Tory comic Ken Dodd's tax probe ('Doddy's Diddles'), among a wilderness of similar, insignificant nonsense.

'Flaming Ada: Dunderdale; that's a name I haven't heard for a while,' said Ringo.

'Do you think he's a relative of *that* Dunderdale?' asked Monica, discreetly dabbing her eye with the sleeve of her cardigan. These days she's always dressed in navy blue cardigans and Chanel neckscarves: apparently they're *de rigueur* for a certain type of health professional. She also weighs in at a hefty size 20, which also seems to be fairly standard in her line of work.

On one level, my mention of Dunderdale was meant as a joke. But it's odd that, as soon as I'd heard his name that morning, part of me had an inkling that perhaps he *was* related to the twat in the torture-trolleys.

'I suppose he could be a relative,' I said. 'Mind you, I've asked around and he does sound remarkably like WANK's own Daniel Dunderdale.'

'And?' asked Monica.

'And nothing . . . Except that one of my fellow patients told me something interesting: he says he insists on being called mister rather than doctor. He makes a big issue out of it.'

'And?'

'Well, doesn't that remind you of anyone?'

Ringo was immediately on my wavelength. '"Thrash me, doctor; hurt me, doctor." Yes, status seemed to be an important factor in *our* Dunderdale's sexual thrills. I remember it well. Maybe it's a family trait.'

'So, what exactly are you saying?' Monica asked. She knew how easily I could construct unlikely stories out of the kernel of half a fact (or less). She once said that if my imagination had hands it would throttle me to death.

But I didn't really know what I was saying. As an experiment I asked, 'Did they ever find Daniel Dunderdale by the way?'

Monica's hand went to her eyes again. She shook her head and laughed. 'Don't start, Dave McVane,' she said.

So I didn't start.

I changed the subject. We spoke for another fifteen minutes or so about who'd be covering my subbing and how the next edition of the *Reflector* was shaping up. Then we were interrupted by a nurse who'd come to do my observations. Ringo and Monica made room for her at my bedside and stood patiently as she took her readings. She was a tall, wiry RGN named Ruth. She smelled of tobacco smoke and had golden nicotine stains on her fingers. She was also faintly redolent of Blossom Hill Red: one of the stronger Californian table wines. This woman couldn't be bothered to hide the fact that she liked to relax.

'Your temperature is a bit high, Mr McVane. I'll get you some paracetamol to bring it down. Your blood pressure has risen too.' She glanced at Monica and Ringo and said, in a joky way, 'Your visitors aren't over-exciting you I hope?'

'How exciting do they look?' I quipped.

Ruth glanced at them and Ringo grinned.

'By the time you're forty,' said Monica, 'you get the face you deserve and the visitors you deserve.' I'd come in for lots of ribbing when I'd turned forty, mainly from Monica. She was just a year away from this milestone herself, and it was obviously preying on her mind.

'I must've have been a Walsall town planner in a previous life,' I said. 'Either that or the midwife who delivered Yoko Ono.'

'Nurse,' I said, as Ruth was about to leave, 'could you tell me Mr Dunderdale's first name?'

Ruth thought for a moment. 'I have to say I haven't a clue – he hasn't worked here long.' She called to Deekus who, visitorless, had just begun to make his way off the ward for a fag. 'Deekus,' she said, 'you know as much about this place as anyone; what's Mr Dunderdale's Christian name?' Deekus glanced at her with contempt and continued on his way with his nose in the air. Clearly Ruth had offended him in some way.

'I've already tried him,' I told her. 'He doesn't know.'

Just then Droppy Collins, who'd been in the toilet for about an hour, walked back onto the ward.

'Ah, Droppy, you'll know,' said Ruth. 'What's Mr Dunderdale's Christian name?'

'Now, then, arr, I 'ave 'eard it.'

He thought for so long I was about to tell him not to bother when, suddenly, he clicked his fingers.

'Daniel,' he said, 'arr, that's it. I remember cus I thought he should be thrown to the lions.'

'Fuck,' I said.

'Flaming Ada,' Ringo said.

'Now there's a coincidence,' Monica said.

When Ruth left I could tell Monica and Ringo were waiting for me to raise the issue again. How could I not?

'That's bloody uncanny, isn't it?' I said.

'A coincidence, yes,' said Monica.

'A coincidence of course,' I said. 'But . . .'

'But what?' Monica couldn't help laughing again.

We looked at one another in silence for a moment and then all started to laugh.

'It's him!' I said. 'The bastard's come back to haunt me. He's stalking the corridors in his hessian under-crackers.' We all buckled with glee.

'Check your arse for a Staffordshire knot,' said Ringo.

We laughed some more. This was cheering me up.

After our mirth subsided we were quiet again for a few moments before I said, 'What are the chances of it actually being *him*, Mon? Just assuming he didn't drown in the Tame. It's a serious question.' She looked at me as if I'd asked if her tits were made of marzipan.

'Is this the drugs talking or just your stupidity?'

I thought she was being unnecessarily harsh. 'Hang on, none us know what happened to Dunderdale. Couldn't he have retrained or something? I'm just asking, hypothetically if you like, what are the chances?'

'None,' she said, 'zero, zilch, so don't start thinking it.'

'Flaming Ada, you really think it's the late WANK Head of English! Are you still bloody drunk?'

It's funny how you can dig your heels in over something your reason tells you is stupid when someone points out just how stupid you're being. That's what I did now. 'He's not the "late" lecturer – as far as I know they never found his body. Unless you've heard different?'

Monica sighed and Ringo shrugged.

'Besides,' I continued, 'we are talking about a bloke with a history of duplicity; someone who has made bogus claims to professional qualifications he hasn't got. Go on, tell me I haven't got a point, I dare you!'

Monica: 'What job do you do?'

Me: 'I'm a journalist, as you well know.'

Monica: 'Well, you wouldn't be a very good journalist if you'd missed a story like a suicide returning from the dead, would you?'

Me: 'I'm *not* a very good journalist. Besides what do we know about it? For all we know he could have swum to the river bank, climbed out and have been living happily with his wife for the past sixteen years.'

Monica: 'Don't you think the news would have reached WANK? Gossip spread like chickenpox in that place.'

Me: 'It would hardly have been front-page news. It's not as if we're talking about John Stonehouse, Lord Lucan or that bloke from the Manic Street Preachers. Dunderdale was an obscure academic.'

Monica: 'Dave, this is no time to start looking for the kind of excitement that will fuel your paranoia.'

Me: 'What do you mean excitement? Do you think my

consultant calls himself Dunderdale just to give me something to talk about?' I was beginning to raise my voice.

Monica: 'Stop it, Dave.'

Me: 'We don't know what became of him is all I'm saying. It's just possible he's still alive!'

Monica: 'Take some deep breaths.'

I took some deep breaths. Monica tends to give good advice on health matters, which is one of the reasons Ringo is so smitten with her. But I wasn't sure how or why Dunderdale had become such an issue. I realized I was being silly. I suppose I was over-emotional – maybe the fruit-flavoured Rennies had tipped me over the edge.

'Is there anything you need from home, Dave?' Monica asked, changing the subject.

'Just some stuff to read, I suppose,' I said, trying not to sulk. 'The latest *Enquirer* and this week's *Heat*. I'm pretty sure both are on my coffee table. Use the spare key I gave you.'

'No need, I can bring you my copies. No Bukowski?'

'Better not: I'm trying to keep my mind off booze.'

In the depths of my mind, or even in the shallows, I knew the two Dunderdales couldn't be the same bloke. How could they be? But part of me – the gossipy part desperate for titillation, the paranoid part fed by my vulnerability, or even the masochistic part craving the adrenalin kick of fear – couldn't help thinking it. I remember wondering if maybe my illness or the drugs meant I wasn't thinking rationally. At least that was Monica's diagnosis, and I'm sure Ringo agreed. Nevertheless, by the end of their visit I was pleading with my old Dutch mate to find out what he could about my surgeon.

'Put one of our reporters on it,' I told him. 'It shouldn't be that hard to check his background. Even if he's got nothing to do with Dr Daniel Perv, he might well be news. There are whispers about him. People here don't like him. There could be a tie-in with the mortality rate story.'

Ringo gave me an exasperated glance and then turned to Monica for approval. She shrugged her shoulders.

'Don't look at me,' she said. 'If you want to pander to his fantasies, please yourself.'

'Please,' I said to Ringo, 'do it for a dying man. Besides you owe me: you stole my lover.' The latter was a standing joke between us. In reality, Monica had taken up with Ringo two years after my relationship with her was officially over.

'But you'll probably see him for yourself tomorrow. You'll see how stupid you've been for imagining such nonsense.'

'The people in the know say he hardly ever shows his face,' I said. 'Besides, I'm keen to learn something about the guy who might be slicing me open. Get one of those J2O drinkers to sniff around him.'

'Hmmm,' he said, 'I must admit, I'm a bit intrigued myself, now you've tickled my fancy. The mortality rate story is a big one. Maybe we could try for an interview with Dunderdale: surgeons always give better copy than managers on the rare occasions they've got the guts to speak out.'

'And Dr Perv? Do you think it's worth checking if his body ever turned up?'

'Flaming Ada, Dave, we'd have heard about it!'

'We might not have – and I'm curious to know for sure.'

Ringo held his hands in the air, palms towards me. 'OK, OK, I'll check.'

My visitors rose to leave as the bell rang for the second time. Just like in a pub: you ignore the first but the second is when it gets serious.

'Will you both come and see me tonight?' I asked,

putting on a pathetic voice and poking out my bottom lip. 'It might be your last chance.'

'We might,' said Monica.

I knew at least one of them would.

'Bring a bottle of brandy with you,' I shouted, as they departed.

# Paranoid Pisshead

Could this Dunderdale be the same guy? It was impossible. Or was it? Dunderdale was dead, surely. As far as we knew he was last seen jumping into the Tame. But was it possible that he didn't drown? It's not much of a river – barely a match for the piss-stream of a Staffordshire Bull Terrier. And we never heard anything about the police finding a body; we never heard anything at all, come to think of it. For all we knew he could have re-emerged through the plughole of the Mayor's Jacuzzi, complete with pink leather harness and torture-trolleys. Despite what Monica said about the wildfire gossip at WANK people hardly mentioned Dunderdale after the first few days of that second term. How would we know if he'd somehow survived? He'd severed his links with the college, after all. But even if *had* survived and we'd missed the news, it was madness to think he could crop up, fifteen years later, as a consultant surgeon! He'd have been in his thirties when he went missing and that was too old to retrain, wasn't it? Could he have gone to medical school? Surely not. Unless it was an overseas college? Is that possible? No. Yes? No.

Of course, there was an alternative.

Perhaps he was posing as a surgeon the way he'd posed as an academic. I'd once reviewed a film called *Paper Mask* in which Paul McGann passes himself off as a doctor. At first, he's quite successful, but he cocks things up in the end. Actually I'd heard of that happening. Some freaks have a pathological need to pose as people of power and authority. In my copy of *The World's Greatest Frauds* there's an entire chapter devoted to bogus doctors, which I dig out occasionally to beef up my column with references to show that any twit can be a doctor. But, even if he *was* still around, Dunderdale wouldn't be posing as a surgeon in the town he'd taught in for years, and using his old name to boot. Surely not. He'd have to be crazy to do that. Wouldn't he? Yes. No? Yes.

My head felt strange.

I tried to settle down for a nap: my rhino was subdued, but I still felt exhausted and ill. I'm not sure how long I'd been dozing when I heard a troubling conversation. At the sink just around the corner from my bed I could hear Ruth swilling something out and chatting to one of the junior doctors, Dr Chance. I'd seen him earlier in the day fall asleep listening to one of Deekus's diatribes. He'd been sitting at the side of his bed and I'd watched him wilt slowly until his head was on the mattress and he was snoozing peacefully. Deekus made a big show of pointing this out to everyone as an example of the Wesley staff's outrageous lack of commitment. I was impressed to see that Chance was still on duty. He and Ruth were conversing in hushed tones.

Chance: 'Ruth, that boring bastard Deekus keeps asking me for drugs, what should I do?'

Ruth: 'Tell him to fuck off. He can have his pethidine when he's due; nothing else.'

Chance: 'Could I give him some paracetemol?'

Ruth: 'No, not with the state his liver is in.'

Chance: 'OK. That bloke Droppy Collins keeps demanding painkillers too, what I should tell him?'

Ruth: 'He can fuck off too. He's swallowed again and we

can't administer any drugs that might inhibit peristalsis.'

Chance: 'You mean painkillers might stop him from shitting?'

Ruth: 'Correct.'

Chance: 'Cheers, Ruth. Another question [sound of Ruth sighing]. That Baggies fan, Gulliver, keeps going on at me about his chances of being discharged before the weekend.'

Ruth: 'Tell him that if he gets his test appointment before Friday then yes; if it's scheduled for next week then we might be able to give him home leave for the weekend as long as he stays nil by mouth from midnight on Sunday. The tests are expensive so he'd better not fuck it up.'

Chance: 'And Donovan's stones – he wants to know if it's possible to have them broken up with a laser.'

Ruth: 'Depends on their size and precise location. It'll be his consultant's decision. Tell him surgery is most likely, anything else will be a bonus.'

Chance: 'Cheers, Ruth. I don't know what I'd do without you.'

Ruth: 'Get sued.'

Chance: [Laughing uncertainly] 'Probably.'

Ruth: 'Is that it?'

Chance: [After two or three seconds of silence] 'Mr Dunderdale gets a lot of bad press around here, doesn't he?'

Ruth: 'That's understandable, don't you think?'

Chance: 'I suppose. That bloated, bald chap, David McVane, keeps grilling everyone about him.'

Ruth: 'Yes, watch him, he's a journalist. Classic Langerhans patient: alcohol-related pancreatitis – although he's a lot chattier than most.' Ruth's voice dropped to a whisper and, though I strained to hear, I could only make out three words: 'pisshead' and 'paranoid' and 'cunt'.

# I Was the Man Who

Monica and I split up in the year of our graduation. During our finals, in fact: May 1989. By that stage I'd become a serious boozehound. Still under the influence of Charles Bukowski, I'd claim I could only really understand literature when I was off my paps – something I genuinely believed, too. And it's true that drunkenness gave me moments of insight that eluded me when sober. But whenever I tried to articulate these moments in the form of an essay they came out as incoherent bollocks. Luckily, the incoherent bollocks was enough to maintain a D-pass average at WANK. I graduated with an embarrassing third, the only person in my year to achieve such a poor degree. But, pissed or not, at least I passed; at least I stayed the course. Maintaining a relationship with Monica wasn't so straightforward. My list of drunken, relationship-shattering transgressions didn't end with fish massacres.

I was excellent, for instance, at passing out pissed. Here are some places I've passed out pissed: in the toilet of Sandeep's Most Excellent Balti Palace; in the boot of a Mark 4 Sierra; in a porch owned by cartoonist and TV celebrity Bill Tidy. After the first I woke, pissed, in Sandeep's Most Excellent Balti Palace; after the second I woke, pissed, in the boot of a Mark 4 Sierra; after the third I woke, pissed, at Green Lane Police Station. There I was forced to explain why I'd been found sleeping in a porch owned by cartoonist and TV celebrity Bill Tidy. If you're interested I'll tell you: I was pissed.

And, speaking of police, I was the man who didn't believe it was possible to be too drunk to drive the morning after a night out until I was charged with being too drunk to drive the morning after a night out. I'd borrowed a car to go to a funeral in Knutsford. My old mate, Knocky, had been mown down by the Birmingham InterCity service to Wigan. He was dragged for thirteen miles and, when they found him, he could only be identified by his dental records. His death had depressed me, which meant that I'd been off my dingers the night before. The rozzers pulled me over doing thirty-four miles an hour up the M6, well half up the M6 and half on the hard shoulder of the M6. I think I'm one of the few people to actually use the phrase, 'Yesh, offisher.' I was dismayed to hear myself sounding like Dudley Moore in *Arthur*, still more dismayed to be driven to the cop shop in a state-of-the-art rozzer-wagon. That was 27 April 1988. In the evening Monica had arrived home with two choice bits of scandal. Her friend, Petra, was having an affair with Waldo, the sixty-year-old manager of a municipal tip and, if that wasn't enough, David Scarboro – the original Mark Fowler from *East-Enders* – had chucked himself off Beachy Head.

'I think I'll join him,' I'd said.

I was the man who was always drunk. Worse, I was the man who, when drunk, always behaved like a fuckwit. As Monica would say (or scream), 'It's *always* fucking you. If someone says, "Hey, there's a bloke on the dance floor with his strides on his head," I don't have to look: it's always you. If someone's on top of the bus shelter singing "Frankly Mr Shankly" at three in the morning, there's no point opening the curtains: it's going to be you; if someone's pissed in the wardrobe and puked in the bread bin, ditto; if someone's killed my fish; if someone's on the front page of the local rag with a dildo on his fucking stupid head. It's going to be you. It's always fucking you!' That was one of our last arguments. Well, it wasn't an argument; it was a litany of my drunken transgressions woven into a ferocious and protracted monologue, to which I had no answer. Then again, I *did* have an answer. The song I'd been singing while pissed on the bus shelter was 'Bigmouth Strikes Again', but I was too scared to correct her.

In a sense, I drove Monica away quite deliberately. I'd like to say that mine was a heroic, Bogartesque gesture where I sacrificed the girl I loved because I knew she'd have a better life without me, but that would be bollocks. I think I *did* love her, in a way, but I loved booze more. I just drank and drank knowing that, eventually, she'd tell me to fuck off and, eventually, she told me to fuck off. If I'd wanted to keep Monica, you see, I'd have had to have given up drinking and who in their right mind would want to do that?

I don't want to claim that boozing makes me a better person, but I have to because it does. Here, for instance, are some things I can do when I'm drunk that I can't do when I'm sober: dance; speak French; tell people I love them; refrain from murdering Daniel O'Donnell. See, if I'd opted for Monica over booze I'd have been forced to kill an Irishman.

# A Visit from Brad Pitt

Brad Pitt came to visit me about half five that afternoon. He came in the form of the Reverend Bradley Pitt, a Walsall parish vicar doing his weekly round of the hospital. He was a shortish, plump, bald gentleman in his late forties.

'Hey, I'm Brad Pitt,' he said, beaming. He was obviously used to getting a startled and/or humorous reaction to this.

'No offence, but you've gone down the pan since *Fight Club*,' I said.

The Reverend Pitt laughed a little too loudly. He was the kind of guy who likes to let you know that he has a sense of humour.

'So is there anything I can do for you,' he said, glancing at his list of patients, 'David?'

'I don't think so, thank you, vicar.'

'I see you're C of E.'

'Er, no. I don't have any religious affiliations. I'm not religious.'

'Oh, if you tell them that they just tick the C of E box on your admissions form.'

'Of course,' I said. This seemed typical of Walsall.

The Reverend Pitt beamed at me some more. He seemed like a nice chap and, despite my irreligious views, I didn't want to upset him, so I smiled back. He took this as an invitation to hang around.

'There is much comfort to be had from God at times of crisis,' he said.

'Thank you, Reverend, but, as I say, I'm not religious. In fact, I don't believe in God.'

'Aha,' he said, rising to the challenge, 'how do you know his name then?'

'I know the name of Father Christmas but I don't believe in him either.'

The vicar's eyes widened and he thought for a moment. 'Did Father Christmas die on the cross for our sins?' he asked at last.

'No, but he's got a red-nosed reindeer.'

'I sense that you're a bit of a cynic, David.'

'I'm as optimistic as it's possible for someone to be who's just boozed himself onto the Lost Islands of Langerhans. I have a tube hanging out of my cock in case you hadn't noticed.'

The vicar flinched at the word cock, but the mention of booze seemed to increase his determination to lecture me. 'In my experience people turn to alcohol because they are unhappy, David.' He looked across at Deekus's bed when he said this, but Deekus didn't notice because he was working on a complaint letter to Walsall MP, Bruce George. 'Don't get me wrong,' Brad Pitt continued, 'I have no wish to judge you personally, but in my experience people who drink too much do so as a form of escape, because they can't face the real world; they are frightened of reality. Would you agree with that?'

'Yes. And people turn to religion for the same reason,' I said. 'The distraction of intoxication and the fantasy of religion serve the same purpose. They are ways of coping with the dumb meaninglessness of existence and the absolute certainty of death.'

I've always found it rather pointless to argue with strongly religious people. Their ability to cope with the world, their sanity if you like, depends so heavily on the rightness of their faith that they're psychologically incapable of questioning it. Their belief system becomes their thought system; it becomes *them*. For such people, seeing the logical flaws in their argument is like trying to see round their own eyeball. But I'd hit a nerve with Brad Pitt. His faith was shaky.

'I think you might be right.'

I chuckled, a bit shocked not to be getting the standard response. 'I don't think you should be saying that, Reverend Pitt, even if you think it.'

'That's the trouble,' he said, 'I've been thinking it for years now.' Suddenly his eyes were full of tears. 'I've been working here for five years,' he said, blubbing, 'in Walsall. At this hospital. Week after week it's the same. Death, suffering, misery. I don't see God here.' He put his hands to his face and started crying. Though he was grizzling quite loudly, no one turned to look at us. It made me wonder if these tears were a common occurrence. One thing was for sure, the chaplain wasn't proving to be much of a tonic.

'Cheer up, vicar,' I said, feeling guilty. 'You provide comfort for lots of people; you're doing a useful job; people need religion when they're ill.'

'Yes,' he snivelled, 'that's the only time they *do* need it. As soon as they leave here they forget about God. Until the next time. It's got so I can't stand to listen to them.' He glanced furtively over at Deekus again, who was now rolling himself a fag ready for his next smoke excursion.

'God can see what you're doing,' I said, the bullshit coming as readily to my lips as it does to my pen. 'He's grateful.'

'But you don't believe in God. And I'm not sure I do any more.'

'You can't take any notice of me. What do I know? Besides, I read somewhere that the need we have for God is an innate craving and human beings have no innate cravings that can't somehow be satisfied.'

Brad Pitt looked puzzled and so I explained, all the time wondering what the fuck I was talking about. 'When we're hungry, we can satisfy that with food; our thirst with drink; our loneliness with love, and so on. All the fundamental needs we are born with can be satisfied by things that exist. You were born with a need for God, weren't you?'

He nodded, drying his eyes.

'Well then, it follows that something exists that can satisfy *that* need. Doesn't it?'

'Where did you read that?' asked the chaplain, blotchy-eyed.

'Er, in an issue of *Spiderman*,' I admitted.

'Ah.'

'But the main thing is that it's true. At least it sounds true and that's the best we can hope for.'

'Really?' he said, sounding like a child in need of reassurance.

'Maybe,' I said.

'Thank you,' he said. 'Now I suppose I'd better go. Is there anything I can get you?'

'No thank you, Reverend Pitt.'

'Well,' he said, taking my hand and shaking it, 'I hope I've been of some, erm, or that in some way I've . . . or boosted your . . . Anyway, I hope you get better soon.'

Christ, I thought, as he stuffed his hanky away and stood to leave, look what Walsall does to its vicars.

# A Pantheon of Tossers

Monica and Ringo visited that evening. Monica, though she forgot my magazines, brought me a bottle of Robinson's Barley Water. Although I was only being allowed plain water at the moment, she said it'd give me something to look forward to. She was right: the thought of sweetness in my mouth turned my taste buds to fountainheads. Being restricted to one swallow of water an hour makes you appreciate sweet, soft drinks; indeed, it makes you appreciate water. I'd look forward to my thirty millilitres and I'd drink it slowly, savouring it like Chateau Lafitte.

For the sake of appearances I waited as long as possible before asking about Dunderdale. Sixteen, possibly seventeen seconds.

'Dunderdale dissolved,' said Ringo.

'What?'

'Dissolved. I had Miles phone round this afternoon. He's still *officially* missing, presumed dead. But the word is he dissolved. Apparently the stretch of the Tame that Dunderdale jumped into had a pH comparable to fuming nitric acid at the time. Something to do with excessive pollution from Jasper's Extrusions Ltd. The company was fined: forty quid, plus court costs of ten grand.'

'Dissolved!'

'Almost certainly. His wife never remarried but still lives

in Walsall, in Wesley Drive, just round the corner from this hospital. Miles spoke to her on the phone. She's quite ill, apparently, but was happy to talk. Anyway, the upshot is that your consultant is definitely a different Dunderdale, Dave.'

'That's not conclusive,' I ventured. 'There's no proof he dissolved.'

Ringo and Monica groaned.

'OK, OK, you're right,' I admitted. 'It was too good a story to hope for. I was being daft.'

'Dafter than daft,' Ringo said.

'Pity though – think of the headline,' I said.

's&m doc wears pink knickers,' Ringo said.

'Did you get Miles to have a sniff around the other Dunderdale, my consultant?'

'Well . . .' Ringo faltered and glanced at Monica who gave him a hard stare.

'I've asked him not to tell you this but I can see he's going to,' she said.

'Go on.'

'Well, Miles did manage to phone Mr Dunderdale on his home number – don't ask me how he got it. He spoke to him about an hour ago. We told him we might do a piece about the pressure Walsall surgeons are under; I thought we could tie it in with Gordon Brown's announcement about the increase in NHS funding.'

'And?'

'And he declined. I think he thought we really wanted to discuss the business about Wesley-in-Tame's mortality rate.'

'Is that it?'

'Well, no. He was most unprofessional with it. Not to mention abusive and unsurgeonlike. He used the words fuck, cunt, cunting and cuntface.'

'Blimey.'

Ringo hesitated again. 'He's certainly a volatile character. Miles thought he might have been drinking.'

'Jesus fucking H. Get me out of here!' But my fear was mostly an act. I was more intrigued than anything.

'Calm down,' said Monica, 'Miles only spoke to him on the phone, he couldn't be certain of anything.' She narrowed her eyes at her husband. 'Isn't that right?' she said, with menace in her voice.

'Flaming Ada, yes,' he said, hastily clicking off the synthesized 'Vicar in a Tutu' that marked another incoming call. 'It's this business about the mortality rate scandal. It's got everybody here jumpy – particularly around us. But Dunderdale's behaviour has made me all the more determined to check him out for you.'

'Thanks, mate,' I said.


Patients were officially allowed only two visitors at a time, but the ward was packed with people.

Gulliver had what seemed to be the entire cast of a Cecil B. De Mille epic around his bed, all of whom were sporting Albion colours. They teased Gulliver by telling him they'd heard his consultant, Mr Bramble, was a Wolves fan. This was funny the first time they said it. By the thirtieth time they'd revealed themselves to be a bunch of raving tits. Martin had seven or eight visitors around his bed. They all sat and exchanged hospital anecdotes over his mute form, like ghost stories round a campfire. Deekus only had one visitor, his mother. Her official title was that of Deekus's 'carer', which, I suppose, meant she was paid for putting up with the cunt. He moaned in one long, unbroken narrative while she gazed at him. She gazed as you might gaze at a church gargoyle: you know from school there's a point to its existence but you can't for the life of you remember what.

Droppy Collins also had a single visitor: his wife, Ginger.

She was one of the few women I've seen in real life wearing a turban. Everything she said was preceded by the sound *Eeeeeee*. She also had a tendency to overuse the word 'yampi'. She spent an hour scolding her husband for scoffing Googie's name pendant: '*Eeeeeee*, yow yampi bastard,' she said, over and over again.

Droppy wasn't too keen on talking to his wife, though, and he hardly listened to anything she said. Instead, he eavesdropped everyone else's conversations and chipped in whenever he felt inclined. He told Gulliver's crowd that, despite his swallowing skills, the last time he visited the Hawthorns he'd nearly choked to death on one of their dodgy meat pies. He topped the most horrendous stories of Martin's visitors with his own harrowing yarn of brain fluid analysis, which left the entire ward wan and nauseous. Ringo listened with a handkerchief over his mouth. I noticed, though, that Droppy was particularly interested in our discussion of Dunderdale.

'Oh arr,' he said, offering his unsolicited opinion, 'there's summat iffy about that Dunderdale. Am yow gooin to write about 'im in yower paper?'

Ringo and Monica smiled politely at him.

'It's just that we used to know someone by that name when we were at college, many years ago,' Monica told him.

'He dissolved,' I said.

'Well, I wish this un 'ud dissolve.'

Then Deekus was at the foot of my bed again. His mother had seemingly bolted at the first opportunity.

'Dunderdale?' he said. 'Please don't talk to me about him. What's he done this time?'

You could tell they both craved information. Droppy and Deekus's lives revolved around this hospital and they thrived on gossip about the staff, who became the mysterious gods of their limited world. It reminded me of how we'd talk about our lecturers at college. We'd discuss the personalities and abilities of these singularly tedious people for hours on end, feeding and feeding off a campus mythology. The mythology starred what amounted to a pantheon of tossers, but that didn't matter. Who they were and what they did in their private lives took on a ridiculous significance. Of course, in the case of WANK, some tutors *did* become genuinely newsworthy but their renown was short-lived. For the most part our gossip was fuelled by froth and trivia. Who was shagging whom; who was a closet gay; who drank too much. Our discussions often involved some kind of conspiracy: them and us intrigues abounded. For one thing, it was well known that if a student complained about a lecturer, the staff would close ranks. We had it on good authority, too, that if you pissed one of them off the rest would mark you down. For hours on end I'd be involved in such discussions, griping over a bad grade (and *all* my grades were bad). We blamed them and hated them because they had power and we didn't. But we also envied them for exactly the same reason.

'Dunderdale, I'm sure, is as capable as any other surgeon,' I said, rather loudly, in an effort to bring the Droppy 'n' Deekus diatribe to an end. It wasn't that I was changing my opinion to suit the occasion, I was just sick of listening to them.

'Absolutely right, Dave,' said Monica, 'we have the finest health service in the world.'

Droppy and Deekus gave identically pitched, hollow laughs and went off to worry Gulliver with stories about just how painful a camera up the arse can be. Ringo and Monica excused themselves. They apologized for having to leave early but promised to visit me again tomorrow.

'Hey, I'm a big boy,' I told them, although I was sorry to see them go.

I've always prided myself on being emotionally self-sufficient but, the state I was in, I was feeling needy. I was also sorry to see them go because this left me alone with Droppy's abandoned wife, Ginger. I could feel her looking at me and I braced myself.

'*Eeeeeeeee*,' she said, ''aven't I seen yow in a Daniel O'Donnell video?'

That's sixteen quid, I thought.

# Fuck, Yea

I loved Ringo and Monica regardless of the reasons I had to be jealous of them: their relationship; their career successes; their ability to walk around without a tube in their bladder. However, any comparison between myself and them tended to depress me somewhat. What had I done since leaving WANK? Apart from lose my hair and gain weight, not much. OK, I was a sub at the *Walsall Reflector*, but that was only because my best mate got me the job. If not for him I'd probably be unemployed by now; or at best still hoofing around as a junior reporter. I think Ringo was hoping the sub's post would help me get off the booze. Certainly, I had fewer opportunities to drink in the daytime these days because I was stuck in the office. Thus, despite my higher salary, I had mixed feelings about the job.

Just in case you don't know what a sub does, I'll tell you: fuck all. Or at least practically fuck all. It was my job to lay the pages out. For this I'd been trained to use a software package called PageSpeed. This allows you to move things around, arrange columns of text and photos to make them look neat – or at least, not too scruffy. I had to make sure that the stories flowed logically and were as snappy as possible. I also had to come up with headlines, which was my favourite part of the subbing job. WALL OF SILENCE SURROUNDS COUNCIL'S OPEN GOVERNMENT POLICY;

COMMUNITY SPLIT ON SOCIAL INTEGRATION PLANS. You know the kind of thing.

Ringo, with his easy-going manner and sense of humour, would let me get away with the ironic ones. I suppose I was the subbing equivalent of the wag who named Vulture Ward. One of the attributes you need to stay sane in Walsall, apart from money enough to get shitfaced, is a sense of irony. Hence: WALSALL SCOOPS UGLIEST TOWN IN THE COUNTRY HONOUR.

Mainly, though, I was a shit sub. I didn't give a toss about accuracy, grammar, punctuation or, for that matter, the news. When journalists submitted copy I rarely noticed any problems with it. Occasionally I'd slice out a paragraph or tweak a sentence to justify my salary, but that was about the limit of my subbing skills. Facts is Facts was popular with readers, but any whining drunk could spew that out once a week. Hardly an achievement to be proud of.

Nor were my relationships with women. These were never successful because any half-astute woman could see I was a bad catch. I was always moaning, always drinking, and always waking up with a rainbow over my bed. I tended to structure my social life around the pub or nights in with a twelve-pack and *Inspector Morse*. Once a week I'd go to Monica and Ringo's for dinner and they'd politely listen to me bleat about the price of fags and booze, and the lack of discernment among contemporary females. I'd return the favour by politely listening to Ringo worry about his latest rash, dizzy spell, chest pain or imaginary lump. Then, of course, we'd turn to gossip: work gossip; play gossip; celebrity gossip. The names changed but the themes remained the same.

I'd think about seeking adventure, but never really get round to it. Averageness had me by the ankles. In 1994 I embarked on an ill-fated fortnight's holiday in Hong Kong, only to get mugged by a monk. I can blame that on the devil's juice too. I was on the small island of Cheung Chau and I'd necked eight bottles of Tsingtao beer at a roadside cafe. There I'd entertained everyone by trying to order a plate of noodles in Cantonese. Apparently my order translated as, 'My uncle requires a watering can full of shoelaces.' They found me so funny they insisted I have another six bottles of beer on the house. Later, when I was trying to find my way back to the ferry terminal, the monk jumped me. The bastard took advantage of the fact that I was off my paps. I had to phone Ringo from Kowloon to wire me some money.

'I need you to send me some money,' I said.

'Tory MP Stephen Milligan has been found asphyxiated with an orange in his mouth,' he replied.

'I've been mugged,' I said.

'He was wearing women's clothes,' said Ringo.

'By a monk,' I said.

Ringo still takes the piss whenever Hong Kong, Buddhism or monks come up in conversation.

My only hobby is booze-related, too: collecting Charles Bukowski first editions. I have many autographed texts, some with the little drawing he'd do of himself drinking a bottle of beer. I even have a letter he wrote me in 1993, the year before his death. I'd been sending him fan mail for five years, always with a SAE. One day he replied with a handwritten note which said:

> I probably wouldn't like you
> you probably wouldn't like me
> > fuck, yea,
> > > Hank.

He didn't sign it Charles, you notice, but Hank. His informal name. I treasure this note and savour its gnomic wisdom.

# Naffing Nora

After visiting time, the staff came round with the trolley and dished out cups of tea, coffee, Ovaltine and Horlicks.

'What do you fancy, love?' asked a woman in a tabard and a hairnet.

I nodded in the direction of my Nil by Mouth sign.

'Oh sorry, love, perhaps tomorrow.' As she wheeled away her trolley of delights my heart sank.

Previously the idea of a cup of Horlicks would have had me honking up my nads but, after nothing but water, I ached for its sweet maltiness. How was it that for so many years I'd ignored the simple pleasures to be had from tasty things? Now my taste buds yelped for them. Is it that I'd always been too pissed, too fogged with nicotine to remember how lovely Horlicks is? Or a doughnut? Or a lemon bonbon? Hadn't I used to enjoy those things? And whatever happened to fizz bombs? I loved them when I was a kid. The sugary explosions of taste that burst from their gritty surface like moondust. That's what I needed now: a good old-fashioned fizz bomb. I'd hold it in my mouth and let my saliva soak it; my senses would reel at the *ting ting ting* of the taste so familiar in the sober, salad days of my childhood: the fiendish fizzbursts would be a match, surely, for the heady effervescence of triple-strength lager.

Just before lights out Nurse Frigata came to do the drugs round.

'Any pain?' she yelled to each of us in turn.

Deekus, of course, answered yes and demanded some pethidine. She told him it hadn't been long enough since his last lot and he would have to make do with aspirin.

'How's your rhinoceros?' she asked me, her thunderous voice rattling the single-glazed window.

I wasn't feeling witty. I shrugged and said nothing, but she began preparing an injection.

'Pancreatitis, eh?' she said, in a much softer voice than usual, although it was still clearly audible to every deafpost within a hundred yards. 'We see a lot of that here. It hurts, doesn't it?'

I nodded. I felt as if was talking to my mom and I said, 'Yes, nurse,' rather pathetically. I tried to remember what I hadn't liked about her the night before, but couldn't.

'This will ease the pain,' she said, 'and help you sleep.' She gently, almost lovingly, administered the drug and I remember thinking what a fool Señor Frigata had been to run off back to Bilbao in the fantasy biography I'd imagined for her.

I felt Deekus's envious eyes burning into me as I drifted off. I wondered how it was possible for him to feel so much contempt for these nurses who regularly displayed genuine care and compassion.

Was Wesley-in-Tame really such a bad place?

In my helpless and sentimental mood my thoughts turned to Walsall's heroine Sister Dora who, in the nineteenth century, selflessly nursed the smallpox-ridden people of the Black Country without a thought for her own sainted, alabaster skin.

Nurses; what would we do without them?

*

I hate these fucking nurses, I thought, when the nicotine-caked Ruth ordered me out of bed the next morning.

'We have to change the sheets,' she barked.

I groaned, still only semi-conscious as she unbuckled my urine-bag from the side of the bed and began using my catheter tube as a lead to encourage me on my way.

'Fucking hell, nurse,' I said, 'watch what you're doing with that tube!'

'And get yourself round to the washroom,' she said, 'you're beginning to stink.'

What a bitch.

When she'd gone Deekus was at my side again in a flash. 'I wouldn't let her talk to me like that. It's an affront to your dignity as a human being. The problem is, you see, you give them a bit of power and they abuse it. You've heard the expression "little Hitler"? This place is full of them, mate. There are complaints procedures, you know. Mind you, as I've said before, it never does any good. They close ranks. The first thing they accuse you of is trying to screw them for compensation. All *I've* ever asked is adequate recompense for injuries suffered at the hands of incompetents, but have I received any? Have I naffing bollocks.'

'I don't think I'm due any compensation for being asked to get out of bed, Deekus,' I said.

'I expected more from Dave Ichabod McVane,' he said. 'You always stick it to 'em in your column.'

It's just that when I meet people like you I can understand their point of view, I thought.

'I'll just be glad when I can leave,' I said but, distracted by the arrival of the tea trolley, he didn't hear me.

'I hope you've got something better than malted milks this time,' he told the tea lady. 'Has the Health Service not heard of custard naffing creams?'

'You don't get biscuits at breakfast,' she told him.

'And that's another thing. The NHS costs the working man naffing millions and you can't even make the effort to serve us a breakfast biscuit. I mean, naffing Nora, would it kill you?'

Eventually, his words became a meaningless drone of naffing this, naffing that and naffing the other.

# A Visit from Dunderdale

I wanted to get back into bed again as quickly as possible. For one thing, it was quite painful being in anything other than a supine position; for another, I was completely shagged out. I'd been disturbed every few hours in the night because my urine emissions had to be monitored regularly. Sometimes nurses would need to adjust the angle of the catheter tube so that the piss volume could be measured properly. A heavy-handed nurse could make this a very painful procedure. Thus I tended to sleep with one eye open and, the second I heard a nurse coming, I'd hold my catheter tube hard against my leg to keep it firmly in place.

'I'm just protecting Big Mac and the twins,' I said, when one of the nurses queried my behaviour. I'd been a little insulted by the volume and duration of her laughter.

As a result of my constant paranoid surveillance, my eyes kept shutting involuntarily and, as soon as the nurses had changed my bed, I was back in it and asleep. But it wasn't a sound sleep and, at some stage, I tuned into the murmur of muted, indistinct conversation. It didn't really register with me at first, but hearing the name Dunderdale a few times pulled me from my slumber. I woke to see a group leaving the Islands of Langerhans: a nurse, Dr Fostus, three or four junior doctors or students, and another guy: a big blond chap who looked oddly familiar.

'Yow've missed 'im, wack!' cried Droppy Collins when

he saw that I was awake. "'E only appears once in a blue moon and yow've missed 'im. Yow woh see 'im again now all wik.'

'Dunderdale?' I said.

'Arr.'

'Why the bloody hell didn't they wake me?'

Deekus scampered over, the wheels of his drip-stand squeaking furiously. 'Why should they want to talk to you?' he said. 'You're only the patient, after all. What do you matter? They've decided you're for the chop and that's that. They won't bother informing you. Oh no, that would be too naffing considerate; that would be too much like providing a service!'

'What,' I asked Droppy, 'does he mean by "for the chop"?'

'It sounds like Dunderdale wants to fiddle with yower innards, wack,' said Droppy, 'but Fostus wants a CAT scan fust. I 'eard 'em.'

'Arguing?'

'Arr, they doh see eye to eye if yow ask me.'

I thought about chasing after Fostus and Dunderdale to ask what they had in mind, but my limbs were leaden and my piss-bag would be like a ball and chain. So I pressed the call button for the nurse. Nothing happened so I pressed it another four times.

Ruth arrived at my bedside after about fifteen minutes.

'My consultant was just here and I missed him,' I told her.

She looked at me as if I'd dragged her to my bedside to inform her that my piss tasted of piss.

'And?'

'Well, I'd quite like to speak to him,' I said.

'You'll have a chance when he does his rounds again then, won't you?'

'But he never does his rounds, does he?'

'If he never does his rounds how come you've just missed him?'

'Do you know who I am?' I asked in desperation.

She looked at my white board. 'You're David McVane?'

'I'm David *Ichabod* McVane who writes for the *Reflector*,' I said, raising my voice, 'and if you don't get me Mr Dunderdale then the next piece I write will be about you.'

I heard Deekus whoop and clap.

Ruth smiled and shrugged. 'I've always wanted to see my name in the paper,' she said, and left.

'Wooooo,' said Deekus, 'she's asking for it.'

I lay there fuming. I was ashamed of myself for my pettiness, but I was livid – mostly, I think, because I was so impotent. My threat had been hollow: even if I wrote about the incident, I couldn't mention Ruth by name. I lacked power in every sense. The state I was in she could have whopped me in a fight. One pull on my catheter tube and I'd have been as subdued as any slave in Penny's Punishment Palace.

But my complaining did have some effect because a few minutes later Dr Fostus appeared.

'I want to see Dunderdale,' I said, still angry.

'I'm sorry you missed him. He's in surgery for the rest of the morning so I'm afraid he can't come back and speak to you today. But I can tell you anything that you want to know.'

'Why were you arguing about what to do with me?'

Fostus looked shocked, which in his case meant his left eyebrow rose one-sixteenth of a millimetre. 'I can assure you we were not arguing. Mr Dunderdale and I are a little concerned by the results of your ultrasound scan. We merely debated which of the various tests available to us would be the most effective. But there were no arguments, Mr McVane.'

'Someone said you'd discussed operating.'

Fostus glanced disapprovingly at Droppy who was

pretending to read his *Black Country Bugle*. 'We prefer non-invasive treatment for your condition. Surgery is very dangerous in the presence of pancreatic inflammation.'

'Am I going to die?' I said, sounding as pathetic as I had last night while talking to Nurse Frigata.

'Not if we can help it.'

'This hospital has the highest mortality rate in the country.'

'There are reasons for that.'

'Because the place is full of quacks?'

'The care you will receive here is equal to that in any hospital in England.'

'How come everyone's always moaning about the NHS?'

'Because no matter how good we are we can never be good enough.'

'What about my Islands of Langerhans?'

'Believe me, we'll do everything we can to save them.'

'What about Harold Shipman?' Fostus turned and walked away. I was never going to get a rise out of him.

I don't deserve to die, I thought as, later, I lay waiting for another shot of pethidine to kick in. Lots of people do, but I don't. At least I don't think I do.

Or do I?

It's something you ponder when confronted by your own potential demise.

And morality is something else. I tried to recall what might qualify me as a good guy, worthy of a few more years. I thought for what must have been twenty minutes.

Here's something I came up with. Yesterday I played God's advocate with Brad Pitt because I didn't want to see the vicar upset. Isn't that a good thing to do? That makes me a nice person, doesn't it? I bet someone like Deekus wouldn't be so considerate. It'd never occur to him because he's not as sensitive to other people's feelings as I am.

I thought for another ten minutes without coming up with anything else. Still, the Brad Pitt episode was enough to convince me: I deserve to live longer than someone like Deekus.

Not only am I more worthy than Deekus in a moral sense, I'm also more prepared to take responsibility for myself and my condition. If I survive with my pancreas intact, I'll do everything to help myself stay healthy. I'll never drink again. I can do that – perhaps even without murdering Daniel O'Donnell. If Deekus were discharged tomorrow, he'd be back in this place within a year. I definitely wouldn't be. Deekus would do nothing to help himself, I'd do whatever it takes to stop me ending up in here again.

So I concluded that I deserve to live more than someone like Deekus. I hope the God I don't believe in agrees.

# f.ada

The phlebotomist, Nosferatu, came again at about eleven that morning and took some more blood. As he did so a chap in a well-tailored suit walked onto the ward, looked around, scribbled something in a notebook and left. I noticed Nosferatu glance at the suited guy and mumble something disparaging under his breath.

'Who's he?' I asked.

'A cot-counter.'

'?'

'He counts beds.'

'What for?'

'Because he gets paid thirty grand a year for it.'

'What does he do with his information?'

'He tells us what we already know.'

'Which is?'

'We haven't got enough beds. We never have enough beds on Langerhans. If it wasn't for his salary, though, maybe we'd be able to afford a couple more. But then, what do I know? I'm just a lowly bloodsucker.'

'What about the increase in spending that Gordon Brown's just announced? Is that going to help things?'

'I've heard it all before. The only difference it'll make around here is there'll be another job for someone like him.'

In my experience the equivalent of the loathsome cot-counter can be found everywhere. Superfluous middle management is a legacy of the Thatcher years that persists under New Labour. Even at the *Reflector* Ringo is always fighting with managers who want to replace Facts is Facts with more advertising, despite the fact that my column is the only thing Walsall people read (and I don't just mean in the paper). The worst thing about it is that the middle managers know this too and so always let Ringo win the argument. But they keep raising it as an issue because they have to be seen to be doing something to justify their jobs. If they suggested they got someone more talented (and/or cheaper) to write the piece they would have a stronger case. And they wouldn't have to look very far: Walsall is full of drunken cynics.

I heard my mobile beep in my locker. Nosferatu tutted and shook his head.

'You naughty boy,' he said, 'that's supposed to be off. Don't let the nurses catch you.' Then he winked and moved onto Deekus, who instantly began moaning about the bruising he'd suffered thanks to the incompetent way his blood sample was taken yesterday.

I surreptitiously looked at my Nokia beneath the bed-clothes. I had a text message from Ringo.

> f. ada.
> big shock 4 u
> if u r still alive
> will b there @ 2

Shock? I thought about phoning Ringo back for elaboration but decided against it. He'd be pretty busy at the paper. Besides, I knew the text was just a teaser to get me going and I didn't want to spoil his fun.

Ringo and Monica were the only visitors I was likely to get regardless of how long I lay in Wesley. I had other friends, but none who'd bother visiting me while the pubs were open. I had relatives too, but most of them kept their heads down where I was concerned. My parents lived abroad: they'd emigrated to Fuerteventura where they owned a modest villa. There they spent their days fussing over an ill-tempered Chihuahua named Rhett. I wasn't going to contact them. They'd insist on coming home and that wouldn't do me any good either physically or psychologically. The last time they visited they refused to change out of the purple and gold caftans they'd purchased on a weekend excursion to Marrakech. The Chihuahua had one too, the size of a bobble hat. No one wore such garments in Marrakech, let alone Walsall. No, they needed to be kept away at all costs because if the pancreatitis didn't kill me, parent-generated mortification surely would.

# Ay Means Is Not

At twelve, Ruth came and told me that I was going to have my CAT scan. Apparently there was a long waiting list but, owing to a cancellation, and because my case was considered extremely urgent, I'd been moved to the front of the queue. Lucky me.

Ruth gave me a litre of badger's piss and told me to drink it. It wasn't actually badger's piss, of course. It was poodle's piss.

'It tastes like poodle's piss,' I moaned.

'How do you know what poodle's piss tastes like?'

'It's what I turn to when I run out of meths.'

'Well, you have to drink it because it helps with the imaging. And put this gown on.' She tossed me one of those smock-like garments that lace up at the back.

Ruth drew the curtains and helped me into the gown: there's no way I could have donned it without assistance. It's not easy to dress when your hand is attached to a drip and your cock is attached to a piss-bag. Even after the pethidine it hurt me to move. My rhinoceros was still there; I could feel him. He was sleeping less soundly now. His ears were twitching; he gave an occasional snort. Soon he'd be struggling to get back on his feet.

Every time Ruth leaned into me I could smell the nicotine of a heavy smoker on her. I was more aware of it than I'd normally have been because I hadn't had a fag since the night of my admission. Mind you, I didn't fancy one. Amazingly, I didn't fancy a drink either – not the taste of one at least. Alcohol, such an old and reliable friend, had become my enemy. The thought of my favourite tipple, triple-strength Dutch lager, made my rhino frisky. In fact, the mere idea of booze made me queasy and never before, not even with my worst hangover, had I felt this way.

But, despite this, part of me still craved alcohol. It's weird. If someone had offered me a consequence-free pint I'd have guzzled it in a trice. I would have quaffed through the queasiness to the delectable, transcendent hit of the alcohol itself. It would be like that lovely, almost sexual feeling you get from scratching an itchy rash or scab: that fleeting, guilty ecstasy we all pursue despite our better judgement.

From the smell of her, I was willing to bet that Ruth knew all about that ecstasy.

'I bet this is a stressful job, isn't it, Ruth?'

'Tell me about it.'

'Why do you do it, if you don't mind me asking?'

'I wanted to be an undertaker,' she said, 'but they discriminate against women.'

'You're joking, of course.'

'The porter will pick you up in half an hour,' she said and left.


The porter came on time.

I was wheeled through Langerhans and out into the corridor with my file of charts on my lap. It was quite a way to the scanner and I was taken through parts of the hospital I'd never seen before. Every now and then bleary-eyed house doctors would zombie past, their stethoscopes swinging from their jacket pockets. It meant we were close to wherever it is they're allowed to lie down and close their eyes for thirty seconds before being woken to commit manslaughter again. As we were approaching a door marked

Theatre 3, I once more glimpsed the guy I'd spotted earlier among Dunderdale's entourage. I was positive he was someone I'd seen before. In my years as a journo, though, I'd met many people and, given the havoc booze had wreaked on my brain cells, I occasionally had trouble placing faces. Still, this bloke looked very familiar. He was a big chap: blond and well built. Was he a doctor? Could it be Dunderdale himself? Perhaps I'd seen him on the telly? Local consultants often featured on the regional news, not to mention programmes such as *Central Weekend*, where they fuelled the public's obsession with health or, more precisely, illness.

The porter responsible for transporting me this time was called Vernon and he had a hacking cough. Several times we had to stop while he was doubled up with a coughing fit. He had to be careful when he coughed, he said, because he didn't want to aggravate his 'double rupture'.

At one point we paused beside a room in which a teaching session was in progress. A dozen or so students – mainly women – were being instructed by a guy wearing a collarless shirt and leather waistcoat. The students looked to be from the Far East – principally, I'd say, the Philippines. The teacher would speak and the students repeated what he said.

Teacher: 'Ay means is not.'

Class: 'Ay means is not.'

Teacher: 'Day means did not.'

Class: 'Day means did not.'

Teacher: 'Yome means you are.'

Class: 'Yome means you are.'

And so they went on, and I stared, amazed, while Vernon hacked his ring up behind me. When he finally composed himself, we moved on and I asked him about the class.

'Oh yeah,' he said, mopping his lips with his sleeve, 'he's teaching them Black Country English. It's to do with the recruitment crisis. They're having to go further and further afield to find staff. They can all speak great English but they still haven't a clue what we're talking about in Walsall.'

'Figures,' I said, wondering how long Vernon had to live and concluding probably a fortnight.

# Yower Feyther Is Jed

I was wheeled into the CAT-scan waiting room which, thankfully, wasn't too crowded. The guy I was placed alongside was chatty, and a bit too posh for Walsall. His name was Charles.

'What ails you, my friend?' asked Charles. Unlike most people, who ask something along these lines as a way into a discussion about themselves, he seemed merely to be making conversation.

'Pancreatitis.'

'Ah,' he said, screwing up his face, 'not a pleasant condition; but an increasingly common one I believe.'

'How come everyone is more informed about pancreatitis than me?' I asked. So far I hadn't spoken to a single person who didn't know at least something about my new illness. I'd previously never heard of it.

'My Uncle Bernard's next-door neighbour developed it after a bout of the mumps,' he replied. 'It killed him actually. Poor chap.'

'Ah.'

'He developed complications, though,' Charles added hastily, 'and he drank like a fish.'

'Whereas I haven't been pissed for almost two days,' I said.

'Sorry,' he said.

'No problem. Was he a patient here?'

'Yes, quite recently as it happens. His consultant's name was Dunderdale.'

'That's my consultant's name too.'

'Oh dear, I'm not doing very well here, am I?'

'Please don't worry about it,' I said, while thinking: Jesus H. fucking Christ!

'Have you been waiting long for your scan?' Charles asked, desperate to change the subject.

'Yes,' I said, 'all morning.'

Charles laughed.

'I had a cancellation,' I said.

'That was a stroke of luck for you; most people have to wait at least a week; outpatients wait six months. The lady I've just been speaking to has waited a year and she's in constant pain.'

'How about you?'

'I'm lucky, I'm private. They booked me in straight away.'

'But this is an NHS hospital.'

'They hire out their equipment to BUPA.'

'*Really?*'

'Here I am.'

I'd heard that this kind of thing went on and now here was Charles confirming it. If it *was* true it would make an excellent basis for a scathing Facts is Facts. I made a mental note to look into the matter if I ever saw the outside world again. When I say 'look into' I don't mean research. I'd do what I always do: offer anecdote and hearsay as fact. Mind you, one seldom needed to be scrupulous in stories about the health service, particularly about Wesley. The bonus with slagging off the NHS is that the public sector seldom sue.

'So what's *your* problem?' I asked Charles, just to be polite.

'Oh, slight stomach pains. It's probably dyspepsia again.'

'Again?'

'Well my last three CAT scans have shown slight abdominal bloating. I always seem to get it after too many truffles.'

I wasn't altogether certain if he was joking but, nevertheless, I could feel my column beginning to take shape: *Pain is to poverty what cash is to healthcare it seems. As the less fortunate suffer, the Health Service prostitutes itself to the privileged few . . .*

Charles was taken in before me and I waited, my bladder bloated with poodle piss, for the doctors to call me in. Various magazines and papers were lying around in the waiting area, and I tried to distract myself with them. One men's magazine from earlier that year had a story about Jamie Theakston's alleged visits to a Soho spanking palace. I'd argued with Monica over this one at great length. She fancied Theakston and maintained that the story couldn't possibly be true; I, meanwhile, thought he was a pointless streak of piss and was certain it was completely accurate. The magazine also carried a piece about the conspiracy that supposedly lies behind the death of Princess Di. The article blamed the death on everyone from Interflora to her jug-eared ex-hubby. This story is another I'd discussed in meticulous detail with my ex and her husband (and another, incidentally, that inspired me to use the phrase 'pointless streak of piss'). There was also an out-of-date *National Enquirer* lying among the pile of *People's Friend*s and *My Weekly*s. The Van Freeks and I both subscribed to this, the daddy of all scandal rags. I recalled that this particular issue carried a story about a Siamese twin being tried for manslaughter following a botched suicide attempt.

Having skipped through the pages of old-hat scandal in five minutes flat, every fibre of my body was on the verge of throttling itself with boredom when, forty minutes later, a nurse finally wheeled me in. I was placed on a table and injected with a solution that gave me an intense, warm feeling in my stomach and made me worry about my bowels becoming too relaxed. Then the three staff members present ran to hide in a little glass cubicle, presumably to shield themselves from the brain-mincing rays thrown off by the scanner. Someone threw a switch and I began to move into a structure shaped like a giant doughnut. When I came to rest a recorded voice clicked on and said: 'When you see a smiley face on the panel above your head, please hold your breath.'

Sure enough the image of a smiley face appeared on a panel above my head. I held my breath. The face clicked on and off several times. Obedient patient that I am, I held my breath each time.

After the scan I waited half an hour for a porter.

As I was being wheeled back to Langerhans we passed a poster advertising an appeal for a new CAT scanner. So far they'd raised a hundred grand and they had another hundred grand to go. On the same noticeboard was an advert for BUPA: 'Freedom and Choice: It's Your Health'. Was that guy from admin taking the piss again, or was the NHS beginning to lose faith in itself?

We went via the teaching room on our way back. The chap in the collarless shirt was still doing his stuff.

Teacher: 'Now we're going to deal with phone calls from relatives.'

Class: 'Aah.'

Teacher: 'Ow is me feyther? means How is my father?'

Class: 'Ow is me feyther?'

Teacher: 'Excellent. Now we respond as the situation dictates. So: Yower feyther is wusser, means Your father is worse.'

Class: 'Yower feyther is wusser.'

Teacher: 'Yower feyther is jed, means Your father is dead.'

Class: 'Yower feyther is jed.'

We'd passed the room before they got to 'Yower feyther is better,' assuming they bothered to learn that scarcely uttered phrase.

# Ruud Van Door

It was after two p.m. when I arrived back at my bed, and Ringo was waiting for me. He was looking a little pale because he'd spent five minutes listening to Droppy explain about the various brain cancers thought to be caused by mobile phones. When, inevitably, 'Vicar in a Tutu' sounded, Ringo held his phone at arm's length to switch it off.

'Flaming Ada, where have you been?' he asked, seeming much more agitated than usual.

'CAT scan.'

'Have you seen Dunderdale?'

'Yes and no. He did his rounds this morning but I was asleep and didn't get a chance to talk to him.'

'You'll never guess where I've been,' he said. His tone suggested he was harbouring a delicious morsel of intrigue.

'Do tell.'

'All this talk of Dunderdale got me thinking about Ebola and the odd occurrences during our first term at WANK.'

'And?'

'I paid a visit to Penny Stroker and Dionne Splendour.'

'Good grief, are they still around?'

'Alive and kicking and in business together. They run an S&M brothel in Balsall Heath.'

'How did you find them and, if it's not a stupid question, why bother?'

'Our advertising sales people were approached a while back with a dodgy advert: *Penny and Dionne's Dungeon of Delight*. It struck me at the time that this must be the same Penny, but we were so hectic at the paper it went out of my mind. This Dunderdale business reminded me. I dug out the ad, gave them a call and she invited me over for a chat. Like you, I haven't seen her since before the fire, so I popped over. I had an interesting half-hour there to say the least.'

'Go on.'

'Well, she still calls me Clogs, for one thing.'

'I hope there's more.'

'Oh indeed. You remember what they told everyone about the cause of the fire?'

'They claimed it was Dionne's candles. I, on the other hand, felt Dunderdale tried to kill us. It's a feeling that, as I recall, no one managed to talk me out of.' My memory was hazy, but I could still remember the words I thought I'd heard that night: 'Dunderdale, you bastard, no.'

'Try again. Dionne says it was probably you who caused the fire.'

'*What?*' My exclamation made half the ward turn our way.

'You were staggering around pissed with a joint. And Dionne says the landing reeked of meths.'

'It's true I was out on the landing but –'

'Apparently Dionne spoke to you, she distinctly remembers what she said. She called you a bastard and told you you'd had too much ale; she shouted at you to go.'

My mind perused its cobwebbed and yellowing Memories of the Fire file. 'Dunderdale you bastard, no,' is what I'd heard. 'You've had too much ale, you bastard, go,' is what Dionne had said. Sounds possible, doesn't it? Let's face it, it's more than possible. Is there a score high enough for me on the scale of wankerdom?

'I don't suppose you remember her speaking to you?'

'I can't say I do, but I was off my paps.'

'You probably found it difficult to hear because of the rhino-horn hood. You know, the one we have a snap of in the *Reflector* photo library?'

'Yes, thank you, I remember. But tell me this: why didn't Dionne mention it to the cops and the fire brigade at the time?'

'Your joint. Penny didn't want any mention of drugs, so they made up the candle story.'

'Jesus H.'

'Anyway, that isn't the interesting bit.' Ringo was relishing this; he was enjoying feeding me his information a morsel at a time, just as he always did. It's childish but, hey, you get your kicks where you can in Walsall.

'*What is the fucking interesting bit?*' I demanded. Those on the ward who hadn't been clocking us before were now.

Ringo, shocked at the volume of my voice, checked himself. 'Sorry, I shouldn't be winding you up,' he said. 'Old habits.'

'Just tell me, Ringo.' I was stunned to learn that I might have burned my home down but if there was something even more newsworthy then I had to hear it. 'What?' I repeated. I noticed Gulliver had taken his headset off to listen and Deekus had curtailed a trip to the loo in order hear Ringo's reply. All faces were turned towards us.

Ringo, also noticing everyone paying attention, began to whisper. 'Well, I happened to –' Everybody in the vicinity craned their necks in an effort to hear. Ringo dropped his voice even lower. 'Well, I happened to –' Deekus was practically perched on the end of the bed; Droppy was leaning so far towards us he was in danger of falling off his.

'Is there anywhere private we can go?' Ringo asked.

We scrounged a wheelchair and Ringo pushed me out into a garden. We parked by a bench with several thousand fag butts beneath it. As soon as Ringo sat down, however, his phone sang 'Vicar in a Tutu' again. It was Kenny Prince, the deputy editor, so he took the call and I waited.

I was tense and I made a conscious effort to calm down. It was a lovely mid-April day and I turned my face up to the sun. If I survive, I thought, I'm going to start to appreciate days like this. I'll try to forget booze and concentrate on drinking in the world instead. Sounds corny? Well, having the Grim Reaper grab your nads can turn you sentimental. I told myself I'd never dull my senses again: no fags; no booze. I'm going learn the names of flowers and cloud formations too, maybe. Instead of flicking fag ends at birds, I'll note their plumage and look them up in *A Guide to English Birds*. Instead of pissing up trees on my way home from the pub, I'll learn about those too. Oak, ash, beech. What exactly is the difference? These things are all around me and I haven't got a clue. It's interesting how interesting the world can be when there's a chance it might evict you. It was astonishing how significant questions of value had become: first morality and now aesthetics. Dr Dunderdale would have been proud. It's just a shame they didn't seem as interesting to me when I was studying them at college. Still, you live and learn. *If* you live.

By the time Ringo finished his call I'd managed to calm myself; in fact, I was almost serene. It was as if Julie Andrews had just cooed the lyrics of 'My Favourite Things' into my needy ear.

'When you went to see Penny and Dionne, what?' I asked.

'When I went to see Penny and Dionne I happened to have a photo of Dunderdale with me.'

'Which Dunderdale?'

'Our pervy Head of English. I found it in the *Reflector* picture archive – it's the one they used when he was announced missing. I'd put it in my wallet yesterday to bring here so we could establish once and for all that he's not your surgeon.'

'And?'

'Well, I'm not sure why I decided to show it to them, but I'm glad I did.'

'Go on.'

'Penny and Dionne had never seen it before.'

'So what?'

'Shall I tell you what they said?'

'Please do, Ringo.' He was winding me up again. He couldn't help himself.

'They said: "That's not Dunderdale!"'

'*What?*' I was shouting again. Nurse Frigata wouldn't like what this was doing to my blood pressure.

'Calm down and take some deep breaths,' Ringo said, lapping this up; his eyes sparking with electric glee.

'I saw Dunderdale at Penny's with my own eyes,' I said.

'Eliot.'

'Who?'

'He called himself George Eliot. Penny and Dionne remember him. Not only that, they remember him as a likeable, gentle chap with a fondness for submissive pursuits – especially being forced to wear uncomfortable underwear.'

'Our Dunderdale was their George Eliot?'

Ringo nodded. 'He was a total masochist; no sadistic inclinations at all. He liked to be spanked with a paddle. He never said anything about being an academic, let alone about being a fake one.'

'Then who was *their* Dunderdale, for fuck's sake? Who was the man who claimed to be Doctor Daniel Dunderdale; the hardcore sadist who bragged about having forged his qualifications, who the fuck was he?'

'He was someone else.'

'Somebody stole Dunderdale's name?'

'Used it, yes, it seems so.'

'Who the fuck was he?'

'Ah, well: they described him as a big, blond fellow. Dionne mentioned that she thought he might be foreign. Any ideas?'

'Have you?' I could see that he had.

'The bloke claimed to be working at WANK, remember?'

'It's something I'm not likely to forget, Ringo.'

'Think of the large blond academics teaching at WANK that first term.' Ringo had pulled his knees up to his chest and was rocking backward and forward on the bench, bursting with excitement. He's loving it, I thought, I'm fucking dying and he's having the time of his life!

'There was that Dutch visiting lecturer from . . . Utrecht was it?' I suggested.

'Ruud Van Door. His name was Ruud Van Door.'

'Yes, I remember his name, but you can't think it was him? He was a nice bloke. A great bloke and a brilliant lecturer. He's the guy who introduced me to Bukowski – I have a lot to thank him for. In fact, he gave me my highest ever grade: B+.'

'Dave, when I described Ruud Van Door to Penny and Dionne they said he sounded exactly like their man.'

'Ruud Van Door? If there was ever a bloke less likely to frequent a brothel it would be him, surely.'

'Who can tell? Dunderdale was a nice bloke and a brilliant lecturer, too, but we were willing to believe he was a fraud.'

Then I remembered the fleeting glimpse I'd had of my surgeon and his entourage. 'Ringo, today while Dunderdale was doing his rounds, I spotted a large blond guy who looked familiar but, at the time, I couldn't place him. He was a big fellow with a squarish jaw. Now that you've mentioned Van Door –'

'Flaming Ada, don't start leaping to conclusions.' But I

had the impression that this was a leap that Ringo had already made.

'It couldn't be, could it?' I asked.

'Calm down, Dave.'

'We could have a big story here, Ringo.'

'For God's sake, don't go off on one. Christ, Monica would kill me if she thought I was winding you up like this.'

'Van Door called himself Dunderdale at Penny's; could he be hijacking his name at Wesley too?'

'That's ridiculous, Dave.' I must've been bawling again because Ringo started making calm-down gestures and talking softly to me. 'I'll sort it out for you, Dave. I'll get some enquiries made. You just calm down.'

He wheeled me back to the Lost Islands of Langerhans and, as soon as he'd made sure I was settled, he left. As he exited the ward I saw him punching urgently at the buttons on his mobile.


Back in my bed I had plenty to think about. Could Mr Daniel Dunderdale be Ruud Van Door? My mind kept turning to the blond bloke I'd glimpsed twice. He'd looked familiar but, sixteen years on, I couldn't be certain. I was fogged with drugs, distracted by my rhinoceros and driven mad by my fellow patients.

Also I had the impression that, on top of everything, I might be suffering some kind of withdrawal symptoms. I'd been nearly two days without alcohol. It was a frightening thought, but this was probably the longest I'd gone without a drink for ten years. I drank every day, sometimes just six or seven pints but always *every single day*. And recently? Jesus. What was my enforced abstinence doing to my mind? Was it affecting my reason? Was it making me hallucinate? One thing was for certain, even without pancreatitis, life in Wesley-in-Tame was becoming strange and unsettling.

My uncomfortable reverie was interrupted by a perky South East Asian nurse who'd come to give me a dose of intravenous antibiotics. She had the oddly incongruous name of Mildred.

'I've gorra give yow yower jab, wack,' she told me.

'It's OK, nurse, I speak English,' I said.

'Thank goodness for that,' she answered, 'I'm afraid I haven't got the hang of the dialect yet.'

'I'm sure it's much easier to learn than . . . I'm sorry where are you from?'

'I'm from Hong Kong. My first language is Cantonese.'

'I know some Cantonese,' I said.

'Really?'

'My uncle requires a watering can full of shoelaces,' I told her.

Mildred thought this was the most hysterical thing she'd ever heard. I half expected her to present me with a bottle of Tsingtoa. If she had I'd have breathed in its aroma, but I wouldn't have tasted. Booze had landed me in enough trouble.

When I'd asked Ringo to give me more details about my part in the fire, he'd made light of it. It was yesterday's news, he said. It didn't really matter what had happened because no one was hurt. Dionne hadn't even been absolutely sure if it *was* my fault. Apparently I was clattering about on the third-floor landing and she came to tell me to keep the noise down. Back in the flat she heard a series of bangs and crashes and she came out again to find me on the second-floor landing. The first time I'd had a full joint in my hand, the second time it had gone. And there were bottles of meths around, of course. But nothing was really conclusive . . . Who am I kidding? Perhaps deep down I'd always known it was me, just as, deep down, Daniel O'Donnell must know he's a treacle-titted tosser?

It's strange, but the realization didn't bother me that much. It was a long time ago and time is a bit like booze: it fogs, distances, desensitizes. The fire, if I *had* caused it, was just another listing in a catalogue of catastrophes that can be blamed on the devil's juice. Another load of shit my boozing had landed me in. I'd started drinking because it added something to my life; my tedious, workaday, average life. But, inevitably, all the time it was giving it had been taking too. Home. Girlfriend. Health. Dignity. Was it worth it? Ask me again when I'm better.

# Problem Patient

Dr Fostus came to see me at about five that afternoon with the results of my CAT scan. He looked, as he always looked, like a delivery from Burke & Hare.

'Your pancreas is very badly swollen,' he told me, 'but there doesn't seem to be any obvious sign of necrosis.'

Had I not already been lying in bed I'd have collapsed with relief. 'So I'm going to live?' I said, thinking what a likeable chap Fostus was after all.

'I hope so,' he said, his voice as grave as ever, 'but, despite there being no necrosis, the scan results were inconclusive. It's Mr Dunderdale's view that another procedure might be necessary.'

Surgery, I thought. They're going to operate on me. I felt a sudden absence in the pit of my stomach. 'But why? And when will I be having this "procedure"?'

'As soon as possible. Mr Dunderdale would like to get you in for tomorrow morning hopefully. He feels it is quite urgent . . .'

Fostus talked on, but I found it difficult to catch what he said. I was panicking and his language was peppered with jargon and, as it was hard for me to concentrate, much of it was lost on me. The doctor spoke, as always, in a ponderous, phlegmatic way, but it was his tone rather than his words that affected me. I had a feeling that he wasn't really sure about the wisdom of Dunderdale's conclusions. He couldn't come out and say as much but something made me suspect it. One thing seemed clear, though: if Dunderdale had his way I'd be undergoing surgery the next day.

'Is it normal to operate on someone with pancreatitis?' I asked him.

'I think I've answered that question for you already, Mr McVane.'

'How long has Mr Dunderdale been working here?'

'Several months, why?'

'No one seems to like him.'

'That's nonsense.'

'Is it? What's *your* opinion of the unusually high mortality rate at this hospital?'

'I'm afraid I'm not willing to discuss that with you.'

'Off the record.'

'Sorry.'

'OK, I'll ask you what might sound like a stupid question, but what are the chances of Dunderdale not being a real surgeon?'

'Pardon me?'

'What are the chances of him having faked his qualifications? What are the chances of him being an impostor? What are the chances of him being responsible for the high mortality rate here?'

Fostus came as close as I think it's possible for him to come to laughing. His mouth twisted in a kind of constipated smirk. 'Mr McVane, that is, as you say, a stupid question. I have seen Mr Dunderdale perform numerous operations and I can assure you he is a real surgeon.'

I couldn't help but persist. 'What are the chances of him being just an ordinary bloke off the street, without any proper qualifications?'

'None whatsoever.'

'Really? Could you stake your life on that?'

'Yes.'

Fostus didn't actually come out and say I was paranoid but I know he thought it. 'Liar!' I shouted. 'It's easy for you to say that because you don't have to stake your life on it. I do.'

'I refuse to continue this conversation, Mr McVane. You're upset and you're not behaving rationally.' He began to leave.

'Don't tell me you've never seen the film *Paper Mask*!' I shouted after him. 'It stars Paul McGann and Amanda Donahue, if you're interested.'

Fostus ignored me and walked on.

'What about Harold Shipman?' I yelled once again but, even as I did so, it struck me that, of course, Harold Shipman was a *real* doctor.

I was becoming a problem patient. When the nurses came to do my observations they were brusque, even hostile – the same attitude as they had when attending to Deekus. It was because I'd had a go at Ruth and bawled at Fostus. I could feel the hostility from Annette, for instance, when she came to take my blood sugar. She snapped the prick down hard on my thumb and then pretended she didn't have a big enough smear of blood and did it again. Inevitably, she showed no consideration when she came to measure my urine. I held tightly onto the business end of the tube and I had the feeling that, if I hadn't, she'd have ripped my bladder out.

I didn't want to be a problem patient. I didn't want to behave like Deekus but, by this time, I could hardly help myself.

# Don't Get in a State

Ringo and Monica came to visit me at six o'clock promptly. Ringo, as always in the hospital environment, was jittery. Even as he approached my bed I noticed him run his fingers around his neck, checking his glands for swelling. He thought *he*'d got something to worry about!

It was Monica who spoke first. 'Now, Dave, Ringo has something to tell you and I don't want you to get yourself in a state.'

After my conversation with Fostus I was already in a state. Now I was in a right fucking state. '*What?*' I demanded.

'Promise me you won't freak out,' said Ringo, which was itself a statement certain to make my adrenalin gland squirt like a water pistol.

'No, *what*!'

'I checked out Van Door this afternoon.'

'Yourself?'

'I speak Dutch, remember.'

'Well?'

'It's stunning stuff. WANK was taken over by the Heart of England University, as you know, but they still have Van Door's CV on file from when he taught there in the 1980s. It claimed he was a Professor of American Literature at the University of Utrecht and that he had a PhD from the

University of Groningen. I phoned Utrecht and they'd never heard of him; then I phoned Groningen.'

'And had they heard of him?'

'Oh yes, he used to work there.'

'At least there's some truth in his cv then.'

'Dave, he used to work there as a caretaker.'

'Fucking hell.'

'Before you ask, they haven't been able to find a photo to fax me yet, but it definitely sounds like the same bloke.'

'So,' I said, trying not to get into any more of a state, 'here we have someone with a history of impersonating professional people, who has used the name Dunderdale, and who knows Walsall. Meanwhile, there is a surgeon working in Walsall, who no one seems to trust or like, who is also called Dunderdale. And, to top it all, the mortality rate in this hospital is the highest in the country. Have our chances of having unearthed something sinister here just increased?'

'No,' said Monica.

'I was talking to Ringo.'

'Maybe,' said Ringo.

'It couldn't happen,' said Monica. 'You can't pass yourself off as a surgeon; it takes years of study and practice.'

'No,' said Ringo, exercising the kind of pedantry that on occasions makes him the most irritating person in the world, 'it takes years of study and practice to *qualify* as a surgeon. There's a difference.'

'You know what I mean,' said Monica.

'Well,' I said, 'he managed to pass himself off as an expert in American literature.'

'He read a few books; stole a few lecture notes. It's hardly the same thing.'

'He was one of the best lecturers in the college that term,' I reminded her. 'He obviously has some skills.'

Monica smiled. 'I've just had an incredible feeling of déjà

vu. Didn't we have exactly the same conversation in 1986 when we thought Dr Dunderdale was a fake?'

'So what?'

'So it turns out he wasn't!'

'No,' I said, exasperated by this rather pointless application of non-logic, 'but Van Door *was*. And in his private life he was calling himself Dunderdale!' How the hell did this woman manage to get a first?

'But why would he come back to Walsall of all places?'

'I don't know. Why does he like spanking prostitutes with a leather paddle? Why would he pretend to be an academic, or even a surgeon? Because he loves power; because he likes to be in charge; because he's *barking fucking mad*!'

'Dave, surgery isn't something you can just start to do.'

'Monica, you can't tell me it's never happened. I saw a whole documentary about it on the telly. I've got a book with an entire chapter devoted to the subject. Dozens of people have passed themselves off as doctors over the years. Some as surgeons. One guy had a job as a ship's doctor for twenty years. He carried out shit loads of operations at sea. He'd swot up on the procedure in a text book the night be-fucking-fore!'

'Those people are usually failed medical students.'

'You admit it can happen?'

'OK, OK, Dave,' she said. 'Say by some miracle you got over the first hurdle of interviews and references. Just think about what the day-to-day life of a surgeon involves. He'd have to make diagnoses in front of qualified, experienced colleagues; he'd have to perform complex medical procedures in front of trained theatre staff: nurses, anaesthetists, not to mention fellow surgeons.'

'Have you never seen *Faking It*?' I asked her.

'Yes, but I've never seen anyone conducting fucking surgery on it!' She was getting mad now. 'You can fake being a cook or a nightclub bouncer. Faking it as a consultant gastroenterologist would be like faking it as a professional tennis player!'

'Not really,' said Ringo. 'The latter relies on innate talent; the former does not.'

She shot her husband an angry look. 'You're not really helping, are you, dear?' she said. 'Can't you see the state Dave's in?'

'He's right, though,' I said, 'and I'm not in a state.'

'Well,' sighed Monica, exasperated, 'discharge yourself then, if you're that worried. Check yourself out of here and contact the police.'

I was silent.

'No, you won't, will you, because you know this is ridiculous.'

She was wrong. I was *hoping* it was ridiculous. Perhaps under different circumstances I would have relished the prospect of being involved in the most amazing story the *Walsall Reflector* had ever reflected. Certainly Ringo was fired up by the possibility that we might have happened upon the ultimate NHS scandal. This could be a ticket to the big time: a national story with the *Reflector* right at its centre. But I was pooing my pants; or I would've been had I the courage to defecate.

Anyway, ridiculous or not, I was in no condition to discharge myself.

'I'm a bit scared I must admit,' I said, and then I told them what I could understand and/or remember about what Fostus had said about surgery.

Monica was shocked, and I could tell she was puzzled by the news. 'Surgery is very unusual while a pancreas is still swollen,' she said, almost to herself.

'Really?'

'I'm no expert on pancreatitis, though, Dave.'

'Let's hope Dunderdale is,' I said.

Monica turned to Ringo. 'Seeing as you're the one who's

pushed Dave's blood pressure to crisis point, what are you going to do to put his mind at rest?'

'I've got Miles on the case,' said Ringo. 'He'll do what he can to uncover Van Door's current whereabouts starting first thing in the morning. He'll try to track down a photo too. I'll talk to the most senior hospital manager I can about Dunderdale tomorrow. I'd do it now if they weren't all nine-to-fivers.'

'I think I'm going to be operated on in the morning,' I said weakly. I noticed Monica frown again. She'd begun to fiddle nervously with the gold brooch that held her silk scarf in place. Did even she think something strange was going on?

'I feel a bit melodramatic saying this,' Ringo said, 'but it might help put your mind at rest. If – and even after all we've found it's still a very big if – *if* when Dunderdale appears tomorrow he *does* happen to be Ruud Van Door, just phone me on my mobile before you do anything else.' He winked at me and said, 'I'll be here with a photographer.' Then, as an afterthought, added, 'Oh, and the police of course.'

'The *Reflector* would have quite a story,' I said.

'Exactly.' Ringo giggled, rubbing his hands together.


Monica and Ringo spent the rest of the visit trying to change the subject, but it was difficult; impossible, in fact. I'd insist on changing it back to Dunderdale and my imminent surgery.

They kept telling me to relax; calm down; keep things in perspective. Deep, deep breaths. My friends tried to take my mind off my fears by telling me about the latest national scandal. It involved the England football team manager, Sven-Goran Eriksson, and TV presenter, Ulrika Jonsson. The two Swedish celebrities had been caught shagging. Normally this would have had me rocking with glee but, the state I was in, I couldn't even be arsed to discuss it.

At one stage Monica left to have a word with one of the nurses. I noticed them chatting conspiratorially for a few moments. The nurse shook her head and shrugged her shoulders. Meanwhile, Ringo tried to distract me by talking about *his* latest medical problem: his nipples had turned mauve which, for people of his skin type, is a sure sign of anaemia.

'It's more likely a sign that you buy cheap shirts,' said Monica, when she returned to my bedside.

'What did that nurse say?' I demanded.

'Oh, she didn't know anything, she's only just started her shift.'

I was sceptical.

They both stayed until the end of visiting. On the first bell I made my usual joke about last orders and on the second – the serious bell – it was time for Ringo and Monica to go. I didn't want them to. When the second bell rings in a boozer it means it's time to confront the crap bits of life again: boredom, mediocrity, oneself. It signals the end of that evening's beautiful distraction. It's the same at Wesley-in-Tame. The second bell leaves you alone with the crap. For an instant, the sight of Monica and Ringo departing opened a hole inside me. I knew it was fathomless and I couldn't allow myself to peer over the edge. I pushed it to another part of my mind and constructed an imaginary danger sign at its rim: FOR FUCK'S SAKE DON'T LOOK DOWN HERE it said.

As she turned out of Langerhans Monica looked back, smiled and trilled her fingers at me in a goodbye wave. Ringo just smiled and gave me the thumbs-up. I smiled back.

The next time they saw me I'd be in no position to smile.

# Don't Fall Asleep or
# They'll Steal Your Kidneys

That night I was feeling paranoid and very anxious, and I concealed my mobile under the bedsheets just in case. I had Ringo's number pre-selected and my phone was primed to contact him at the push of a single button. Part of me felt a bit silly doing this, but still.

I kept trying to recall exactly what Fostus had said to me. He'd mentioned a 'procedure' and he'd tossed in a few terms that confused me. I'd have given anything to have talked to him again just to clarify what was in store for me. Surgery, yes: but what was the nature of the procedure? I was completely sober and my memory still failed me. Worse, as the evening wore on, my rhino became aggressive again: nutting me, horning me, tormenting me with its dildo of death. I kept having visions of an enormous, swollen pancreas even though I didn't know what a pancreas looked like. Sometimes I saw a giant rhino horn; sometimes my pancreas was Van Door trying to smash his way out of my chest with a spanking paddle.

Nurse Frigata was on the night shift and she came round with the drugs trolley at about half ten. I was in a lot of pain and needed relief badly. She could see I was suffering and administered the pethidine quite tenderly once more. Within moments my rhino horn was flaccid again and I was floating a finger's breadth off the mattress.

'Thank you, nurse,' I sighed.

She began doing my observations: temperature, blood pressure, blood sugar, piss emissions. I tried to stop myself talking to her because I was embarrassed at how easily paranoia seized control of my tongue. But I couldn't help myself.

'Maud, try not to laugh when I ask you this, but what are the chances of an unqualified person passing himself off as a surgeon?'

Rather than laugh, which is what I expected, she merely raised her eyebrows. 'Are you interested in a professional capacity, *Ichabod*?'

'No, well, perhaps.'

I didn't quite catch what she said next because the drug was making me light-headed. It sounded a bit like: 'I'm wanking a chow,' but that wouldn't make sense, would it? Unless she was a freakishly weird canine fetishist. Could it have been 'It's happening now'? That would make more sense in the current context. But surely that was just my imagination rearranging reality to suit my paranoia? I didn't get a chance to quiz her further because Deekus was demanding his painkillers and explaining to the rest of the ward how quickly nurses become desensitized to human suffering.

Her unclear answer troubled me, but my pain had been troubling me much more so the relief the drug offered was orgasmic to the point of distraction. I abandoned myself gratefully to the experience. I was swimming, every nerve-ending as floaty and relaxed as the tendrils of a drifting jellyfish. Somewhere in my mind Julie Andrews started singing again. The sound of Nurse Frigata's booming voice saying, sarcastically, 'Yes, Deekus, anything you say Deekus,' subsided until it resembled distant thunder. I fell into a deep sleep.

The deep sleep didn't last long. It never does in hospitals. At about three o'clock my glucose drip-bag was changed to something more viscous than glucose and this rapidly made the area around my cannula extremely sore. The back of my hand began to ache and I hardly slept from that point on.

By dawn I was still awake, despite trying practically every position I could think of to get comfortable. At one stage I found myself curled at the top of the bed and looking, for the first time, at the wall behind my metal headboard. A piece of chewing gum had been stuck in a crack in the plaster on the wall. I clicked at it with my thumbnail but it was welded to it like a barnacle. No one had even bothered to try to remove it. There was a good deal of graffiti too. Someone *had* had a half-hearted go at erasing this – it was faint and slightly smeared – but it was still readable.

One piece said: DON'T FALL ASLEEP OR THEY'LL STEAL YOUR KIDNEYS! Yes, I thought, they'll nick anything in Walsall. Even your kidneys. Even your teeth. Even your name. Another piece said: DEEKUS WOZ 'ERE. APRIL 92, FEB 93, JULY 93, MAY 94, AUG 94, JAN 95, MARCH 95, NOV 95, JUNE 96, JUNE 97, DEC 97, JAN 99, MARCH 99, JULY 99, SEPT 99, JAN 00, OCT 00, FEB 01.

It looked as if 1998 had been a good year for him.

# I've Just Shat in a
# Dead Dutchman's Mouth

Dr Fostus came to see me early the next morning. My anxiety had built throughout the night and by the time he turned up my cap was about to snap.

'Mr McVane,' he said, 'I hope you're feeling a little more relaxed. Mr Dunderdale will be here in a couple of minutes to give you all the information you need about your procedure.'

'You mean I'm actually going to see him?'

Fostus thought I was being sarcastic and ignored my question. 'He'll tell you what your procedure will involve.'

'I've been told that someone with pancreatitis shouldn't undergo surgery.'

Fostus looked puzzled. 'Surgery? Er, yes, generally speaking that's right,' he said. 'It's very risky to operate on someone with your condition.'

'What!' I shouted.

'Calm down, please, Mr McVane. Mr Dunderdale will be here in a second and he'll be able to reassure you. It's clear that you won't listen to me.'

'Admit it: you think he's a fucking nutter, don't you?'

'I beg your pardon?'

'Tell me, is he a Dutchman?'

'What? I'm sorry I don't under–'

'*Is he a Dutchman?*'

'Mr McVane, try and get a grip of yourself. Lie back and

take some deep breaths. Mr Dunderdale will be here in a minute.'

I took some deep breaths, clenching and unclenching my fists with each. I managed to relax just a little. I tried to keep my speech measured and restrained as I addressed Fostus. 'Dunderdale. You disagree with him. He's going to mess with my Islands of Langerhans and you think it's a mistake!'

'Mr McVane,' he said, in a tone that was serious but not angry, 'I think you are upset, frightened and paranoid. This is a traumatic experience for you so I'm willing to overlook the absurd and offensive nature of your outburst; not to mention your accusations. Now, I'll repeat: Mr Dunderdale will be here directly. I hope he'll be able to put your mind at rest.'

'You haven't answered my question: is he a Dutchman?'

'I'm sorry, I don't know what you're talking about.'

'I think you do. *Is he a Dutchman?*'

Fostus rose to leave.

'Answer me, quack: *is he a Dutchman? Does he have a spanking paddle with a Staffordshire knot pattern on it?*'

Fostus began to walk off the ward.

'What about Harold Shipman?' I yelled.

Everyone in my ward-bay was looking at me.

Deekus had paused midway through rolling a fag and was gaping. For once, I imagine he was undecided about who should be suing whom: patient or doctor. Even Droppy, a veteran of numerous mental institutions, looked shocked: he had a spoonful of Bran Flakes suspended half-way to his mouth. The spoon's anti-swallow block swung gently beneath his fist. Gulliver and Donovan were also staring, open-mouthed.

'Sorry,' I said.

I tried to compose myself. My nerves were no longer floaty tendrils; now they burned like wire wool in a flame.

I was twitchy and my skin felt too thin, the way it does when you're badly sunburnt.

Ruth arrived at my bedside a few minutes later with what I assumed were my pre-med tablets.

'What are these for?' I asked.

'They're to relax you, Mr McVane. Dr Fostus said you're getting a bit worked up.'

'Give me twenty.'

'I'm afraid two is your limit.'

'When is Dunderdale coming?'

'He was on the ward quite early this morning. I saw him about thirty minutes ago but I haven't seen him since. I know Dr Fostus has mentioned that you're keen to talk to him so I'm sure he'll be here soon.'

The moment Ruth left, Deekus started.

'The staff seem to be getting on your tits, Dave.'

'You could say that.'

'Understandable. Very understandable.'

'I'm having surgery,' I said.

'Oh dear. I wouldn't let that bastard Dunderdale operate on me, not after all I've heard about him.'

'I haven't got much of a choice,' I said, although I was acutely aware of my mobile beneath the bedclothes. If Dunderdale did turn out to be Ruud Van Door, I'd be yelling for Ringo.

'You don't know if he's a Dutchman by any chance?' I asked.

'Eh?'

'Oh, never mind.'

'All I know are the stories. Mistakes. Incompetence. Blunders. Naffing Nora, do you know how dangerous surgery is even when your surgeon is competent?'

'I'm sure you're going to tell me.'

'Ever heard of necrotizing fasciitis?'

'Sounds appealing,' I said. I was beginning to feel a bit

groggy. The pre-med pills were kicking in quickly. My skin began to feel thicker again; my nerves no longer glowed quite so hot and red.

'It's an aggressive infection which destroys the tissue beneath your skin. They sometimes call it hospital gangrene. It's very nasty. It starts with swelling, then you get a fever – a real smoker – then your skin turns purple, although I've seen it go a weird shade of bronze too.'

'Is that it?'

'Nope, that's just the start. Big blisters full of blood start to appear although, at first, the surface layers of the skin stay intact. It's only after about a week that the skin begins to die. That's enough to turn your stomach I can tell you. Christ, the stench. Isn't that right, Droppy?'

'Oh arr, very nasty, wack, very,' said Droppy, although I noticed he wasn't fired by his usual enthusiasm for gruesome medical horrors. He'd set down his anti-swallow spoon even though his Bran Flakes were only half eaten. Perhaps he was feeling a little under the weather. He wasn't the only one. The tablets were affecting me strongly now; I felt simultaneously weightless and leaden, like a floating anvil. Mind you, on the plus side, I was wonderfully relaxed. My muscles had begun to unknot and, as often happens when I'm hit with a tranquillizer, I farted. It was a protracted cheese-cutter that seemed to take an inch off my abdominal bloating and was audible around the ward-bay.

Deekus gave me a thumbs-up sign and Gulliver shouted, 'One nil!' Embarrassed, I closed my eyes and pretended to be settling down for a snooze.

One thing I hadn't done since they fitted my catheter was have a shit. As I said, I'd been too scared to defecate. There were a number of reasons for this. One was that the thought of straining with a catheter fitted filled me with scrotum-clenching dread. The tube, though theoretically removed from the bowel, was nevertheless inhibiting. I don't know about you but I need to be comfortable and relaxed when I'm having a poo, and comfortable and relaxed are two of the things you aren't if you're wearing a catheter. I'd be more relaxed pooing while a jumpy lunatic held a scalpel blade a millimetre from my nad-sack. You're not particularly mobile with a catheter either, which is the second reason I hadn't been. Getting around with a sack of piss isn't easy. You know those plastic bags that goldfish come in when you win them at the fair? Imagine walking around with one tied to your cock. If you're a girl, imagine having one tethered to the most intimate piercing you can imagine. It puts you off.

Now I needed to go. For the first time since my arrival my bowels were sufficiently relaxed to contemplate opening. In fact, they were no longer contemplating; they were insisting. I had to get to the loo; there was no way round it. I eased myself out of bed, stepped into my Homer Simpson *D'Oh!* slippers and carefully stood up. I was a little reluctant to move because, knowing my luck, Dunderdale would turn up as soon as I was out of the bay. Still, I didn't have much choice. I slipped my mobile into my pocket, just in case I spotted him on the way.

It was the first time I'd tried to walk in two days and it wasn't easy. My limbs were weak and I was tired. I held my piss-bag at my right side like a lady with her handbag and, pulling my drip-stand along at my left, I forced myself along. The castors squeaked and I felt self-conscious, like in one of those dreams where you're naked on the centre court of Wimbledon: you don't know whether to butch it out and walk proudly around, or whether to stoop and cower and creep about apologetically. The catheter was uncomfortable at first, jabbing into my bladder with each footfall. After a few steps, however, I found a way of walking which minimized the discomfort: a kind of tentative, bow-legged waddle. Still, it was slow going, like crossing a carpet of glue. I was scared I wouldn't make it to the loo in time to avoid everyone having a peek at my bowels' unspeakable contents.

The closer I got to the shitter the more it felt like I was walking on a trampoline or a mattress. My feet seemed to sink into the ground. But the strangeness seemed normal. Dream normal – like watching your grandad French kissing Eddie Izzard, or finding a beer bottle where your cock should be. I could see previously unnoticed dustmites watching me from the creases in the curtains. I had the impression they were sniggering. I could hear the ghosts of dead patients whispering in their hiding places: under beds, behind lockers. I knew they had holes where their pancreases should be and I knew they had some gossip that I didn't need to hear. I gritted my teeth and ignored them all.

At last I made it to the toilet. I arranged myself in front of it and, with my back to the bowl, pulled up the lid and eased myself gently down. I then tried to relax, but it was hard because part of me felt that I wasn't on a bog at all. Nevertheless, I dropped my shoulders and began rotating my head. There shouldn't be much in the way of faeces, I thought, because I hadn't eaten anything in two days. I was wrong. The pontiff of all logs began sliding out of me. With a satisfied groan, I shut my eyes and let it drop, feeling like the *Enola Gay* over an unsuspecting Hiroshima. Oddly, I didn't hear the splash of toilet water but was aware of the unpleasant stench of turd, and an uncomfortable feeling that my impressive log, if no longer attached to my body, was still a little too close to it.

I stood, gingerly, and then did what I'd told Nurse Frigata I didn't do: I turned to admire my scatological accomplishment. And there it was, standing proudly in the gaping mouth of Ruud Van Door's disembodied head.

My first mistake was letting go of my piss-bag. Where it

went I had to follow and, as it dropped, I was pulled to my knees. The momentum was such that I was propelled forward towards the toilet bowl and its repulsive contents. My second mistake was that, as I fell, I screamed. The scream was the type that you can feel in your head rather than hear but, as Ringo would say, that's not the important bit. The important bit is that my mouth was open. I simultaneously headbutted Van Door and caught a gobful of my own steaming excrement.

Suffice it to say, my experience of the NHS had reached a new low.

I tried to stand, simultaneously spitting, swearing and silent-screaming. I managed to entangle myself in my drip-tube, though, and my weight brought the whole apparatus crashing down. The drip-regulator machine began beeping wildly. I crawled frantically away from the horror, towards the toilet door. As I did so my mobile fell from the breast pocket of my pyjamas. Ringo, I thought. The police; the scoop. Sitting on the floor with my piss-bag leaking urine over the tiles I pressed the button that would put me in touch with the sane world. It rang. No answer.

Impossible; Ringo was never far away from his mobile. I let it ring. Still no reply. Desperate now, I pulled the door open and dropped into the corridor.

'Help!' I shouted.

At that moment there was chaos all around. A number of staff were rushing a patient along the corridor on a trolley. That patient was Droppy Collins. Music was coming from the general vicinity of his abdomen. That music was 'Vicar in a Tutu' by the Smiths.

'Help!' I shouted to anyone who'd listen. 'I've shat in a dead Dutchman's mouth!'

Had someone shouted those words to me they'd have had my immediate attention. I, however, was ignored. People rushed about oblivious to my existence.

'Help! Help! I've just shat in a dead Dutchman's mouth!'
Nothing.

The room swam and I failed to swim with it. It coiled around me, trapping me in a sickening whirlpool. I was corkscrewed into queasy oblivion.

# Face to Face

I blinked the blackness away as I came round, startled. I was beneath the sweat-sodden sheets of my bed. The muted sound of 'Roll Out the Barrel' was audible under the blankets.

Every conscious person on the bay was staring at me once again.

'Am yow all right, wack?' asked Droppy.

'Er . . . I think so.' I eased my hand down the back of my pyjamas to see if I'd soiled myself. I checked tentatively, apprehensively, the way you might check whether a swatted wasp is really dead. Relief: I hadn't been stung by that particular humiliation. That was to come.

'What's all this about a Dutchman's mouth?' Droppy persisted.

'I, er, I don't know. Excuse me.' I dropped beneath the sheets to answer my mobile. I heard someone on the ward – possibly Deekus – say, 'Fucking cracked,' followed by some inaudible mutterings.

As I tried to answer my phone it skittered around like a frog in my sweaty fingers. Despite the perspiration, though, I was freezing cold and had gooseflesh on my arms and legs.

'Yes,' I said when I finally managed to punch the right button.

'Flaming Ada, you took your time.'

'I was asleep,' I said, breathless and shivering, 'I've just had a fucker of a dream.'

'Save it for visiting time, I've got news.'

'Go on.'

'Guess.'

'Fucking hell, Ringo this is no time for pissing about. *What?*'

'All right, all right. Brace yourself: Ruud Van Door's dead! Someone from personnel at Groningen phoned me this morning. They'd heard I'd been asking about their ex-caretaker. The woman I spoke to yesterday was new and didn't know the whole story.'

I was still numb from my dream and woozy from the tablets but, if I had to analyse my feelings, I'd say I felt a mixture of shock and relief. I was finding it difficult to concentrate. The little cave I'd made for myself out of the bedclothes glowed green with the light from my phone, turning the sheets into a surreal landscape that, for some reason, absorbed my attention. Completely distracted, I couldn't stop looking at it. I must have gone a while without speaking.

Ringo broke the silence with: 'Are your teeth chattering?'

'I'm cold. How did he die?'

'He was stabbed to death in a Rotterdam brothel in 1997. The prostitute got off with a verdict of self-defence.'

'That makes sense. Was he calling himself Dunderdale?'

'I've had articles faxed over from the Dutch papers. The story made some of the nationals. You'll like this: *De Volkskrant* say he was using the name Scott Fitzgerald; *De Telegraaf* say he called himself Charles Bukowski. I assume he shuttled between the two depending on which brothel he found himself in.'

'Amazing. Is there mileage in it for the *Reflector*?'

'Hardly; the Walsall connection is too weak and his death's old news. It's disappointing, I suppose. Your surgeon's name is just a coincidence, after all. Have you seen him yet?'

At that point a hand pulled back the bedclothes.

'Switch that bloody phone off, man!' I was face to face with a large blond bloke in his early fifties. He was wearing a Donegal tweed jacket and a green dickie-bow. His name badge said *Mr Daniel Dunderdale*. It was the guy I'd seen twice from a distance but, at close quarters, he looked nothing like Van Door or, for that matter, anyone else I knew. Of course he didn't. How could I have been so stupid?

I switched off the phone without saying goodbye to Ringo. 'Sorry,' I said.

'So you bloody should be. I take it you know that those things interfere with our equipment?'

'I didn't, Dr –'

'Well, they do, and don't call me doctor. I didn't take all those blessed surgery exams for a bet.'

'When do I have my operation?' I asked timidly.

'What? What's he talking about?' He addressed himself to Ruth who, together with six or seven other people, stood quaking in Dunderdale's shadow.

'Mr McVane's been a little distressed,' she said.

'Get a grip of yourself, man,' he told me. 'You're not having surgery, what gave you that idea?'

'I . . . I don't know. Dr Fostus mentioned a procedure. I've had some pre-med tablets . . .'

'We gave him some diazepam earlier,' said Ruth, 'to try and calm him down.'

'Give me his file,' he told her.

Ruth handed him the file a little nervously.

Among Dunderdale's entourage was a number of terrified-looking student doctors. He turned to the closest: a pale, slim young woman wearing trendy rectangular glasses. 'You,' he said, 'how do we diagnose pancreatitis?'

'We erm . . . we –'

'Too late. You,' he said, nodding at a young Asian guy in a very, very clean white coat, 'you with the funny name, help her out.'

'We measure the patient's serum amylase, Mr Dunderdale.'

'Correct.' Dunderdale tossed my file at him. It bounced off his chest and he scrambled to stop it scattering all over the floor. 'And, judging from this data, what would be your prognosis?'

The student scanned my file with wide, panicky eyes. 'His latest blood test shows a drop in amylase,' he blithered.

'And?'

'So . . . he's getting better?'

'Don't look so surprised, sonny; it sometimes happens, even in the Lost Islands of Langerhans.'

He turned to me and softened his voice somewhat. 'I think you've managed to get the wrong end of the stick, old chap.'

My mouth was dry. 'Have I?' I croaked. 'Dr Fostus said I was to have a procedure.'

'Not a surgical procedure, man. Surgery would be a good way of seeing you off! And I don't think the hospital could stand another lawsuit.'

There was a chorus of sycophantic guffaws from the students.

'I wasn't joking,' he said.

The students fell silent. One cleared his throat as if he was going to speak but apparently thought better of it.

'Your bloods show that your pancreas is beginning to function normally again, but I want to do another test – not, I repeat, a surgical procedure – an ERCP.' He turned to a weedy, fair-haired guy who resembled the Milky Bar Kid. 'You, what does ERCP stand for?'

The Milky Bar Kid looked as if he'd been asked to tie a

knot in his dick. 'It's an Endotropic . . . no, Endoscopic Reflex?'

'Can you say, "Would you like fries with that, sir?"'

The Milky Bar Kid nodded, quivering with shame.

'Well, at least you won't be stuck for employment when medicine doesn't work out for you.' He turned again to the Asian guy. 'Funny name, tell him.'

'An Endoscopic Retrograde Cholangio Pancreatogram?' said the Asian guy.

'Bloody smart-arse,' said Dunderdale to me, winking.

I was still too wound up to acknowledge this and the consultant looked at me more closely.

'Actually, you look like shit,' he said. He put a thumb on my right eyebrow and widened my eye; he looked hard at it. 'When did you last have an alcoholic drink?' he asked.

Before I could reply Ruth leaned over and whispered something in Dunderdale's ear. As she spoke the surgeon's eyes narrowed and he started to snort a little. 'Oh really!' he boomed. 'Yes, I've heard all about you. Your cronies keep phoning me up! You're from the bloody rag that keeps printing drivel about us, aren't you?'

'I, er . . . yes.'

'You're quick enough to come here pleading for treatment when it suits you, I notice.'

'I, er . . . yes.'

'I remember that headline: "Sack the Wesley Quacks" indeed! Your column is fatuous claptrap, my friend. Listen: we *do* have the highest mortality rate in the country but I don't suppose you're interested in the reasons why. Are you?'

I nodded sheepishly.

'If you'd bothered to research the matter you'd know we have the highest mortality rate in the country because this God-forsaken dump of a town doesn't have adequate hospice provision. Terminally ill people come to our hospital to die because there's nowhere else for them to go; when people come to your hospital to die you're going to have a high mortality rate, aren't you? It follows, doesn't it?'

I nodded sheepishly again. Is he supposed to talk to people this way? I wondered. The answer is no, he isn't supposed to. But he does anyway.

'Here's some advice: stop drinking. For one thing your pancreas can't take it and, for another, you need all the brain cells you can get.'

He turned to leave but I stopped him. 'What happens now?' I asked timidly.

He turned back to me, a little calmer now. 'OK,' he said, 'this is what happens: it looks as if your pancreas is beginning to function normally again which suggests an acute attack rather than the start of a chronic problem, but you'll have the ERCP to make sure. I couldn't get you in for today but I've booked you in for tomorrow. If that goes OK we'll keep you on the drip for another couple of days but you'll be able to leave as soon as we can get you back on solids. We need the beds, in case you haven't heard.'

'And if it was an acute attack, will it happen again?'

'Listen, I'll tell you this on the off-chance you're not a complete twit. If you stop boozing you'll probably live; if you carry on you'll probably die.'

'Die?'

'You'll either die or you'll lose half your pancreas and then you'll wish you were dead. You'll be diabetic, in constant pain, and you'll have a massively reduced life expectancy. Are you with me?'

'I understand.'

'Well, I'm new to this place but from what I've seen so far, if you *do* understand, you'll be in a minority. They don't call this ward the Lost Islands of Langerhans for nothing. Good day.' With that he breezed out, his entourage scurrying along in his wake.

'I wouldn't let him talk to me like that,' said Deekus, who'd been listening to the entire conversation, 'but he's right about the constant pain.' He began banging on his call button. '*Nurse!*' he yelled.

Straight away I sent a text to Ringo, although it took me a while because I was still numb-noggined from the tranquillizers – where did I get the idea that they were pre-med tablets?

> d.dale ok
> no op needed 2day.
> more tests.
> might even live.
> c u later.

Despite the way he'd spoken to me, part of me liked Dunderdale. Not just because he'd given me good news, but because he was a 'no bullshit' sort of person. You could see straight away why he rubbed people up the wrong way, of course. He was the quintessential prima-donna surgeon – like something out of *Doctor in the House*. He was brusque, arrogant and opinionated, but he exuded an air of authority that you couldn't help but be impressed by.

It was obvious why he was gossiped about; why he was developing a reputation around the hospital. People like him always do. Chinese whispers distort them. Gossip deifies or demonizes them: whatever makes the best story. Facts are irrelevant. People crave hyperbole, not reality. Dr Dunderdale would bang on about it in his 'Learning to Evaluate' class.

'It's human nature to inflate things,' I remember him saying, 'it makes the tedium of existence more bearable. We demonize and vilify, we lionize and deify because ordinary people aren't interesting enough. When we're bored by religion we invent aliens and crop circles; when we're bored by history we invent conspiracies; when we're bored with the news we have the *National Enquirer*, the *Sun*, the *Mirror*. Fantasy, fantasy.' He'd bash the lectern with his blond-knuckled fists. 'This,' he'd say, 'this is why more people read Danielle Steele than Chekhov!' He may have worn hessian-lined knickers, but he'd got that right. He was a living example of the all-too-human need to escape the mundane. Van Door was another. *I* was another. Look how I'd perversely fed my own paranoia over something that, let's face it, could only ever have been a fantasy. How could Ruud Van Door ever pass himself off as a consultant surgeon? An academic, maybe: what's a doctor of philosophy if not a doctor of bullshit? (Sorry, Monica.) You don't escape from reality by becoming a doctor of medicine. Quite the opposite.

There are two primary escapes from mind-shrivelling reality: bullshit and booze. I fed one to my readers and the other to myself. I resolved that from now on I would do without both. I would give up writing bollocks in my column and, more importantly, I would stop getting off my paps every day of the week.

Was that feasible? Was it possible to face Walsall sober? I remember Van Door telling us that Ernest Hemingway shot himself after six months of sobriety. Is that the only way to go when the second bell calls time on the distractions of the devil's juice for ever? Will soul-sapping mundanity, cock-wilting averageness drive you to the bullet if you can't have the bottle? Maybe. But then Van Door was a caretaker: there's a fair chance he didn't have a clue what he was talking about. A caretaker. The bloke who'd given me the highest grade I ever achieved was a fucking caretaker.

# From Bad to Worse

I slept away most of the morning. Despite my good news, I wasn't feeling at all well either physically or psychologically. I had lucid episodes mixed with quite alarming moments when I had to fight to keep control of my faculties. Twice I woke and was completely unaware of my surroundings. I'd lie still, frightened. I'd see my fellow patients eyeing me suspiciously and, though part of me recognized them, it'd be a while before I remembered exactly who they were. Also, my muscles kept tightening painfully. When Dr Chance paid me a visit at about half eleven I mentioned this and he told me not to worry. Later, I overheard him ask Ruth what to do about it but I didn't catch her reply.

It was a good job I wouldn't be having any visitors today. Ringo was putting this week's *Reflector* to bed and Monica was at a conference in Reading. At around two o'clock, however, Gulliver came over to me. He'd come to say goodbye, cockahoop because he was being discharged. His camera-up-the-arse test had been postponed. Now he would get to see the Albion play their crucial decider.

'There was a mix-up with the dates,' he said. 'Someone else has my slot. They reckon they might be able to do the test later in the year. Deekus says I ought to sue, but it couldn't have worked out better. I'm going to see the Baggies get promoted.' He offered me his hand to shake.

This is something people do when they're discharged from hospital.

'Good luck,' I said, impressed with my ability to speak. It was a peculiar experience, though: I felt distanced from the exchange, as if I was observing the conversation rather than taking part in it.

A little later Donovan also came to shake my hand. He, too, was being discharged. They'd determined that he needed surgery for his kidney stones. Now it was just a matter of getting a date.

'They reckon three months at the outside,' he said, 'but Deekus tells me it will probably be more like a year. He thinks I ought to sue for trauma.'

'Good luck,' I said.

'Actually, I don't think they meant to discharge me but I happened to be in the loo when the cot-counter came round and he reassigned my bed.' Donovan gestured towards a comatose gentleman who now occupied his position on the Langerhans ward-bay. 'I returned from the shitter to find him there!'

I must have been asleep during the admission because the arrival of this new guy was a surprise to me. I wasn't sure what to say to Donovan, but he was looking at me expectantly so I felt I should come up with something. In the end I said, 'Dunderdale wasn't Dunderdale. Dunderdale dissolved. Nor was he a Dutchman. He was Dunderdale. A different one. It was me who burned down the brothel, you know.'

'Good for you, mate,' he answered, backing away from me with an odd look on his face.

# A Room of One's Own

That evening I was taken off my bay in Langerhans and placed in a side room. Nurse Frigata was the staff nurse in charge for the night shift and I heard her tell one of the students that I was being moved because I was disturbing the other patients.

Now I had a little room to myself, with my own personal telly. The news was on when they wheeled me in and I recall that the NHS spending story had been superseded by the one Ringo had mentioned about Sven and Ulrika, in which the couple were caught 'romping naked' by Ulrika's nanny. It wouldn't have been a good day to break a counterfeit surgeon story, after all. I tried to get excited about the Swedish scandal but somehow I couldn't manage it.

I was looking forward to seeing Ringo and Monica the next day, though. I wanted to tell Ringo of my decision to reinvent my Facts is Facts column. As soon as I was well, I'd be writing a piece about Wesley-In-Tame Hospital. What I'd seen so far had been quite enlightening. There was bad *and* good here. Naturally, there was plenty of mileage for a negative piece. But that would be to ignore all the positive things. The staff worked hard and had a lot to put up with. Would *you* like to push a suppository up my arse after ten Settlers, six Deflatines, five fruit-flavoured Rennies, a bottle of Gaviscon and forty shots of brandy? If so, then you're either a dedicated health professional or you work for Penny Stroker. The hospital itself had a lot to contend with. The Droppys and Deekuses of this world are a drain on resources and patience. Their problems are, in a sense, self-inflicted but the hospital can't turn them away. I think for once in my journalistic career I was going to write, wait for it, a balanced article.

I felt a bit ashamed about the rubbish I'd written in the past. I'd made most of it up, or at least I'd exaggerated where necessary and never bothered to check facts. I didn't know anything about the hospice problem, for instance; mind you, even if I *had* known about it I probably wouldn't have mentioned it. I always went for what was shocking, controversial, funny. I pandered to the popular need for the lowest form of stimulation.

No more. If it was mundane to write a piece about a hospital in which dedicated people worked hard in difficult circumstances, then so be it. If I lost readers like Deekus by being factual rather than sensational, then tough.

But I'm not sure if my new-found respect for the nurses was reciprocated. I'd exploded at Annette earlier and couldn't even remember why. I recall Deekus coming over to congratulate me on the vitriolic spirit of my attack and I'd thrown a plastic beaker at him. He scampered away, yelping and threatened to sue me, the *Walsall Reflector* and the National Health Service.

It was frightening.

Since being moved to my private room I'd tried various relaxation techniques in an attempt to calm myself. One method, learned from a woman I knew into Transcendental Meditation, involved adopting a particular breathing pattern while chanting a mantra. The mantra I'd always used in the past was Hank, my hero's informal name. 'Hank, Hank, Hank,' I'd repeat, all the time thinking about the rhythm of a giant turtle's heartbeat. However, when I tried it now the word Hank kept changing to *rank*, *stank* and *wank*. It ruined my concentration.

Nurse Frigata came to see me just before lights out. She brought another pethidine injection and I was looking forward to it. I'd begun to feel sick and my cramps were worse. The weird thin-skinned feeling had returned too; I felt raw and taut and my pyjamas were like sandpaper against my skin. Dr Dunderdale would have paid good money for the sensation.

'The hypodermic looks a bit bigger than usual,' I said, as Nurse Frigata approached. Actually, it looked twice as big. Maybe she was just going to fill it with half as much drug?

'Don't worry, Mr McVane, it won't hurt.' She spoke quietly. Nurse Frigata was speaking quietly. Was there something wrong with my ears or something wrong with her throat? She sounded almost sexy, like Felicity Kendal advertising Cadbury's Buttons.

'Are you OK, nurse?'

'What do you mean?' She was still speaking quietly as she eased the needle into my leg. It hurt a bit more than usual.

'Ouch. That hurt more than usual.'

She slowly and deliberately withdrew the needle and then dropped the hypo paraphernalia into a kidney bowl on my locker. I had the odd sensation of ants crawling through my vein from the place where she'd injected me.

I began to feel a little scared. Despite her soft voice, Nurse Frigata had taken on a sinister aspect.

'Why did you move me to a private room?' I asked her.

She didn't answer. She walked to the window and gazed out. There wouldn't be a very good view. I guessed it over-looked the visitors' car park: several square acres of tarmac perpetually jammed with seventh-hand cars.

She returned to my bedside.

# Third Person

In the side room Dave McVane lay on the bed, his face pale and panicky. Nurse Frigata was calm.

'Why did you move me to a private room?' Dave repeated, a little louder this time. Nurse Frigata had moved closer to him; she was close enough to whisper.

'It gives me the chance to kill,' she told him. 'The injection I've just given you will stop your heart.'

'What?' A dead feeling was creeping through his arms and legs. Slowly it invaded his groin, stomach and chest.

'You ruined my life,' said the nurse.

'How?' He was terrified, his mouth was dry, and he could only speak with effort.

'It was thanks to you that he left. The truth is that he fled from you.'

'Who?' Dave asked.

'Dunderdale.'

'The surgeon?'

'The academic. The WANK Head of School. He is my husband.'

Dave seemed to ponder this for a while; as he did so he sucked hard on his bottom lip. 'Your name is Frigata?' he said at last.

The nurse looked puzzled. 'It's my maiden name,' she said. 'I'm Dunderdale' s wife and it's your fault we're not together.'

Again, he struggled to make sense of this. Nurse Frigata was Dunderdale's wife? He recalled Ringo saying she was still alive. Hadn't he also said that she lived near the hospital? Suddenly he was very frightened.

'I'm not responsible for your husband's death,' is all he could think of saying.

'My husband's still alive.'

'What?'

'My husband's still alive. He vanished, but he's back, posing as a consultant.'

'Mr Dunderdale is not a fraud. That's what *I* used to think. He really *is* a surgeon!'

'That's what he wants you to think. Yes, he is my husband and the only thing that's stopping him admitting it is that you're still around to expose him.'

'What?' Dave was beginning to see she was unbalanced.

Her eyes were abnormally wide and her gaze drilled into him. 'When you're gone he'll come back; he'll have no need for brothels and whores.'

'Brothels . . . whores?'

'Like the one I burned down. Like that bitch Ebola Barker who would play his kinky games when I refused.'

'You set fire to Penny's? You killed Ebola Barker?' As he spoke, Dave struggled to rise again.

The nurse put her hand on his forehead to keep him down. As he pushed against it she gently but firmly kept him in his place. 'I made it look as though you caused the fire; I made Barker's death look like suicide.'

He could see the woman was barking. He tried to lift himself off the bed once more and, though Nurse Frigata had removed her hand, it was as if he was tethered to it by unseen restraints.

Nurse Frigata stood and left the room, her shoes squeaking. Dave lay on the bed wearing the wan, shocked face of a man who knows he's going to die.

He could hear hospital business going on as normal just a few yards away from where he lay. He tried to call out but his cry, though loud in his mind, reached his lips as an ineffectual splutter. It was like the final air bubble to break the surface of a glass of flat lager.

McVane soiled his pyjamas.

\*　　　\*　　　\*

In the side room Dave McVane lay on the bed, his face pale and panicky. Nurse Frigata was calm.

'Why did you move me to a different room?' Dave repeated, a little louder this time. Nurse Frigata had moved closer to him; she was close enough to whisper.

'Because you're ill,' she told him. 'The injection I've just given you will slow your heart.'

'What?' A dead feeling was creeping through his arms and legs. Slowly it invaded his groin, stomach and chest.

'You're ruining your life,' said the nurse.

'How?' He was terrified, his mouth was dry, and he could only speak with effort.

'Be thankful for the life you have left. Ruth said what he told you.'

'Who?' Dave asked.

'Dunderdale.'

'The surgeon?'

'He can't work magic, but he's no fool. He's one of the best in the land.'

'Your name is Frigata?'

The nurse looked puzzled. 'My married name,' she said. 'Dunderdale was right. Take control of your life, pull yourself together.'

'I'm not responsible for your husband's death.'

'My husband's alive.'

'What?'

'My husband's alive. He's Spanish. He works as a financial consultant.'

'Mr Dunderdale is not a fraud. That's what *I* used to think. He really *is* a surgeon!'

'That's what you used to think? Yes, he acts very grand but he knows what he's doing. I don't mind admitting that I'm glad he's around. We need more like him.'

'What?'

'I'll do your obs when I come back; you look worse than you did before.'

'Brothels . . . whores?'

'I'll get something to calm you down. I think today you're a little confused.'

'You set fire to Penny's? You killed Ebola Barker?' As he spoke, Dave struggled to rise again.

The nurse put her hand on his forehead to assess his temperature. As he pushed against it she gently but firmly kept him in his place. 'My goodness, you're on fire; you're burning up inside.'

He tried to lift himself off the bed once more and, though Nurse Frigata had removed her hand, it was as if he was tethered to it by unseen restraints.

Nurse Frigata stood and left the room, her shoes squeaking. Dave lay on the bed wearing the wan, shocked face of a man who knows he's going to die.

He could hear hospital business going on as normal just a few yards away from where he lay. He tried to call out but his cry, though loud in his mind, reached his lips as an ineffectual splutter. It was like the final air bubble to break the surface of a glass of flat lager.

McVane soiled his pyjamas.

# A Tangle of Tiny Scorpions

I woke trying to scream and breathe at the same time. I sucked and blew but all I managed to do was emit a rattling, choking sound. Nothing entered my lungs. I struggled to pull in some air but my chest failed to inflate; a wave of panic coursed through me. I tore at the blankets and swung my legs out of bed. I tried to breathe again and the tiniest fart of air managed to squeeze past whatever was blocking my windpipe. I was sitting at the side of the bed now, my hands on my knees, my head turned skyward like a howling wolf, sucking desperately at air. Another fart's worth bubbled into my lungs and eased my panic a little; it eased the dizziness too. I sucked again and there was a noise like the squirt of a draught beer tap when the barrel needs changing: another, bigger fart of air. Then another; then another. After a few seconds I was drinking air more freely, gasping it in. I knew what had happened because, as with most drunks, it had happened to me before: I'd breathed vomit into my lungs. But this time it was different: though the panic and the dizziness subsided as my breathing resumed, fear still gripped me and the world seemed vague and incoherent.

Nurse Frigata had tried to kill me and I'd soiled my pyjamas.

At that point she entered the room. She was smiling, pushing the observations equipment in front of her.

'Time for your obs,' she said, 'and I've got something for your temperature.' Her smile was somehow too big for her face, like a portrait of Will Young painted by Edvard Munch. It seemed to throb, expanding and contracting like a lung. Terror swelled within me and I pulled the drip-tube out of my cannula and dropped to my knees. A crimson jet of blood arced from my vein, splattering my locker, my water jug and my Blue Stratos toiletries bag. I felt the tug of the catheter tube as I began rolling under the bed, away from Frigata. I gripped it with my left hand and pulled. The tube came away from the piss-bag. Urine streamed out together with a dozen goldfish which began flick-flacking pathetically on the dusty tiled floor.

'I didn't kill your husband,' I screamed, 'I swear I didn't kill him. For Christ's sake, leave me alone!'

'Calm down, Mr McVane,' I heard her say. 'My husband's alive and well. Like I say, he's a financial consultant.'

'He dissolved!' I bawled.

'What?'

'Dunderdale!'

'Mr Dunderdale? Come out from under the bed, Mr McVane, please!'

'What about Harold Shipman!' I screamed.

I wasn't trying to faint but, somehow, I did.

I woke dithering. I don't know how much later. Hours? My stomach was knotted and I had the urge to vomit. In the upper corner of the room I saw what appeared to be a sparrow flittering about, seemingly trying to find a way through the ceiling. I watched it fly at the roof several times before moving away from the corner and beginning to circle the room. The bird was flying in a strange way, as if its wings were too small, or weirdly constructed. Occasionally it would lose height and become laboured in its flight, like a smoked bee or a wasp in winter. After a few hard-fought laps of my room it began to fly towards me, losing height as it did so. It was moving slowly and, as it neared, I noticed that it wasn't a sparrow but a locust. I watched transfixed as it approached, its wings a blur and making a clicking sound like a cigarette card in the spokes of a bicycle wheel. It had eyes like tiny jet ball-bearings. It had mandibles. When it landed on the sleeve of my pyjamas it was almost weightless; but not quite. I would have thought my scream was so high-pitched that only dogs and sperm whales could have heard it, but it brought people running into the room. Ruth and Dr Fostus.

'Locusts!' I screamed.

'Calm down, Mr McVane, there's nothing to be afraid of. There's nothing there. Ruth, prepare another dose of benzodiazepine.'

'Nurse Frigata tried to kill me!' I yelled, and I began crawling backwards up the bed. I felt a tug at my cock, pulled up the blankets and saw a snake hanging like a black and yellow noodle from the end. I screamed again, grabbed my bottle of Robinson's Barley Water from the locker and began beating my genitals with it.

Fostus wrestled the bottle from me and shouted, 'Mr McVane, try to calm down. I'm going to give you a drug that will help. We suspect you are suffering from the effects of alcohol withdrawal. Delirium Tremens. No one has tried to kill you. There are no locusts.'

'Kiss me softly, Amy Turtle!' I screamed. '*Kiss me softly, Amy Turtle!*'

Fostus shook his head in pity and dismay.

As I looked at him I noticed that his eyebrows weren't made of hair but were a tangle of tiny scorpions. I tried not to scream again and made a whimpering sound instead. Fostus put his hand on my forehead.

'Scorpions,' I said.

'He's still hyperpyrexic,' he told Ruth. 'Put a fan on him

269

and get him some paracetamol.' He then inserted a syringe into my cannula and injected a liquid.

The effect was rapid: I was under warm water, breathing effortlessly; I was weightless; someone would have to tether me to the bed to keep me down. In the far distance I heard Fostus say, 'We're not equipped to deal with this. If he doesn't calm down we'll get him sectioned.'

# The Amsterdam Experience

I woke, opened my eyes and had to stifle a yelp as I saw my reflection in the mirrored ceiling. I would never get used to my new body. It was like a tightly knotted pair of white bootlaces.

My mobile was ringing. It no longer played 'Roll Out the Barrel'. I'd reprogrammed it with D:ream's 'Things Can Only Get Better'. You might even call this an example of optimism.

The screen said: 7.45 a.m. Ringo. The clock on my mobile needed adjusting: I was an hour ahead of GMT at the moment.

'Hello, Ringo.'

'How's Amsterdam?'

'The pavements are covered in vomit and there are condoms in the canals; it reminds me of Walsall. I'd think I was still in my hometown but the people here speak better English.'

'And the room?'

'Above a brothel! I knew I could rely on you to fix me up with something appropriate.'

'I thought you'd appreciate the irony.'

An old mate of Ringo's was letting me stay here rent-free. The room was quite nice once you got used to the red wall-paper and, of course, the mirrored ceiling. Every time I looked up I scared the bejesus out of myself.

'We've had a lot of letters complaining that you've stopped writing the column.'

'I'm sure Deekus will do you proud.' I'd recommended Deekus as the *Reflector*'s new Facts is Facts columnist when I decided to leave the paper. Who better?

'You were right: he does seem rather suited to the job. His copy takes a lot of editing – it's always twenty times too long – but he appears to be hitting the right note.'

'I guessed as much.'

This week's *Reflector* lay on my bedside table – I'd picked it up on my way to the airport the day before. Deekus's latest Facts is Facts column slagged off Wesley and made specific reference to his last sojourn there. It opened:

Such is my desire to avoid draining NHS resources I seldom consent to hospitalization. However, despite my best efforts, my physician insisted I be admitted to Wesley-in-Tame in April of this year. Sadly it confirmed my worst fears about the state of the Health Service in this country. Can you believe I found myself on the same ward as a patient who spent his days screaming about Dutchmen and claiming the nurses were trying to kill him? Admittedly he was probably right about the latter, but you'd think the hospital authorities would be a bit more sensitive to the needs of other patients. They should show more consideration when it comes to dealing with the mentally ill: a surgical ward is no place for nutters. The television was barely audible over his screams. It's just another example of this hospital's lamentable lack of concern for . . .

Ringo would probably have added the word 'lamentable': he had a feel for alliteration. Deekus was as big a bull-shitter as me and certainly his whining tone would be lapped up. I knew from experience the kind of readers' letters this diatribe would provoke. Most would sympathize with his shabby treatment; a few would undoubtedly complain about his use of the word 'nutters' – not because it's an insensitive way to describe the mentally ill – but because they'll feel it should've been spelt with a *k*.

'People are asking about you,' said Ringo, his voice tinny and distant in my mobile. 'Should I tell them where you are?'

'Tell them I've gone to the Islands of Langerhans.'

'And what should I tell them is the nature of your business?'

'Conservation.'

Ringo chuckled. 'I have an exciting piece of gossip by the way.'

I groaned. 'I promised myself I'd get out of the gossip racket.'

'You know you love it.'

'If it's about Jade from *Big Brother* Monica's already told me: her mother's a one-armed lesbian.'

'No, no, that's yesterday's news. This is bigger. And more important. Before she died Ebola Barker was working on a memoir, the book she mentioned when we knew her. It's about to be published by a small local press. I have a proof copy in front of me: the publishers are hoping for an advance review.'

'Jesus. Is it any good?'

'It is actually: it's astonishingly well written. It clears up a few mysteries about her, too. She was profoundly depressed, obsessed with her weight, constantly contemplating suicide. You can see why they wanted to publish it: there's always a market for breakdown memoirs. Her barbiturate overdose doesn't seem to have been planned, as such, but she knew she was overdoing it. She didn't care.'

'I see.'

'But that's not the interesting bit.'

'Do go on.' I could imagine Ringo's face: his eyes incandescent with delight, savouring his knowledge; his moment; his power.

'Apparently for years Ebola's mother has been unwilling to let it be published. She's been waiting.'

'Waiting for what?'

'In the book Ebola says she was having an affair with a colleague and Ebola's mother didn't want to publish while the wife of that colleague was still alive . . .' Ringo, as is his way, trailed off mysteriously.

'For bollocks sake, tell me!'

'Mrs Daniel Dunderdale lost her fight against cancer three months ago.'

I wasn't going to tell Ringo about my Nurse Frigata hallucination. So what if the Barker–Dunderdale association is one my subconscious had tormented me with? It meant nothing and, besides, I was embarrassed about my DTs. Both Ringo and Monica had visited me at the height of my withdrawal symptoms and seen me screaming and crying and mistaking them for scorpions. I just wanted to forget it.

'I don't suppose *Mrs* Dunderdale left a memoir admitting to burning down Penny's Punishment Palace by any chance?'

'Flaming Ada, what makes you say that? You're not back on the sauce, are you?'

'No, mate, just clutching at straws.' I was happy in my role as the cretin responsible for the fire; every time I thought about it it reminded me how dangerous it is for me to drink. I needed reminding.

'Well, Ebola's book is enough to be going on with. It's a hot one on top of everything else: there are long, racy descriptions of her and Dunderdale's S&M sex sessions. She was his dominatrix. It's called *The Silent Scream* and it reads like a cross between *Prozac Nation* and *Venus in Furs*.'

'Never heard of them.'

'Anyway, it's interesting how Dunderdale and Barker had antithetical personalities: the passive and the aggressive; the humanist and the poststructuralist.'

'Yow wot?'

'Never mind.'

'I'll certainly read the book when I get back.'

'Make sure you do, Dave. You could learn a lot from it.'

'Does Ebola avoid becoming a reductive stereotype?'

'Do any of us?'

'As a drunken journalist I suppose it's hard for me to answer that. Does she mention us?'

'A sentence or two. She talks about visiting Penny's to get a deeper insight into the psychology of extreme sex. She calls me the brainy Dutch boy.'

'And me?'

I could hear Ringo tittering.

'Well?'

'She calls you the mouthy drunk who's going bald.'

'The cheeky cat.'

'Don't think too badly of her. You and she have a fair bit in common.'

'Like what?'

'I'll leave you to work it out.'

I wasn't even going to try: my IQ wasn't up to it.

We spoke for another ten minutes. Ringo could afford this because his mobile account was covered by expenses. Mind you, I'd also dropped on my feet financially. When Allied Midland Newspapers were looking to make redundancies Ringo wangled me a healthy package. It was good for them, because they saved my sub-editor's salary. A significant saving given my non-existent subbing skills. My only real contribution to the paper had been Facts is Facts and now they got this freelance for a snip. In fact, for less than a snip: Deekus refused payment in case it affected his benefit. He did it for fun.

Before I left the *Reflector* I did get around to writing my balanced piece about Wesley. I thought it would be nice to go out on a high note professionally. Titled, 'Wesley-in-Tame: Dedication Against the Odds', it received more complaint letters than anything I've ever written.

# Runners, and People Who Jog

The DTs didn't fully get a grip of me until my third day in hospital. I'd drunk so much trying to kill my rhino it had sustained my physical dependence through the Tuesday and the Wednesday. I suppose the paranoia over Dunderdale was the first symptom of my withdrawal, then my confusion over surgery and who had said what. Ringo feels guilty about inadvertently fuelling this with his revelations about Van Door – they didn't help, of course, but I'm glad the truth came out.

It was after I'd seen Dunderdale that I really began losing it. By Thursday evening I was off my swede. I narrowly missed being sectioned, but it was the weekend before my mind was functioning normally. My recollection of events becomes clearer and more confident from then on. However, for the rest of my two-week stay at Wesley, I couldn't be in the same room as Nurse Frigata without feeling uneasy.

A psychiatrist later told me that my hallucinations were both classic and unusual. It's apparently common to see insects but, in his experience, fairly rare to see quite as many scorpions as I did. And who, he'd wanted to know, was Amy Turtle?

I came through it, though. I survived my cold turkey and I survived pancreatitis. My pancreas deflated and is now its old self. My Islands of Langerhans are safe. They tell me things will stay that way if I stay off the booze. 'Not so much as a wine gum,' Dunderdale warned.

It was eight o'clock GMT; time for my run. I pulled on my shorts and marvelled once more at my flat stomach and fat-free legs laced with hard muscle. My God: I'm starting to look like Paula Radcliffe. I rolled on a pair of double-lined anti-blister running socks and then laced up my pair of Nike Air Pegasus. I dampened the sensors of my heart-rate monitor with several smears of saliva and then fixed them into position on my chest with their elastic straps. I adjusted the monitor's wrist unit to beep if my heartbeat fell below 145 b.p.m. I needed to stay around this rate to increase my aerobic fitness. I stuck a pair of corn plasters on my nipples and slipped on my running vest.

As I left the flat and descended the stairs my monitor beeped to tell me that my heart rate was too slow. Out in the hallway it was still beeping. When I reached the street I started to trot, slowly at first to warm up, then more quickly until I hit my running rhythm. The beeping stopped as my heartbeat reached the required frequency.

I ran, noting the street names as I went: south along Zeedijk to Waag, then down Bloedstraat. From there I turned right and crossed two bridges to Oude Kerk. I lapped the old church noticing two or three hookers in their booths despite the early hour. Were they the early shift or the late shift? One of them, a black woman in a white basque, tapped her window at me and gave me a big sexy smile. 'Let me rub your head, baldy!' she shouted.

Many people, including me, would feel sad for this woman. But she looked happy and, above all, safe, in her little cubicle. She wasn't like the women who still haunt the streets of Caldmore. I didn't worry about this Dutch girl the way I worried about them. Ringo had made the point that, if a Walsall prostitute had stabbed Van Door to death she'd have a hard time pleading self-defence. Why? Because she's a criminal to begin with.

I'd be spending a fair bit of time around Amsterdam's red light district. Having given up subbing I'd returned to what I do best: fetish leathercraft. I had a suitcase full of samples and a wallet full of addresses. I'd come to Amsterdam to drum up orders. Rotterdam and Utrecht were on my itinerary too. My latest specialist item for masochists was called a Wesley: a hand-tooled sharkskin catheter. Only joking.

I ran on. I passed the bars with their signs for Amstel, Christoffel, Dort, Egelantier, Heineken, Grolsch, La Trappe, Natte, Oranjeboom, Sjoes, Trippelaer, Zatte. Christ: who'd have thought there was so much beer in the world? Some of the proprietors were out hosing down their steps and, as I passed, I'd glance into the bars' brown-stained interiors; they looked sad in the morning with their empty, echoing quiet and chairs stacked on tables.

I generally only saw bars from the outside these days. When Bukowski left hospital he'd gone straight into one. Despite the time he'd just spent on the charity ward with bleeding stomach ulcers he was determined to drink on. Not me. I've become that most tedious thing: a teetotal non-smoker.

It's been hard, of course. Now I can't dance, speak French, tell people I love them and, if Daniel O'Donnell ever crosses my path, he's one dead Irishman. It's hard partly because it's easy to forget about my rhino. From this distance he looks tame – a gerbil-sized rhino that you could take liberties with. I can't see his horn from here. Sometimes I'll be alone in my flat and I'll almost crack. All around, Walsall will be stewing in its own bland juices. There'll be nothing on the telly but a repeat of *Quincy*. Everything in the paper will be pointless. At times like this I'll think: just one glass of Grolsch won't hurt. I can imagine a foaming, golden pint sitting on the coffee table. I could cool my lips in it and stay calm for ever. It howls and yelps and yaps to be tasted. I'll have three or four wanks in a row (I can do that these days), but they fail to distract me. And after each one *Quincy* looks less and less attractive. I'll eat an apple and an orange; a Go Ahead diet bar; a tomato; a carrot slice; ten slices more. It fails to distract me. I'll thumb through my *English Birds* book. With a wave of despair I'll concede that nothing in the world will help me forget. And then I'll forget. For a bit. Something like this sequence happens every day, twice on Sundays. I haven't cracked yet. But it hurts.

*Yaaaaaa, haaaaaaa.*

As I ran up Warmoesstraat I passed a couple of old ladies. They were like old ladies everywhere: they both wore hats and overcoats despite the summer heat. I noticed the one on the left regarding me closely as I approached and I waited to hear what 'Haven't I seen you in a Daniel O'Donnell video?' sounded like in Dutch, but they passed without comment. Had Daniel made it across the North Sea? Even for a country that had produced the Vengaboys this would be a new low. When I think of myself on that live video, of the photo of me on the cover, I cringe. I look happy, but I know I'm putting it on after a skinful in the NEC bar. I was trying to be ironic, but the irony was on me.

I continued up Warmoesstraat in the direction, the signs suggest, of Munt Plein. My lungs were functioning nicely after four months without a fag. I no longer coughed up yellow mucus; I was beginning to lose all trace of my smoker's rattle. And, as I say, I'd lost a staggering amount of weight: down from fifteen stone to eleven. I'd lost two stone in Wesley and I'd shed half a stone a month since. I was a gazelle; a remarkable assemblage of sinew and muscle. I was javelin thin.

This was my first morning in Amsterdam, but I knew

roughly where Vondelpark was. I was going to work my way up to it for some serious running.

I was a serious runner rather than a jogger, you see.

A serious runner is massively different from a jogger. You can tell them apart before the running begins. A jogger, for instance, doesn't worry whether or not he will have an opportunity to jog, he just jogs when he can. A serious runner always worries. If there's any possibility of missing a session, a serious runner will get jittery. He will set his alarm. He will rearrange meals, meetings, flights, anything, to make space for a run. Here's another difference. If you stop a jogger on the street to ask him directions he will interrupt his exercise to assist. A serious runner won't do this; a serious runner will ignore you and, if you persist, he will knee you in the nads.

Here's another. A jogger won't wear a heart-rate monitor to ensure he is exercising at a sufficient intensity; a serious runner will. If he hears the monitor beep a warning, he will speed up, because a serious runner wants to improve, to cover his route more quickly and efficiently. He relishes his victories over distance and time.

But the most telling difference is this. If a jogger develops an injury, like the ankle strain I have this morning, a jogger will take the day off. A serious runner won't do that. He will stupidly risk just another run, then another, then another, then another, till he finds himself limping into an x-ray room, with a Nike Air Pegasus in his clammy, trembling hand.

*Also available from Tindal Street Press*

# THE AFTERGLOW
## Anthony Cartwright

'An excellent read, told with style and pace'
*Alan Sillitoe*

Whether at work at Paradise Meatpacking, out on the town with Jamie, playing snooker with the unnerving Risley, or back in bed with his ex-fiancée, the guilt of a family tragedy haunts Luke. Years after the event, he still can't piece together the details of that terrible day. And summertime tensions mean that pints shared with mates turn to punches thrown; unemployed days are eked out with mundane tasks; and dreams of escape might stay forever unfulfilled.

'Anthony Cartwright has an instinctive talent for using description to create subtle shades of mood'
*Carol Birch*

'This painfully honest and accomplished first novel . . . penetrates beneath the skin of young and old. We are given no more than the remnants of the old working-class world of warmth and solidarity, one that has now had its heart torn out, but what afterglow there is comes from the portrait of the mother, Mary, and her "little victories of life over death"' *Philip Callow*

ISBN: 0 9541303 6 7

*Also available from Tindal Street Press*

# GOING THE DISTANCE
## edited by Alan Beard

'Triumphant proof that the short story
is alive and kicking in the UK'
*Peter Ho Davies*

All the way from Birmingham to Trinidad, Colombia
and Canada, by way of Wales, Essex, Liverpool and
London, *Going the Distance* offers 20 'honed and
accomplished' short stories to enjoy. Be enticed by a
heartbreaking tale of an illiterate couple told as a raw
and insistent letter from a prison cell; a spot-on
portrait of a girl on the verge of losing her virginity; a
beautiful, poetical allegory about a man's love affair
with the bottle; plus 17 other deft, vigorous stories.

'Annie Murray's "The Tonsil Machine" is written
with a delicate but edgy lyricism that evokes the
flowering of revulsion in a child's mind'
*Birmingham Post*

'"Homing Instinct" by Maria Morris is
outstanding. Every word carries the perfect weight,
each image is as vivid as if it were your own
memory' *Time Out*

'Always powerful, original, perfectly understated,
each voice strong and enticing' *Laura Hird*

ISBN: 0 9541303 5 9

*Excellent contemporary fiction from*
*Tindal Street Press*

**WIST** by Jackie Gay
ISBN: 0 9541303 4 0 * £7.99

**WHAT GOES ROUND** by Maeve Clarke
ISBN: 0 9541303 3 2 * £7.99

**ASTONISHING SPLASHES OF COLOUR**
by Clare Morrall
*Shortlisted for the Man Booker Prize 2003*
ISBN: 0 9541303 2 4 * £7.99

**BIRMINGHAM NOUVEAU** edited by Alan Mahar
ISBN: 0 9541303 0 8 * £7.99

**BIRMINGHAM NOIR**
edited by Joel Lane and Steve Bishop
ISBN: 0 9535895 9 5 * £7.99

**A LONE WALK** by Gul Y. Davis
*Winner of the J.B. Priestley Fiction Award 2001*
ISBN: 0 9535895 3 6 * £6.99

**SCAPEGRACE** by Jackie Gay
ISBN: 0 9535895 1 X * £6.99

**THE PIG BIN** by Michael Richardson
*Winner of the Sagittarius Prize 2001*
ISBN: 0 9535895 2 8 * £6.99

All Tindal Street Press titles are available from good
bookshops, online booksellers and direct from
www.tindalstreet.co.uk